The Novice's Tale

MORE BY THIS AUTHOR

Historical Fiction

The Testament of Mariam

This Rough Ocean

The Chronicles of Christoval Alvarez

The Secret World of Christoval Alvarez
The Enterprise of England
The Portuguese Affair
Bartholomew Fair
Suffer the Little Children
Voyage to Muscovy
The Play's the Thing

Oxford Medieval Mysteries

The Bookseller's Tale

The Fenland Series

Flood
Betrayal

Contemporary Fiction

The Anniversary
The Travellers
A Running Tide

The Novice's Tale

Ann Swinfen

Shakenoak Press

for

Two dear Oxford friends

Frances & John Walsh

Chapter One

Oxford, Summer 1353

The sun had broken through at last, dispersing the veils of river mist which so often hang over Oxford in hot weather. As the last wisps drifted away, Jordain Brinkylsworth and I carried our tankards of ale out into the small orchard behind my bookshop and settled ourselves on the bench under the pear tree. A dappled shade was cast by the branches, now beginning to put forth fruits no larger than a thumbnail, where only a few weeks before they had been starred with blossom. The orchard trees mitigated the heat somewhat, for when Oxford makes up its mind to summer, cupped as it is deep in the valleys of two rivers, it can become too hot for comfort, just as in winter it may turn itself into a pocket of ice.

Our hens had retreated into the shade of the bushy fig tree I grew against one of my boundary walls. The children were playing with Jonathan Baker, who lived on the other side of the High Street, and my sister Margaret had gone to visit her friend Mary Coomber, who kept the dairy. House and garden slumbered in unaccustomed quiet. Even the bees were somnolent, only a few valiant souls venturing forth from the skep to visit the bean flowers.

Jordain drank deeply of his ale, then, with a sigh of contentment, set down his tankard beside him on the bench and stretched out his legs.

'Have you given your men a holiday, Nicholas?' he said. 'I saw no one in the shop.'

'Roger asked leave to visit his mother, who lives over toward Otmoor. She has been ailing of late. And since there was so little business doing, I told Walter he could take the rest of the day off. We have enough *peciae* in hand, and most of our orders are complete. This is poor weather for scribing, as you must know yourself. Your sweaty hand sticks to the parchment. It's all too easy to smear the ink, and the ink itself can run too fast from the quill. Better to give them time away from work than have them spoiling good parchment. Besides, there's little doing, with term over and most of the students away home.'

The heat was making me sleepy, and I yawned till my jaw cracked. 'How did your students perform in their end of year disputations? I know you were doubtful about some of them.'

'Well enough. I have two still staying on in Hart Hall for the summer. Having failed their disputations they have had a proper fright – and high time, too! They are hard at their studies at last, hoping to pass in the autumn. I had warned them both that they risked failing, but did they listen? Too much misplaced confidence cometh before a fall.'

I smiled. 'I wonder, are they the same two who acted as my bodyguards? Handy with a sword, but ill-suited to the scholar's life.'

'Aye, one of them is. 'Tother scraped through his disputation. He's said farewell to Oxford and is off back to his father's manor. That's the life he is truly fit for. He will soon forget most of his studies, the philosophy and the ancient authors, but he will be better able to oversee the manor's accounts than his father has been. And if he never reads another word of Tully, at least he will be able to make some sense of any Latin deeds and charters that come his way.'

'Surely most manors keep a lettered steward, do they not?' I pointed out. 'To deal with such matters?'

My own family's farm had never required the services of such a steward, and besides, it was in my cousin Edmond's keeping now, and of no concern to me.

'There can be no harm in the manor's lord possessing enough learning to keep a weather eye on the estate books,' Jordain said earnestly.

'I suppose not,' I agreed.

I smiled to myself. He had the right of it, certainly, though he himself came from a family of poor tenant farmers who had never had to worry about managing an estate. Enough for them to grow and harvest and store sufficient food to survive the next twelvemonth. It was Jordain's own exceptional abilities which had brought him first as a young student to Oxford and then raised him to the position of Regent Master and Warden of Hart Hall.

'So, you are a free man this summer,' I said idly, sipping at my ale.

The puppy Rowan, who had declined to go with the children to the Bakers' house, preferring to keep out of the heat, came wandering into the garden from the open kitchen door and sought refuge in the shade under our bench.

'Aye, except for keeping those two lads to their books,' Jordain said, 'and pursuing my own studies. At least, when it is not so hot.'

Indeed, he was looking the worse for the heat, and wiped his face on the trailing sleeve of his academic gown. I was grateful I was no longer obliged to wear one as I went about the town. I had even thrown aside my cotte and sat in nothing but shirt and hose.

'However, it is not all idleness,' he said, 'and that is why I have come round to see you.'

'Indeed? I thought it was for the pleasure of my company and my learned discourse.'

'That too, of course, although I am glad of a respite from learned discourse. Nay, it is the matter of William's mother and sister.'

'Mistress Farringdon? But has she not returned home to Berkshire?'

'Aye, she has. But you will remember that with her husband's death and the loss of the pension granted to him by the king, she has been forced to give up the tenancy of their farm. Their lord has turned them out. Had William not been killed by that devil Allard Basset of Merton, their lord might have allowed them to stay until William took up his junior Fellowship and could support them. However, as he now sees no prospect of the rent being paid even in the future, he has proved quite ruthless. They are without a home.'

'How do you know this?' I asked.

'Oh, not from Mistress Farringdon herself. She has too much pride to beg for help. It was the girl, Juliana.'

'That young girl? She has written to you for help?'

He grinned. 'Aye, she has. You will remember that she was not afraid to speak her mind. It was she told us of her cousin Emma Thorgold, Sister Benedicta at Godstow Abbey.'

'I remember,' I said.

'Perhaps you also remember that there is another child, a little girl – she must be of an age with your Rafe, four or five. Mistress Farringdon's granddaughter, child of her son and his wife who died in the Great Pestilence. They left the child behind with a neighbour when they came to Oxford after William was killed.'

'I had forgotten there was another child,' I admitted. 'A woman and two young girls, and no menfolk to support them.'

'The nearest man is the second husband of Mistress Farringdon's dead sister, but there is little love there, I understand. He has means enough to support them, I gather, but there has been no offer forthcoming from him, and, I fancy, little willingness on her part to accept his charity.'

'She may be forced to plead for his help, if they have no roof over their heads.'

'For the moment they are living with the neighbours who cared for the child, but from what Juliana has written to me it cannot be for long. These good people have little enough means of their own, and the house is very small. Mistress Farringdon and the two girls must find somewhere else to live.'

'Is this why Juliana has written to you?' I looked at him in concern. I knew that Jordain would give away every penny, but he did not have the means to support this family.

'She has not asked me for financial help,' he said hastily. 'Nay, quite the opposite. Where they live is but a small village, half the population dead in the Pestilence. Juliana thought there might be more chance of their earning a living for themselves here in Oxford. She was somewhat hazy as to how they might do so, but she wanted to know whether it would be possible to find lodgings here.'

I looked at him dubiously. 'I suppose some of the townsfolk who let rooms to students might take them for the summer, but they will want the lodgings free when term begins again. Besides, have they the money for rent?'

'Again, she was not very clear, but they have a little, it seems. How much, and whether it would suffice for lodgings, I cannot say.'

'There was that woman from Banbury who sold me her husband's books,' I said. 'She and her daughter are keeping themselves by making lace and braid. I suppose there is work unprotected women can do, who are gently bred. The Farringdons could not work in an alehouse, or a laundry.'

'Certainly not!' He looked horrified. 'At the moment, I am not concerned about how they would earn their bread. My only interest is in finding them somewhere to live. This is where you come in.'

'Me? I would like to help, Jordain, but we have no room here.'

'Nay, nay. That is not what I have in mind. William was to have taken up his Fellowship at Merton. And he was killed by a Fellow of Merton, or at any rate on Allard

Basset's orders. Do you not think that Merton has a debt to William's family?'

'In justice and mercy, aye, you have a point. Whether they will see it that way themselves . . . they are more than a little tight fisted, I fear.'

'So this is where you come in.'

'I do not follow you,' I said.

'Who exposed the thief and murderer in their midst? Who recovered their most valued treasure for them? Who kept the scandal quiet, so that the college's name was not befouled? You did.'

'But–' I said.

'Merton is a rich college. They could compensate William's family in coin. They have also bought up a great deal of property in Oxford since so much was left abandoned after the deaths from the plague. Might they not have a small house somewhere in town? One that Mistress Farringdon and the two girls could occupy?'

I was beginning to see where this was heading. 'They might,' I said cautiously, 'but Merton's bursar is a man who holds the purse strings in a tight grip. I'd not expect any kindness from him.'

'Did I mention the bursar? You should go to the Warden himself, William Durant. I have no claims there. I can do nothing. But it was you who laid the Irish Psalter safe back in his hands. You are asking nothing for yourself, nor would you ever do so, but I think he would be shamed if he refused any help to William Farringdon's family. They thought highly of the lad at Merton, he had great promise. It is the least they could do.'

Presented thus, it was very persuasive.

'It might be worth the try,' I said, still cautious. 'But you forget, I also have an unfortunate history with Merton. Just before I was to take up my own Fellowship there, I abandoned my academic career to marry Elizabeth. I think it is still held against me in the college.'

Jordain waved my words aside. 'That was seven years ago. There was a different Warden heading the college then, Robert Trenge. The present Warden may not even know of it. And the man who held it most against you was Master Allard Basset himself, that same thief and murderer. I am sure that recent events have much greater value than all that ancient history. Will you at least make trial of it?'

What could I say? Mistress Farringdon and the two girls were in desperate need. It was their poverty which had driven William to accept the work of scribing a copy of the ancient Irish Psalter. And because he was an honest, decent young man, when he discovered the criminal nature of the scheme, he refused to continue. It had cost him his life. Surely I was not such a coward that I could not do this for his mother?

'Very well,' I said. 'I do not relish such an interview with Warden Durant, but I will do my best.'

'Excellent!' He thumped me on the shoulder, nearly spilling my ale. 'None of us can do more than our best.'

We sat for a while in the drowsy afternoon silence, broken only by the occasional murmur from the hens, and those few determined bees flying between their skep and my rows of beans. These had nearly finished flowering, but their sweet fragrance still hung in the air, a scent to surpass any apothecary's perfume compounded for some great lady. Once, Rowan woke, gave an explosive sneeze, then slept again.

'Did you not say that you had a book to show me?' Jordain asked.

'I have. And I will bring us more ale. This weather makes for a great thirst.'

I got up and went back into the kitchen. Margaret kept the barrel of ale in the coolest corner of her stillroom. When I had filled a flagon, I went through to the shop, where the closed shutters made it clear that I was not open for business. Although it was dim in here, I could put my hand on the book at once, where I kept it safely hidden away on the highest shelf. My scriveners, Walter and Roger, knew that it was not for sale, but I wanted to be sure that no customer, idly examining my books, would pick it up and handle it. I carried book and flagon out to the garden, but set the flagon down at a slight distance in a shady clump of long grass.

'You shall have more to drink,' I said, 'but best to keep it well away from this.'

I laid the book in his hands. It was small, barely four inches wide by six inches tall, bound in pale blue calfskin. The cover was tooled and ornamented with gold leaf, but it was not studded with gems, as some more ostentatious books are. I preferred it so. It fitted neatly into the hand, smooth and silky to the touch. Bookbinder Henry Stalbroke had chosen exactly the right binding to suit the contents. The edges of the pages were gilded. It looked rich, but restrained. Elegant.

Jordain opened it. 'A book of hours?'

'Aye.'

'But not the one you starved yourself to buy when you were a boy?'

'This is new made.' I still loved my first book of hours, bought from Humphrey Hadley – who later became my father-in-law – partly because it reminded me of his daughter Elizabeth. But this book was of a different order.

He began to turn the pages.

'This is very fine.'

'It is.'

He chuckled. 'And an artist with a clever, subtle, sense of humour.' He looked up at me and smiled. 'There is no harm in a little leavening amongst the solemnity of prayer. I think anyone who used this for daily devotions would perform them all the more warmly, for the kindliness of the illustrator.'

He said no more until he had turned over every page. Then he handed the book back to me.

'And where did you come by such a treasure? That is not Roger Pigot's work, nor yet Walter's.'

'It is not.' I ran my thumb gently along the spine of the book. 'I saw it first in Henry Stalbroke's workshop, where he had it in for binding.'

'It was locally made?' he said in surprise. 'I thought perhaps it had come from France.'

'Locally made indeed.'

'Not in your bookshop, and no other bookshop in Oxford has men who could produce that quality. Nor, I think, any of the colleges. And anyway, these days they mostly work at copying the major academic texts. That is their greatest need.' He eyed the book, loosely clasped between my hands. 'It must come from one of the monastic houses.'

I nodded.

'But which? I have not seen work of that quality from any of them. Such fine detail. And the colours are used with an expert eye for beauty. Nay, it is too much for me!'

'It was made at Godstow Abbey.' I was unable to keep a certain triumphant note from my voice. 'At first they were reluctant to sell, but Henry Stalbroke persuaded them that such works of devotion would be as worthwhile a source of income for them as the fine embroideries they deal in more commonly. I had told him I would buy it if they would sell.'

'It was made by a *woman*!' He made no attempt to conceal his incredulity. 'I would never have believed it! Well, you will be able to sell that for a fine price to some nobleman.'

'I shall not sell it.'

He looked at me speculatively. 'Do you know who made it?'

'Indeed I do. It was Emma Thorgold, William Farringdon's cousin.'

'Indeed?' He smiled. 'I remember you were much impressed by William's beautiful cousin when you visited her at Godstow.'

'Beautiful, intelligent, and resourceful. Had she not kept Merton's Irish Psalter safely hidden, I should not have been able to return it to Warden Durant. So, by your reasoning, that is another member of William's family to whom Merton owes a debt.'

If I hoped by this to divert Jordain from discussion of Emma Thorgold, I was unsuccessful.

'I know that you had a meeting with her, when you took her the word of William's murder, and another when you retrieved the Psalter.'

'That second time was hardly a meeting,' I said. 'She simply handed over the book to me at the gatehouse. I did not even enter the abbey.'

'And have you seen her since?'

'Briefly.' I felt uncomfortable even recalling it. 'I had promised to let her know what was the end of it all, so I rode out there the day after I returned the Psalter to Warden Durant. I was permitted to have a meeting in the parlour of the guest house, but this time we were chaperoned by Sister Clemence. We barely spoke.'

He nodded his understanding. 'Well, you can hardly take it amiss. Three visits by a young man to a novice in their care, within the space of less than a week? And you not even kin to the girl? Little wonder you were chaperoned! I would have demanded it myself.'

'Do not talk such foolishness, Jordain,' I said, annoyed. I got up and refilled our tankards from the flagon in the grass, then carried the book of hours back to the safety of the high shelf.

'Besides,' I said, as I rejoined him on the bench, 'neither Emma Thorgold, *Sister Benedicta*, nor the guardian dragon Sister Clemence, could possibly regard me as a young man.'

I found I could not leave the subject alone.

'A widower with two children, an Oxford shopkeeper? I am no threat to one of the holy lady nuns of Godstow, who all come from good families.'

'And does Sister Benedicta come from a good family?' he said. 'We have been speaking of her aunt Farringdon's poverty.'

'As far as I can make out, Mistress Farringdon married somewhat beneath her birth, though her husband was a good man of the minor gentry. Her sister, Emma's mother, married above her rank, in her first marriage. Her first husband, who was Emma's father, was the younger son of a knight. The second marriage, to Emma's stepfather, was less fortunate.'

'Less fortunate in many ways,' he agreed, 'if all we are told is true. It resulted in the lady's death from an unsought late pregnancy and the forced entry of her daughter into a nunnery.'

He looked at me thoughtfully. 'You seem to have learned a good deal about the family. Was this during the time when you barely spoke?'

'We had a few minutes alone before Sister Clemence took up her post. Like you, I was concerned about the family and sought to know more about them.'

'Hmm,' he said. 'And did you learn more of the girl herself? It must be a full year ago that she was sent to Godstow. According to her cousin Juliana, the stepfather despatched her with an attendant company of six armed men of his, to ensure *she did not escape*. Juliana's words. When is the novice to take her final vows?'

'Sometime later this summer. As I said, we had the chance to speak only briefly before her guard arrived.'

'You contrived to discover much in a short time.'

I shrugged. Our conversation had been driven by some urgent but unspoken need for haste, our words tumbling over each other. I suppose we had both realised we might not have another meeting. I had been promised the opportunity to bring her word of the outcome of the pursuit of William's killers, but I did not think the abbess would admit me again. As Jordain pointed out, I was no kin to Emma Thorgold. *Sister Benedicta*, I corrected myself.

'She has still no vocation for the monastic life?' Jordain said. 'I had thought she might have become reconciled by now.'

I shook my head. 'As much reconciled as a singing bird would be reconciled to a cage in a dark room. She desires her freedom with a fierce passion. If they try to force her to make her final vows, I think she would take to her heels and flee the place.'

'Surely they would not do such a thing? They are holy women, not monsters.'

'What if it has been made plain to them that it is the wish of her family?'

'Mistress Farringdon is her only blood kin,' he said, 'and she would not force her.'

'I think her stepfather assumes that he has rights over her. It was he who wanted her put away there. Perhaps he has also made it plain that he wants her secured there for life.'

Jordain looked alarmed. 'What do you mean?'

'Come, Jordain,' I said, 'you cannot be that innocent. He may have offered them a substantial benefaction if they keep her.'

'But why? It makes no sense to me. If he has promised money, he could have used the same to dower her in marriage. Why force her?'

I shrugged. 'I do not know. I do not think Emma herself knows, but we had no chance to discuss it. She did say that the man has three daughters of his own, by previous marriages, and sons, too. Perhaps he sees her as a cuckoo in the nest, an unwanted appendage to her mother. He married the mother solely to provide him with a woman to manage his household and care for his children, as well as to warm his bed. Emma was of no use to him. It would not be the first time an unwanted girl has been shut away in a nunnery.'

'Juliana did mention in her letter,' he said slowly, 'that the man plans to marry again.'

'There you are. Emma would not fit in with his plans.'

'It is a sad situation, but there is nothing we can do about it.' Jordain shrugged, but I saw that he looked regretful.

'I suppose there is not,' I said reluctantly. 'Besides, Godstow will be all the more eager to keep her, now that she has produced that book of hours. In worldly terms, they must see her as a financial asset.'

'I expect you paid a great deal for that book. It is truly beautiful.'

'I paid a fair price,' I said firmly.

'Do you really think she might run away? It would be a grievous sin.'

'Not every novice takes final vows. If the abbess were to agree to release her, she could walk away with no shame or guilt.'

'And then what?' he said. 'Join her aunt and cousin in their poverty? Surely she would not want to return to her stepfather, even if he would have her. 'Tis a pity she is a girl. Were she a man, you could employ her as a scrivener, and make your fortune, producing books like the one you showed me.'

It was clear that he was doing no more than teasing me, yet even so . . .

'Aye,' I said, quite seriously. 'I would be happy to employ her, but it would almost certainly lead to trouble.'

Our conversation was interrupted by the return of the children, Alysoun and Jonathan half leading, half carrying Rafe between them. The right knee of his hose was torn and blood was pouring freely down his leg.

'Rafe fell on a sharp stone, Papa!' Tears were running down Alysoun's face. 'He did not mean to do it.'

'Of course he did not,' I said, lifting Rafe up, but doing my best to hold the bloody knee away from my clean shirt. 'Aunt Margaret is still away to the dairy, but I know where she keeps her salves. Come, my fine man, we shall soon have you bandaged up.'

Rafe nodded. Tears were also making pathways down his dirty face, but he was biting his lips to keep himself from crying out. Even at four years old he tried to show the courage demanded by his masculine pride. I felt pity like a deep ache in my stomach. A child of four should not need to play the man

ॐ∞ॐ

Four miles north of Oxford, Godstow Abbey occupied an island in the many-branched Thames, and was reached by a bridge, which gave it something of the appearance of a fortified manor, an appearance further strengthened by a handsome gatehouse of two storeys and a substantial stone wall enclosing the monastic buildings. Although it lay some distance off the main thoroughfare from Oxford to the royal palace at Woodstock, there was a well-used trackway leading west from this road to the abbey, through the small village of Wolvercote and the even smaller hamlet of Godstow, which provided housing for the abbey's servants.

One of the few wealthy nunneries this far north, Godstow had been well endowed since Henry II had granted it funds and property, for it was the resting place of his mistress, Rosamund Clifford. A series of shrewd and practical abbesses in subsequent years had increased its endowments, so that it was now also a favoured place of withdrawal or retirement for great ladies who had seen enough of the secular world and sought the peace and tranquillity of Godstow as guests of the nuns. These noble ladies, however, did bring with them a certain whiff of the worldly life outside the abbey walls, which was not always welcomed by the stricter and more conventional of the sisters. Indeed, the bishop had been known to wax severe on the subject, although there was not a great deal that either Abbess Agnes de Streteley and her obedientiaries or the bishop himself could do to prevent, if some lady of noble or royal blood took it into her head to favour Godstow with her presence.

It was perhaps irritation at the arrival that morning of

yet another secular lady to take up residence in the guest quarters that made Sister Mercy, mistress of the novices, more than usually short tempered. Or perhaps it was the stifling heat trapped within the walls all day, unrelieved by any breeze. Sister Mercy did not bear the heat easily, and an enveloping monastic habit of black wool is no garment for summer weather. Whatever the cause, Sister Mercy's temper – never of the kindest – was frayed beyond control.

The novices under her governance, all six of them, had been set a particularly grim passage from St Jerome to parse and translate, before writing a commentary on it, which was to demonstrate their certain grasp of his arguments. Moreover, of the girls sent to school with the nuns of Godstow, the two eldest were deemed sufficiently apt in their grasp of Latin to be set the same exercise as the novices, while Sister Mercy (who undertook much of the teaching of these paying pupils) dealt with the younger girls in another room, hearing and fiercely correcting their exercises in the French language.

The eight older girls, novices and pupils alike, sweated over St Jerome in an airless room, the window tight closed, for Sister Mercy believed in shutting out all distractions, and for some time since the dinner hour no sound had disturbed their toil other than the scratching of quills, until one girl flung down her pen and leapt to her feet. Seven heads went up in alarm, and seven hands stopped writing.

'Sister Benedicta! What are you about?'

It was Sister Ursula, like Emma Thorgold eighteen years old and on the point of professing. Unlike Emma, she had come to Godstow by choice. Given to sudden raptures and fainting fits, at other times, when she was in sober control of mind and body she regarded herself as the leader of the novices, by reason of both her age and genuine vocation. Her face was rigid with disapproval, but the others regarded Emma with interest, for one could never be quite sure of what she might do. Sometimes her demeanour was tightly controlled and submissive. Sometimes it was not.

Emma gave Ursula a look which was part pity, part impatience.

'I have finished the exercise. I do not intend to sit here a moment longer.'

'How can you have finished?' Ursula protested, though without absolute conviction. She knew, as they all did, that Emma was a better scholar than Sister Mercy, and many of the other nuns.

Emma did not bother to answer, but slipped out of the door, closing it softly behind her. The rooms where the novices and schoolgirls were taught opened directly on to the cloisters, and, by turning away from the room where Sister Mercy was teaching the younger girls, she could make her way unnoticed to the outside day stair leading up to the dortoir.

Like many nunneries, Godstow permitted its inmates to keep pets, provided they observed the strictures which forbade taking them into the church during services. Emma's dog Jocosa had come with her into the abbey the previous year, for she had refused to leave the animal behind, fearing what her stepfather might do to the creature once she was gone. Had Godstow banned dogs, Emma would probably have smuggled Jocosa in anyway, but the small dog, one of the fluffy, white, Maltese type, was well behaved and acceptable. The abbess had granted permission without hesitation, perhaps because she realised just how unwillingly Emma had been brought to the abbey.

At the top of the stairs, Emma gave a short two-note whistle – something she was forbidden to do within these decorous walls – and Jocosa bounded off her mistress's bed, skittering across the polished wooden floor with a clattering of claws. She hurtled down the stairs ahead of Emma and made instinctively for the gate leading through the wall and into the abbey's vegetable garden.

The stifling heat had driven the nuns indoors from weeding amongst the rows of cabbages, beans, and peas, but half a dozen of the lay sisters had no such freedom and were hard at work, while two of the male servants were digging over a bed from which early lettuces and carrots had already been harvested.

Emma was popular with the lay sisters, treating them with more consideration than did most of the nuns, so they smiled and nodded as she passed. It was clear that she was playing truant, for at this hour she should have been at her lessons, but they were not likely to betray her.

Beyond the end of the vegetable garden, which was enclosed with a wooden fence, a meadow lay within a curve of the river, providing grazing for a small herd of goats. Milked by the *deye* or dairy woman, these goats were the source of the small, strong cheeses sent weekly to Oxford market, while the abbey's flock of sheep and herd of cows were kept at the home farm on the far side of the bridge, adjacent to Godstow village.

The dog ran joyously across the meadow, taking care to avoid the goats, known to be of uncertain temper, not unlike Sister Mercy. She wove a zigzag course through the grass, stopping from time to time to explore enchanting smells. On the bank of the Thames Emma kicked off her sandals, kilted up her habit, and waded into the shallows of the river under the shade of a spreading willow tree. In its shadow the water was cold, making her gasp at first, but bringing relief from a day of oppressive heat. In defiance of all the rules, she snatched off her veil and wimple, and felt the faint stirrings of cool air through the stubble of her hair, as she stood here in the river. She ran her hand over her head, ruffling hair which was nearly half an inch long. Soon the razor would be taken to her scalp again.

The story the novices were told was that a shaven head would bring their thoughts and prayers nearer to God, but Emma wondered whether Jesus had ever decreed that his women followers should be so treated. Surely the women of Judah had worn their hair long? She suspected, instead, that it was merely one more humiliation intended to break the spirit of any woman entering the conventual life. Instead of a full head of glorious hair, a temptation to men and an invitation to vanity, every novice and every nun was reduced to hideous baldness. Even monks fared better, for they retained a fringe of hair circling their tonsure.

The river had hollowed out a miniature cove between the roots of the willow, where the water lay almost still, only shimmering faintly from the current flowing along the main course of the river. So clear was the water and so tranquil that every pebble on the bed of the river in this cove showed in glowing detail, and a school of minnows hung motionless near Emma's feet. As she stepped cautiously forward toward deeper water, the fish moved as one, a cloud of creatures with a single mind, turning with a flick of their tails and disappearing under the arch of a watery root.

She waded a little further out into the river, until the water reached her knees and flowed rapidly, spinning an occasional fallen leaf past her like a miniature boat. The Thames led south from Godstow, eventually twisting past Oxford in a maze of waterways, serving as a means to carry goods up and down river. Supplies for the abbey often arrived by boat, for it could prove an easier route than transporting loads by cart along roads regularly broken by rain and frost.

Emma had often wondered whether she might escape her prison by this unguarded way, but the river was usually deep here and she could not swim. However, the prolonged period of hot, dry weather had caused the river to shrink. Ahead of her a bank of gravel, halfway across, had risen above the surface of the water.

Deliveries of those goods that came by boat were landed on the other side of the meadow, where a solid wooden landing stage had been built. She could hardly beg passage in one of the boats, marked out as she was by her monastic clothes. Somehow – and soon – she must find a means, before she could be forced into making her final vows.

When the bell rang from the abbey church for Vespers, Emma knew that she must return and face her punishment. She thrust damp feet into her sandals, and did her best to secure her wimple and veil, though they were lopsided and creased. Slowly she dragged herself back through the vegetable garden, empty now of any workers, and joined the end of the procession of novices into the church. Ursula glanced at her with pursed lips and a faintly sanctimonious smile. The dog, knowing her place, retreated to a corner of the cloister.

During the service, Emma closed her eyes and allowed herself to sink, mindless, into the music. Sister Mildred, the precentrix and librarian, was a true musician, and the only solace Emma had found here in Godstow, apart from her work of scribing and illumination, was the music. She herself possessed a rich singing voice in the upper register, and joined happily into the music of the service, ignoring the nervous glances of the other girls and the knowing looks from Ursula.

To her surprise, Sister Mercy did not summon her after Vespers to answer for her defection from lessons. To herself, Emma argued angrily that Sister Mercy had nothing to teach her, and in any case she had completed the work set on St Jerome. Nevertheless, she was uneasy, and went to bed wondering why she had received no punishment exercises or penance. She slept at last, rose for the night-time services, and greeted another scalding dawn at Prime.

It was after Prime that retribution came at last.

'You are summoned to Chapter,' Ursula said, in tones of considerable satisfaction. 'You did not think you would go unpunished, did you?'

Emma looked at her steadily. 'No doubt you took pleasure in telling Sister Mercy that I left, once I had finished with St Jerome.'

'The first rule of the Benedictine Order,' Ursula said piously, 'is obedience.'

Emma was not sure that this was true, not that it was the *first* rule – surely that was to serve God? – but would not demean herself to argue. She strode away firmly to the Chapter House, although she felt a certain sickness in her stomach.

The sisters were ranged in a circle on the stone seats around the perimeter of the Chapter House, the abbess sitting on a large throne, slightly raised, facing the door as Emma entered. One nun was standing. Sister Mercy.

'This is the delinquent novice, Reverend Mother,' Sister Mercy said, addressing the abbess and not troubling to look at Emma. 'She left her lessons without permission, went out beyond the enclosure, even beyond the gardens, and was seen in the river in a state of partial undress.'

So Ursula spied on me, Emma thought. All the better to ingratiate herself with Sister Mercy.

'What do you have to say for yourself, Sister Benedicta?' the abbess said. She was a fair-minded woman, but she would not brook disobedience.

'It is perfectly correct that I left the schoolroom,' Emma said, not deigning to make excuses. 'However, I had completed all of the work assigned to us. It was very hot and I went only to cool myself by the river. I did remove my sandals. I returned as soon as the bell rang for Vespers.' She closed her lips firmly. She would take her punishment and not plead further.

'This is by no means the first time Sister Benedicta has shown herself disobedient, self-willed, and impertinent,' Sister Mercy said, her lips thin with anger. 'She has also failed to admit that she removed her veil and wimple, shamelessly baring her head. Mild words and simple punishments have proved of no avail in the past. I request permission to inflict a whipping.'

There was a stir and a murmuring amongst the sisters. Whipping was permitted in the Order, but was usually only carried out for serious crimes. Many of those sitting in Chapter may themselves have also felt a longing for cool air and an escape through the meadow grass in the present heat.

The abbess studied the mistress of the novices, then turned her eyes to Emma, who raised her chin defiantly.

'Very well,' she said at last. 'Twelve strokes.'

Sister Mercy turned to Emma. 'Lower your habit to the waist.'

Emma's face flamed with shame. She was to strip here, in full view of all the nuns. She struggled to untie the strings at the neck of her habit and to draw her arms out of the sleeves. The irritating rough cloth stuck to her hot skin, but at last she was free of it and naked to the waist.

'Bend down.' From somewhere Sister Mercy had produced a thin and whippy birch rod. She must have brought it with her to Chapter, in confident hope that she would get her revenge.

Emma bowed over, clenching her teeth, determined to make no sound. She clutched her knees to steady herself. However severe the beating, she would not fall to the ground.

The birch descended with a sound like ripping cloth and pain like fire burned into Emma's back. She could not suppress an involuntary gasp, but she would not cry out. Again the whip struck. Again. And again.

It was over.

Somehow she managed to pull her habit up over her back. There was blood running down it, soaking into the folds where her rope girdle gathered the cloth together at her waist. The rough fabric clawed at the raw flesh of her back.

'You are dismissed,' the abbess said.

Emma turned slowly, finding that the Chapter House dipped and swayed around her. Everything seemed to have drawn very far away, the edges of the carved stonework shimmering like water, the nuns' faces blurred and unrecognisable. Only Sister Mercy's face was clear. Emma stared at her, and the woman took a pace back, but the novice made no move toward her. The door was there. She had only to walk through the door. It was becoming impossible to breathe here. Emma walked to the door, fumbled for the latch, and then she was through.

Chapter Two

Having promised Jordain that I would approach Warden Durant of Merton, I made my way along the High the next morning, soon after settling my two scriveners to their tasks. Despite the weather, hot and heavy, the work of the shop could not be deferred for more than one day. Walter Blunt was engaged in recording our current stock of secondhand books in the ledger, while Roger Pigot would continue to add the final colours to the illustrations for the collection of traditional tales he had copied from one of the books I had bought a few weeks ago from Widow Preston of Banbury. The original book had been cobbled together from an assortment of small books, differing in size and quality. Ours would be a great improvement on this original, written on good quality parchment, with a full page illumination at the start of each tale.

Roger's penmanship was precise and careful, and if his illustrations had any fault, it was because they also were precise and careful. They would do very well for my prospective buyer, an elderly gentleman possessed of a small manor over near Witney. What they lacked was the freedom, the originality, and the joyous observation to be found in the work of Emma Thorgold.

As I turned down Magpie Lane and headed toward Merton, I considered the possibility of commissioning more work from her. The approach would need to be made through Abbess de Streteley. Sometime within the next few days I would ride out to Godstow and seek a meeting with the abbess, purely on a matter of business. The great abbesses may live cloistered, but they manage estates quite as large and demanding as those of any secular lord, and like secular lords they must learn to handle complex matters of property and finance. I would put it to her as a profitable transaction – book production which would bring an income for the abbey merely at the expense of the novice's time. I was unlikely to have the opportunity of seeing Sister Benedicta, but if the abbess approved the plan, it would be necessary for me to consult the novice about the work in future.

It must needs be work of a religious nature – prayer books, Psalters, books of hours, meditations, and lives of the saints – though I smiled to think what the gifted novice would have made of secular material, like the illustrations for Roger's book of famous tales. That could be no more than a fanciful dream, for the abbey could not be expected to provide books of a worldly nature, even those with an uplifting moral.

However, I would have no difficulty in finding purchasers for religious books of the quality Emma Thorgold would produce. Since the Great Pestilence, most men's minds had veered off in one of two irreconcilable directions. Some had been terrified into intense religious observance, hoping by their prayers and their gifts to religious foundations to ward off another visitation of all-consuming death as terrible as the one we had endured four years ago. Others had lost all faith in a merciful God, for how could such a Deity have slain so mercilessly, cutting down the innocent as indiscriminately as the sinful? Why trouble to lead a virtuous life here on earth, when there was no prospect of eternal life hereafter in a blissful Heaven under a benign God?

The pious would provide themselves eagerly with holy books. However, there were stories whispered abroad that those who had abandoned God had turned to the Evil One, burning religious works and reciting the Mass backwards, amongst other vile practices, yet I could not believe any such existed in Oxford. A town of the learned might become pompous and complacent, but it was surely not so misguided as to turn aside on such a devilish path.

I frowned. How had my thoughts strayed into these dark regions? I clung to my own faith in a loving Christ, although the death of my wife had come near to shattering it. For the sake of my children I must live, and pray, and believe that goodness still survived in our torn and broken world. Although the dead no longer lay in the streets or in houses marked with black crosses, the memory could never be quite wiped out from those of us who had lived through it.

My errand to Merton today was an assertion that goodness did indeed survive, if I could persuade Warden Durant to come to the aid of the Farringdon family. I must shake off the dark thoughts which still ambushed me unawares and concentrate on what must be done now, today, in this present world which we were trying to rebuild.

The porter at Merton sent his boy to enquire whether the Warden was free to receive me, and he returned with an invitation to me to join Master Durant in his private lodgings. The last time I had come here was to return the precious and ancient Irish Psalter, the college's greatest treasure. Now I came empty-handed, to ask, as I put it to Warden Durant, a favour in return.

'I am not sure whether you were aware of William Farringdon's family circumstances, Master Durant,' I said. 'Following the death of his father, shortly after Christmas, William was left as the sole support of his mother, his young sister, and the orphaned daughter of his brother, who had died, like so many, of the plague.'

'You mentioned,' he said, 'that young Farringdon had undertaken to copy the Psalter in order to earn enough to support his mother until he took up his Fellowship.'

'Exactly,' I said, relieved that he had provided me with a way to introduce my request. 'Once he had entered into his Fellowship here, he would have been able to support them. Not lavishly, but adequately. His mother was gently born, but unassuming. There is no other male relative.'

I decided to avoid mention of the former brother-in-law.

'After William was murdered by a Fellow of this college, his family was left destitute.'

He stirred uncomfortably at the mention of murder, but I had no intention of sparing him the truth.

'It seems to me,' I said, 'that Merton has an obligation to the young man's family, since a member of this college deprived him of life and his mother of a son on whom she was dependent.'

'I cannot see where your argument is taking us, Master Elyot,' he said, somewhat stiffly. 'The college was hardly a party to the killing.'

'No indeed.' I inclined my head in acknowledgement. 'However, it would be an act of mercy, of justice even, to make some provision for them.'

'Times are hard, Master Elyot. Since the Great Pestilence, the income from our endowments of land has shrunk to barely more than half. Villein labour on our manors is in short supply. Many of our tenants are either dead or without their own labourers. The college can barely meet its own needs.'

All very well, I thought. A sad story. It does not hide the fact that Merton has been able to buy up much abandoned property, both in Oxford and elsewhere.

I made a sympathetic noise, but kept these thoughts to myself.

'William's family are homeless,' I said, 'having been turned out of their farm by their overlord, as they are unable any longer to pay the rent in labour and coin. They wish to make their home in Oxford and find some respectable means of earning a living. What they need here is a house, and preferably a house on which they need pay no rent. Now I know that Merton has been able to purchase a number of houses and shops throughout Oxford. Might there be one which you could make available to them, rent free? It would be an act of charity, and a great kindness in memory of a young scholar who would have found his future here among you.'

Master Durant shuffled a pile of papers on his desk, avoiding my eye, and said nothing for some minutes.

'I believe there is a house in St Mildred Street,' he said finally, 'for which we have not yet found a tenant. There is some work still to be done on it. I understand that the roof requires repair and some of the shutters are broken. Most of the properties we have been able to rent have a shop attached, but this one does not. I assume that Mistress Farringdon would have no objection to the lack of a shop?'

'I am sure she would not,' I said, pleased that he seemed to be agreeing so readily. 'But these repairs? The college would undertake them before making the house available?'

'I will need to consult the bursar,' he said. 'We have a considerable programme of work in hand here in the college.'

'They will need to move very soon. It does not sound as though these repairs will take long. Might the house be ready, perhaps, in a week's time? And it will be rent free?'

'As for the repairs, I will need to consult the bursar,' he repeated. 'But I believe we could allow Mistress Farringdon to have the house without rent. I am as aware as you are, Master Elyot, that Merton has in a sense an obligation to the young man's family. I will speak to the bursar and send you word as to when the house will be ready for occupation.'

'I am grateful for your kindness,' I said, 'as I know Mistress Farringdon will be. Most grateful. Where in St Mildred Street is the house?'

'South of Exeter College,' he said. 'Two doors this side of St Mildred's Church. It is a modest house, two storeys, but with a substantial garden behind. That is much overgrown and neglected, I fear, for the house has been uninhabited since the Pestilence. I am afraid I cannot spare any servants to tend the garden.'

I could hardly expect more. Perhaps Jordain could set some of his students to work. I thanked him again, and made my way out of the college with a lighter heart than when I had entered it. Just beyond the gatehouse, I encountered Philip Olney, *librarius* of Merton. We greeted each other warily. Since our encounters in the spring we had observed a neutral attitude to each other. I knew much about Olney which could damage him, should I make it public. I had no mind to do so, but I think he was not quite sure of my silence and discretion.

'Were you looking for me?' he asked. Fair enough question, for I often sold him books for the college collection.

'Not today. I have been with the Warden.'

I saw him stiffen. He was still anxious.

'I have been seeking some help for William Farringdon's family,' I said, to reassure him. 'Merton is to let them have a house in St Mildred Street, as they are coming to live in Oxford.'

'I know the house. Be sure that it is made watertight. It is damp and draughty. Not the best of our properties.'

'The Warden has promised to see to the repairs.' That was not quite what the Warden had said, but I chose to take the more optimistic view. 'As for the rest, I expect many will be glad to lend a hand to make all comfortable for them – a woman, a young girl and a small child. All who can help will be welcome. All.'

Olney was not entirely without blame in the affair which had cost William Farringdon his life. I gave him a knowing glance, at which he looked alarmed, but without further words I bade him good-day. As I walked away back to the High Street, I contained my laughter. It would be good to see Philip Olney, who was somewhat too fussy about his person, clutching a brush loaded with lime wash in his hand.

On my way home I decided to see for myself this house the Warden was prepared to make available for

Mistress Farringdon and the girls, so I headed west along the High, and between All Saints Church and the Mitre Inn I turned up St Mildred Street. This narrow lane, hardly deserving of the name 'street', led directly north past St Mildred's Church and the newly built Exeter College to reach the town wall at a postern known as the 'twirling gate'. Similar to the lych gates leading into some churchyards, it was a turnstile which permitted the passage of pedestrians, but of no animal larger than a dog. Horses and carts must use one of the larger gates to pass through the wall, and it also served to keep stray cattle out of the town. Some called the gate 'the hole in the wall', reckoning it not truly a gate, but it was useful for those who did not want to walk as far as the North Gate.

Two doors this side of the church, the Warden had said. There was no mistaking it. Timber framed, like many Oxford houses, this one was more ancient than many, its jettied upper storey dipping somewhat perilously to the left, the window frames skewed out of true. As the Warden had said, the shutters were missing – all of those on the ground floor, probably stolen for firewood, only one gone from the upper floor, where they were more difficult to reach, but the rest broken or hanging askew. The windows were unglazed. The street was too narrow for me to stand back and assess the state of the roof. The plaster laid over the wattle and daub, which filled the spaces between the timbers, had fallen away in some quite large patches, and could not have been given a fresh coat of lime wash for ten years at least.

The house huddled close against the buildings on either side, a cordwainer on the right, to judge by the ancient boot hung up for a sign. On the left, it must be a herbalist or apothecary, indicated by a newly painted sign depicting a mortar and pestle. Standing as it did between two shops, it was curious that the house had no shop front itself. Perhaps at some time in the past it had served to accommodate a large family from one of the adjacent shops, too large to fit into what must be their very small living space.

I noticed that the door was not quite closed and gave it a gentle push. The rusty hinges squealed in protest, but the door swung grudgingly open and I stepped through. What greeted me was not unexpected in a house that had stood empty for four or five years. It was surprising that Merton had done nothing to restore it, but perhaps the college had concentrated all its resources on the properties which had the best chance of attracting a tenant. The apothecary's shop looked fresh and neat; perhaps it was another recent acquisition by Merton.

The ground floor of the house consisted of two rooms, that at the front for daily living, and behind it a kitchen, which was squalid and filthy. The floor throughout was strewn with dead leaves which had drifted in through the unshuttered windows, and in one corner of the front room there was a pile of ragged brychans hopping with fleas and a sack part-filled with straw, indicating that at some time recently a vagrant had bedded down here. The hearth in the kitchen possessed a rusty grate and a hook to suspend a cookpot, but nothing else. In the far corner a stair which was hardly more than a ladder led to the upper rooms.

With some caution I climbed this, expecting at any moment to put my foot through rotten wood, but to my surprise I reached the upper floor unharmed. There were two rooms here, one facing the street, one overlooking the garden, both empty but showing stains on the floorboards where rain had leaked through the thatch of the roof. That was one repair the college must complete before anyone could live here.

From the room at the back I was able to look out over the rest of the messuage. There appeared to be a generous garden, but Durant's description of it as 'overgrown' seemed an understatement. Nettles as tall as a man's chest, interlaced with bindweed and sprinkled with thistles, flourished in the hot summer sun. It would be no simple task to bring that under control. No wonder the Warden had been in haste to declare that he could not spare servants for the garden. What was needed was a herd of very hungry goats to work their way through it all.

Downstairs again, I managed to push open the outside door from the kitchen, only to be met by this solid wall of vegetation. Well, that was not the first concern, which was, as Olney had said, to make the place weatherproof. The house did not feel damp at the moment, no doubt due to the summer heat, but as soon as it rained, or the season turned to autumn, it would be like living half outdoors.

There was not a scrap of furniture, nor even a dented cookpot or a broken cup, anywhere in the house. The former inhabitants, dead in the plague, must have owned possessions, however poor. Once the fear of contagion had passed, people had come here looting and taken every movable object, apart from that verminous bedding, which I suspected must be a fairly new addition or the fleas would have migrated to a more promising home. I was tempted to carry it into the garden and set fire to it, but that was a task for Merton.

Out in St Mildred Street again I stood and surveyed the house. No doubt it had once been a pleasant enough home, though small, but a great deal needed to be done before the Farringdons could move in. I wondered whether they had any furniture, something which had not occurred to me before.

'Partial success,' I said to Jordain, who was supervising the work of his somewhat reluctant students. 'Warden Durant has agreed to let the Farringdons have a house in St Mildred Street, rent free.'

He jumped up. 'Excellent news! I was sure that you could persuade him, Nicholas.'

'He did not take a great deal of persuading,' I said dryly. 'It is half derelict and they have been unable to find a tenant for it, since there is no shop. Some flea-infested beggar has been sleeping there. Behind the building there is not so much a garden as an impenetrable forest. There are holes in the roof, no shutters downstairs, and I think if Margaret were to see what I assume is meant to be a kitchen, she would faint clean away.'

'Oh.' He sat down again.

'However.' I did not want to discourage him too much. 'I think the college can be prevailed upon to mend the roof and shutters. There is, of course, neither glass nor horn in the windows. The building is far too humble. Warden Durant did not mention the poor state of the plaster on the outside walls, but I think we might insist that it should be restored. Otherwise the building will fall into greater ruin, which surely they cannot want. As for the rest, I think we might muster a few friends to clean the place and apply some lime wash to the inside walls.'

I looked at the two students, who were listening with interest to this distraction from their studies.

'Perhaps if these lads apply themselves diligently to their work, you might allow them time away from their books to help.'

They both looked hopefully at Jordain, who could read the intention behind my words as clearly as if I had spoken it.

'I might consider it,' he said solemnly, 'but only if you do indeed work hard.' He gave them a severe look. 'We shall see. When will the college carry out the repairs, do you think?'

'I intend to send a note round to the Warden today, describing what I have observed, particularly of the plaster work. My impression was that he had not seen the house himself, but merely been given a description of it by the bursar or their master of works. Merton is well supplied with skilled craftsmen, they are forever building. If they will but turn their minds to the work I am sure that it could be completed within a week.'

'Good,' he said. 'Do you write to the Warden urging his first attention to this, and I will write to Mistress Farringdon, to explain that there will be a house for them, once certain repairs are carried out.'

'Do you know whether they possess any furniture and household goods?' I asked. 'The house is empty. Not so much as a cookpot.'

'Surely they must. They have been driven from their home, but their goods cannot have been seized, unless there was money owing to their lord.' He frowned. 'They will require a carter to fetch all to Oxford. Do you think I should–?'

'I am sure Mistress Farringdon is more than capable of managing that,' I said hastily, envisaging Jordain rushing about distractedly, trying to supervise the move. 'And if she is not, that daughter of hers is a fine manager, I am sure. Leave them to arrange their move. We shall be busy enough here, making the house fit to be lived in.'

'You will help?'

'Of course. And I have as good as recruited Philip Olney.'

'Philip Olney?' He gaped at me. 'Are you mad?'

'Not at all. Do you not recall that trim little house where he keeps his mistress and his son, out beyond the East Gate?' I laughed. 'I am sure he will be more than willing to lend a hand, with a little persuasion.'

❧❦

Emma lay face down on her hard bed in the dortoir. Left alone except for Jocosa, she had wept, but her tears were dry now. She was exhausted and numb with pain. On leaving the Chapter House she had come straight here and no one had followed her. Dimly through her misery she had heard the bells to summon all to the services in the abbey church, but she had not stirred. She had eaten no dinner and had not attended her lessons with Sister Mercy. Instead she seemed to exist in a world cut off from the abbey and all its people. Perhaps she would stay here and never move again.

The daylight was beginning to fade when she became aware of a soft step on the night stairs, leading up from the church, not because she was listening but because Jocosa, under her embracing arm, suddenly sat up, tense.

'Sister Benedicta?'

It was no more than a whisper, but she knew the voice. Madlen Sewtry, the oldest of the schoolgirls, near in age to Emma and due to be married in the autumn to some friend of the family.

Emma turned her face toward the door, but did not lift her head from the thin pillow, which had been sodden earlier but had now nearly dried.

'Madlen,' she said dully.

'I've stolen some salve from the infirmary,' Madlen said. 'Will you let me treat your back?'

'If you wish.' Then, thinking that sounded ungracious, 'Thank you. That would be kind of you. You will face trouble, if they discover you have stolen it.'

Madlen shrugged. ''Tis no matter. Me they cannot beat.'

She spoke no more than the truth. Coming from one of the great families in the shire, she was always treated with nervous respect on the part of the nuns. The schoolgirls, although handled firmly, were not subject to the same discipline as the novices.

Madlen knelt down beside the bed and drew a small pot out of the breast of her gown. Peering at Emma's naked back in the dim light she let out a soft cry. 'Oh, this is cruel, Sister Benedicta. How could they treat you so? It was not so terrible, what you did. You had completed the work Sister Mercy had set us.'

'My name is Emma,' she said, and clamped her teeth together.

Madlen had no answer for that. 'I will be as careful as I can, but I fear this will hurt.'

At the first touch, Emma let out her breath in a hiss, but managed to hold back the cry which rose to her lips. Madlen worked carefully, spreading the salve generously over Emma's whole back, and after a few minutes it brought some relief from the fiery pain. When she had finished, Madlen perched on the end of the bed and wiped her fingers carelessly on her skirt.

'Will you take your final vows next month, when Sister Ursula does?'

'Nay,' Emma said shortly.

'But how can you avoid? You have been a novice more than a year now.'

'They cannot force me.'

'Can they not? I do not know what powers the abbess has, but if your family placed you here, with the wish that you should become a nun–'

'It was not my family,' Emma said grimly. 'It was my stepfather, after my mother died. He is no kin of mine.'

'But he is a man, so he must have the right.'

Emma shook her head, as best she could, lying flat on her stomach.

'I do not know the details of the law, but I am certain that no one can be forced into vows they refuse to take.'

Madlen sighed. 'I wish you could come home with me, but I shall be married almost at once, and I do not know my husband's mind well enough.'

'You are kind, Madlen, but I must find my own way out of this tangle.'

'You cannot stay a novice forever. You do not want to become a nun. Could you move into the guest hall, where the visitors live, and the great ladies who retire here?'

Emma shuddered, then laughed. 'That is not the life I seek, Madlen. Besides, I have no money to buy myself a place as a guest. I must leave.'

'But how? Where will you go? What will you do? Have you no other kin?'

'I have an aunt, my mother's sister. William's mother. Do you remember my cousin William, who used to visit me here?'

'I remember. That was terrible, what happened to

him. It was an evil thing. But could you not go to his mother? Surely she would be glad of you, now she has lost her son.'

'Nay, she is penniless. I should be a burden to her. But I cannot stay here. Somehow I will escape. What I shall do thereafter, I do not know.'

From the church came the sound of the bell ringing for Vespers.

'Will you come to service?' Madlen said. 'I can help you with your habit.'

'Nay. Hold me excused. I thank you for your care, Madlen.'

'Do not do anything rash.' She reached out and touched Emma's hand.

'I promise that I shall do nothing without careful thought. Now you must hurry or you will be late for Vespers.'

As Madlen's steps died away, Emma struggled to sit up, although she was stiff from lying in one position for so long, and movement tugged the skin at the raw weals on her back. The other girl had descended by the outside stairs, for if she had entered the church from the night stairs it would have been clear that she came from the dortoir, where she had no business to be at this time of day. Sitting on the edge of the bed, Emma felt weak and dizzy. She had eaten nothing since the piece of bread and beaker of small ale permitted in the morning, and the beating had left her as feeble as a kitten. Jocosa jumped off the bed and whined.

Emma leaned down to stroke her, and gasped as the skin on her back broke from the half dried scabs. 'I'm sorry, little one. You have had nothing to eat, have you? There is no need for you to suffer. While they are all at Vespers, we will see what we can find for you.'

With infinite care, she eased her arms into her habit and tied the strings at the neck. The rough cloth chafed her back, but Madlen's salve gave her some ease. She slipped her feet into her sandals and quietly descended the outside stairs, closely followed by a hopeful Jocosa.

In the kitchen the abbey servants would be preparing the supper, to be eaten after Vespers. With luck it might be possible to beg something for herself and the dog and retreat to the dortoir again before the service in church was ended.

Emma was known to the kitchen servants, for she regularly fetched food for Jocosa, and today it seemed that word of her beating had spread even to here, for the senior cook, a stout and matronly woman called Edith, greeted her with cries of sympathy.

'Come and sit you down here, my pet,' she said. 'Here's a good pottage you may eat this minute, if you do not mind our rough ways here in the kitchen. And little Jocosa shall have her share too.'

Edith worked under the kitcheness, Sister Theresa, but fortunately she would now be attending Vespers with the other nuns. The heat in the abbey kitchen was overpowering, for the two great hearths were heaped high with logs for the cooking, and all the servants were as scarlet in the face as a full-blown rose. From time to time one would rush to the water barrel and dip up a ladleful to drink. Emma wondered how they could endure to work in this heat, but was glad of the chance to eat here, away from the company of the nuns who had watched her humiliation in the morning.. Edith placed a steaming bowl of pottage in front of her, and put a shallow saucer of the same to cool for Jocosa.

'Fresh bread here,' she said, pushing it across the table, and cutting a slice as though she thought that Emma was too fragile to do it for herself.

'I thank you,' Emma said quietly, suddenly feeling a desire to weep. The company of these simple men and women seemed to her far kinder and more Christian than the assembly gathered in the Chapter House, where no single voice had been raised in objection to her beating. Sister Mercy was not liked, yet none had shown the courage to oppose her.

Although she had come mainly to find food for her

dog, she realised that she was hungry herself, spooning up the pottage gratefully, and soaking up the last of it with a crust of bread. Although the strict Rule banned meat for all but those in the infirmary, this clause in the Rule was barely observed, though meat was never served on fish days. Today the evening pottage was thick and substantial, mutton with onions from last autumn's harvest, and the cabbage and carrots newly gathered from the vegetable garden. When Edith ladled a further portion into her bowl, Emma did not object.

Amid all her misery and shame, she had begun to think coldly what she must do. If she was to escape from the abbey before she was forced to make her final vows, she must plan carefully. It would be foolish to attract attention and punishment again, so she must be quiet, obedient, and submissive. Having nowhere to go, she knew that life in the world outside would be difficult, even dangerous, until she could find herself a position, perhaps as a servant.

It would be easier to lose herself amongst the populace of a town, rather than stay here in the country. Oxford was nearest. Perhaps there would be work there. Her ideas were vague, for she had never before needed to fend for herself, but women worked in towns, did they not? They were alewives and bakers, they wove cloth, made cheese. If her year at Godstow had benefitted her in no other way, it had at least taught her some of these domestic skills, for Benedictine nuns were expected to lead a practical as well as a prayerful life. So if she were to undertake a future of physical labour, she must now eat well and grow strong, although it would take some time to recover from the beating.

Time was passing. The service of Vespers would end shortly. Already the servants were carrying the large serving bowls through to the frater for the nuns' supper. Emma thanked Edith, gave Jocosa another slice of bread and tucked one into the breast of her habit. As it was nearing mid summer, the sky was still light as she hurried across the courtyard to the dortoir stairs.

Clothing, she thought. I cannot leave the abbey and make my way to Oxford wearing a Benedictine habit. I must obtain secular clothing. That would be almost as difficult as passing out through the walls, walls which had enclosed her ever since she had been brought here early the previous summer, escorted by her stepfather's men. The steward, handing her over to Abbess de Streteley, had claimed the need for an armed escort in case of outlaws living wild in the wooded lands through which they had travelled, but Emma knew otherwise.

Back in the dortoir she hid the slice of bread under her pillow to share with Jocosa later, slipped her feet out of her sandals, and lay on her bed again face down. It would be days before she dared to lie on her back.

When her stepfather, Falkes Malaliver, had announced that he was sending her to a nunnery, she had pleaded to be allowed instead to join her aunt's family. Their circumstances had been very different then. Her uncle was still alive and in possession of his pension, which not only supported his family but paid the wages of a manager to do the work he could not do himself, and which had formerly been done by his elder son. William had been about to come home for the summer then, before starting his final year as a student. Even last year there had been the prospect of a college Fellowship for him. Her aunt's family would have welcomed her, so why – she demanded – banish her to a nunnery? She had no vocation for the monastic life. She would, she declared, refuse to take the vows. At that, her stepfather had struck her in the face and warned her that she must do his bidding. Her lip had bled, where her teeth had been driven into it.

'I will make certain,' he said, 'that Godstow keeps you in fast hold. You will not so easily slip through their fingers.'

It had made no sense to her then, and although her aunt's life had changed drastically during the last year, at the time it had seemed a solution beneficial to all. Her stepfather would be rid of her (which he clearly desired), she would be happy living with her aunt's family, and they would welcome her, as they had always welcomed her, from the time she was a small child. Perhaps William might have been stopped from agreeing to copy Merton's Psalter.

She felt the tears well up again in her eyes, remembering how things might have been. Ever since the beating she seemed to weep uncontrollably at the slightest provocation. She must not let the other novices, who slept at this end of the dortoir, see her weeping. Angrily, she wiped her eyes on the sleeve of her habit. She must retain her pride. By the time novices, schoolgirls, and nuns came to the dortoir, she was asleep. When the bell rang at midnight for Matins, Emma did not stir, even when Sister Ursula poked her, none too gently, in the ribs.

The next morning, however, Emma rose for Prime. Washed hands and face in the lavatorium, freeing her cheeks from the salt stiffening of dried tears, and fell into the procession in her allotted place. During her prayers, if she did not seek forgiveness for her misbehaviour, but help for her intended escape, no one might have detected it from her humble and demure appearance.

All that day she went about her duties quietly and unobtrusively, worked in the heat of the laundry without complaint, and bowed her head submissively when Sister Mercy scolded her without cause during the novices' lessons. A slanting glance caught the nun's triumphant smile, but even then Emma did not reveal by so much as a set mouth that she had noticed.

Matters continued quietly for another two days, and then Sister Clemence fetched Emma at the end of lessons.

'Mother Abbess wishes to see you, Sister Benedicta,' she said. 'You are to come with me now.'

Emma followed the abbess's private secretary and personal assistant, with her angular heron's gait, from the cloister and across the courtyard to the abbess's lodging, a substantial stone-built house of two storeys and a garret, which would not have disgraced a member of the minor nobility. Sister Clemence led her to the abbess's study and withdrew, closing the door quietly behind her.

Abbess de Streteley was seated behind a large desk loaded with papers and books, but Emma did not look at her. She stood quietly with downcast eyes, her hands clasped at her waist, hidden under the fall of the wide sleeves of her habit.

'Well, Sister Benedicta,' the abbess said, 'I hope your chastisement has taught you better conduct, and that you will not wilfully disobey the mistress of the novices again.'

Her voice was clear and steady, somewhat deep for a woman. It carried no overtones of censure or of satisfaction.

'I stand corrected, Reverend Mother,' Emma said. She did not raise her eyes. The abbess was shrewd and experienced. She might have read something there which did not accord with the humble words.

'You will be well aware,' the abbess continued, 'that you have now served your novitiate for somewhat more than the customary twelve months. It is time that you made your final vows. You and Sister Ursula will profess in three weeks' time.'

Within her sleeves, Emma clenched her hands together. No more than three weeks to complete her plans.

'Mother,' she softly, and with every appearance of a submissive novice, 'I do not believe I have a vocation for the monastic life. I have dwelt amongst you this twelve month. I have kept the offices dutifully, and I have prayed for God's guidance, but I have not been called. I believe my future must lie outside these walls.'

She risked looking up. Abbess de Streteley was regarding with an unfathomable expression.

'I am afraid, Sister,' she said, 'that you have no choice. You have been placed here by your father as an offering to God. Whatever your will, the terms on which you were placed here cannot be overturned.'

This was something which had never before been mentioned in Emma's hearing, and the words fell upon her like the sudden shock of icy water.

'But, Mother,' she said, startled out of her humble pose, 'Falkes Malaliver is not my father. And I was brought here at the age of seventeen, far too old to be offered as an *oblata*, a gift to God.'

She found that she was shaking. Oblates, children given to the monastic life as infants, could not escape, but surely, nearly a woman grown, she was none such.

'Very well,' the abbess said patiently, 'as you wish. He is your *stepfather*, but he is your legal guardian. He signed the papers which gave you to us. I have them here.'

She laid her hand on them, its long elegant fingers quite unadorned except for the simple gold ring which marked her marriage to Christ. Emma fixed her eyes on it. She knew that Sister Ursula longed passionately for her own ring to be slipped on to her finger, and in her fervent moments babbled about her marriage in terms that Emma found repellent. As if a human woman, alive now, could consummate a physical marriage with a Man and a God crucified more than thirteen hundred years ago.

She dragged her mind back from the horror that ring represented to her.

'I signed nothing, Reverend Mother, nor was my consent to this arrangement ever asked.'

'Neither your signature nor your consent was required. Your stepfather acted in your name.'

Emma could feel the blood rising from her neck and flushing her cheeks, as though the very flesh had been set afire. Between them, her hated stepfather and this abbess had treated her with as little regard as if she were a parcel of land or a gift to the abbey of new candle sticks. Why? She had never understood why Falkes Malaliver had been so immovably set on shutting her away in Godstow, but here was an entirely new puzzle. Why had the abbess agreed to it? She had always found Agnes de Streteley fair minded if strict. What could have induced her to accept a reluctant girl of marriageable age as an *oblata*? The custom of taking infant oblates into the monastic system was in order to rear them innocent of the secular world, entirely devoted for their entire lives to the Rule and the service of God, although even some senior men of the Church had come to frown on the practice. A seventeen-year-old oblate was an anathema, a mockery of the whole concept.

She was not sure how long she stood, staring at the abbess, as these rebellious thoughts raced through her head, but at last she clenched her hands together all the more fiercely and managed to assume a look of resignation. Whether the abbess detected its falsity, she could not tell.

'So be it,' she said dully. 'Three weeks, you say, Mother?'

'Three weeks.' The abbess looked relieved. Clearly she was expecting more of an outcry, but Emma had herself in hand now.

'You may return to your duties, Sister Benedicta.'

'Thank you, Mother.'

Emma made her reverence and walked quietly from the room, the very image of a dutiful novice, soon to be a fully professed nun.

Out in the court, she drew a deep breath. More than ever, now, she must maintain her pretence of obedience. But before the three weeks had passed, she would leave this prison for ever.

Chapter Three

There was this to be said for Warden Durant: when he decided upon an action, he wasted no time about it. What passed between him and his college bursar, I cannot say, but, the day after I had first seen the house in St Mildred Street, workmen were already busy about the place. The old thatch was combed free of birds' nests and other rubbish, and new thatch, still golden from the field, laid over it. The shutters on the upper floor were repaired and new shutters fixed to the windows on the ground floor. By the time, three days later, that Jordain had rounded up half a dozen students to help clean the inside of the house, a plasterer was at work on the street front, chipping away the old rotten plaster before he could lay on a new coat. The frontage would have an odd blotchy appearance until the new plaster dried enough to be lime washed, but the house would at least be watertight. For the moment that was not a serious concern, since the hot dry weather continued without remission.

Jordain had secured the services not only of his two failed students who were staying on at Hart Hall, but also of three others who lived near Oxford, together with a former student of his who had taken a position as a clerk in the Guildhall. Like most young men, these six were a great deal happier in the dirt and rough work of repairing the house than in poring over their texts, at any rate while this fine summer weather lasted and they had no wish to be confined to their studies.

It had not been necessary to carry out my threat to recruit Philip Olney.

Merton's acquisitions in Oxford, I discovered, were even more numerous than I had realised, and the college's wealth would certainly prove of advantage to the Farringdons. Probably the advancement of Merton's fortunes was due to the shrewdness and decisiveness of William Durant, so that the college now found itself in a situation much to be envied by the other colleges of the university. Durant's predecessor, Robert Trenge, had survived the plague himself, but had watched the swathe which Death cut through his students and Fellows with growing despair. Already elderly, and a gentle, quiet man, he had become a near recluse, turning his back on life and spending much of his time on his knees, where one day he had simply failed to rise.

Appointed Warden in 1351, William Durant had taken the college in hand, seizing the opportunities offered in the aftermath of the Great Pestilence to buy up properties cheaply in Oxford and in other parts of England. However much he might protest about the lack of villeins to work the land, Merton was well placed to build its fortunes for the future. Between them, Warden and bursar kept a close watch over the college purse. I had been more fortunate than I expected in persuading Master Durant to grant Mistress Farringdon a rent-free house, but it was clear that the more desirable properties in the town had already found paying tenants.

Jordain's students worked hard and willingly on the interior of the house, although it must have been unfamiliar labour for them. Most were drawn from the families of minor gentry, from homes where all manual labour was carried out by servants. What they lacked in skill, they made up for in enthusiasm, and after three days of somewhat chaotic effort, the house had been swept clean and every inside wall enthusiastically covered with lime wash, much of which had found its way on to the clothes and persons of these gentlemen labourers.

'All that is needed now is furnishings,' Jordain said, surveying his students' work with satisfaction the next morning. 'I wrote to Mistress Farringdon as soon as you had the promise of a house, and she responded that the farmer with whom they are lodging will bring them and their goods in his cart once all is ready. I think I may send word now.'

'Aye,' I said, 'I think you may.'

Although the land behind the house was still a wilderness, apart from a narrow path cut through the nettles to the well, the house itself had been transformed from the filthy hovel I had first seen. Although it was small, it should suit the three of them very well. The hearth was now fit for cooking, after one of the boys had poked a broomstick up the chimney and brought down several birds' nests and a barrelful of soot.

'One bed chamber will serve for Mistress Farringdon, the other for the girls,' I said. 'The downstairs room at the front is large enough for everyday living. What I do not know,' I added, 'is what means they will have for living.'

'Let us settle them in a home of their own,' he said, 'and then they may take stock.'

This was an optimistic view, for they might not have long to take stock before the need for an income became urgent, but I thought my sister Margaret might well be of more help to Mistress Farringdon than the two of us.

Having surveyed the completed work on the house, we locked the door, a new lock and key having been provided by Merton, and Jordain turned to walk up past St Mildred's church.

'Do you go my way?' he said.

'Aye, I shall take my dinner at home, then I am going to ride out the Godstow.'

As we turned along Brasenose Lane and past the Hall from which it took its name, he gave me an amused glance.

'Surely you have no more business there?'

'Business indeed I have. I am going to see Abbess de Streteley, to propose the production of more illuminated books, like the one I showed you. Their novice has the skills, I have the buyers, and the abbey will benefit from the sales. I am sure she will find the proposal attractive.'

'You may also take the opportunity to tell Sister Benedicta that her aunt will shortly be here in Oxford.'

'I think it unlikely that I shall see Sister Benedicta,' I said stiffly. 'All I intend is a meeting with the abbess. However, I will leave word for the novice of her aunt's arrival.'

'I am sure she will be glad to know that her kin will be safely housed, and not too far away to make an occasional visit to Godstow.'

'It would not be easy for them. Too far to walk, and I doubt they will have the means to hire horses. Though I suppose carts must travel there from Oxford with supplies for the abbey.'

'Perhaps they go by boat, up the Thames,' he said.

'Indeed they may.'

We had reached St Mary's Passage, where we parted, Jordain to head for Hart Hall on the corner of Hammer Hall Lane, I to turn down past St Mary's to the High Street and my home.

Early in the afternoon I hired my usual mount from the Mitre Inn, a chestnut gelding called Rufus, and set off through the North Gate on the way to Godstow. There was the usual crowd hampering the passage through the gate, augmented today by a group of people shouting protests outside the door which led to the town prison, an unpretentious lockup which consisted of two rooms over the gate. This was generally used to confine aggressive or incapable drunks, or youths caught brawling in the streets. More serious criminals were held with greater security in the castle. From all I could gather, as I forced my way through to the gate, the offenders in this instance were two lads who had smashed each other's faces the previous night outside an alehouse in Fish Street. Their separate partisan bands were now close to coming to blows themselves, so I was glad to escape into the wider reaches of St Giles.

By horse it does not take long to reach Godstow Abbey, but in such hot weather I had no mind to exhaust Rufus by going at more than a walking pace, and I was in no great hurry. My meeting with the abbess – if she would agree to see me – would not take long, so I could be back again in time to close up the shop for the evening. The trees along St Giles drooped in the heat, reminding me that our kitchen garden would need watering if the crops of vegetables were not to wither and perish. There had been no rain for at least three weeks, which might not augur well for the farmers.

The straggle of houses that stretched out from Oxford along St Giles dwindled away as I reached the Woodstock Road. There the road grew narrower, the trees taller, providing some shade. On my left, beyond a scattering of small farms, some of which belonged to the colleges, I could see the gentle slope down to the water meadows and the occasional glint of sunlit water from the Thames. Jordain was right. It was likely that supplies would often be brought to the abbey along this stretch of the river, a reliable waterway except when frozen in winter or over-filled with spring floods. More reliable than the minor trackway which led off from this good road, passing through Wolvercote to the abbey. I had never ridden it in winter, but I could imagine that it became treacherous with clinging mud, slippery ice, and holes deep enough to break a horse's leg.

Today, however, the track was pleasant, especially as much of the way was a tunnel under overarching trees, providing the welcome of a cool green shade. Rufus plodded along, in no more hurry than I was. When the bridge to the abbey enclosure came in sight, he raised his head and quickened his step, as if he recognised it as our goal from previous visits here.

I dismounted and explained my business to John Barnes, the lay servant who was porter for the abbey.

'If the lady abbess can spare me half an hour,' I said,

'I should like to consult with her on a matter of business.'

Barnes knew very well that my three previous visits had been to Emma Thorgold, but if he thought my request to see the abbess surprising, he did not show it.

'If you will bide here in the gatehouse, Master Elyot,' he said, 'I will ask whether Abbess de Streteley is able to see you. You will find a tethering ring for your horse over there, in the shade. Better for the poor beast. I think sometimes they suffer from the heat more than we do. We have the understanding to know that it will end, but how can a mindless beast know that?'

With this piece of philosophy he took himself off.

'Never mind him,' I said to Rufus as I tethered him, as directed, in the shade. 'Mindless beast, indeed!'

Rufus blew a great gust of hay-scented breath in my face, as if in disgust, then dropped his head to sample some tussocks of juicy grass growing close under the abbey wall. I retreated to the cool of the stone-built gatehouse and waited until Barnes returned.

'The Reverend Mother will see you now,' he said, 'though she may not have a whole half hour. Her assistant, Sister Clemence, will come for you shortly.'

Sister Clemence and I were, by now, old if slight acquaintances. I wondered whether she would feel obliged to chaperone my meeting with the abbess as she had with the novice. I had no time to reflect on this, for she followed close on the porter's heels.

'Master Elyot,' she said, frowning slightly as she looked me up and down. 'Do I understand that you wish to see the Reverend Mother? Is this further matter concerning the death of William Farringdon?'

'It has no bearing on the death of William Farringdon,' I said carefully – although perhaps that death had led in a roundabout way to my being here. 'I wish to discuss with the Reverend Mother the production of holy books.'

'Books?' she said. 'I had forgot. You are a bookseller. You have a shop.'

She made it sound like a disease.

'That is correct,' I said politely. 'I both make and sell books. I have already purchased a book of hours made here in the abbey and I am interested in discussing the creation of more.'

I saw no harm in stating my business to Sister Clemence. It was clear that she was in the abbess's confidence, and I wanted to make it quite clear that I was not intent on seeing Emma, for that might mean trouble for her.

I was shown into a lofty, pleasant room whose wide window – glassed, I observed – was open onto the prospect of the abbess's private flower garden, from which scents, drawn up richly by the day-long sun, flowed pleasantly into the room. Agnes de Streteley rose briefly from behind her desk and acknowledged my presence with a gracious nod.

'Thank you, Sister Clemence,' she said, in tones of quiet dismissal. 'Please, Master Elyot, be seated.'

We both sat as Sister Clemence withdrew, closing the door behind her. It appeared that the abbess did not require a chaperone. Abbess de Streteley and I studied each other with interest. She was a woman perhaps in her late forties, not beautiful, but with a strong, intelligent face and sharp eyes which looked as though they would miss little in this world she ruled. I was encouraged. She seemed likely to listen attentively to what I had to say.

'Reverend Mother,' I said, aware that with this woman it would be wise to come straight to the point, 'you will no doubt recall that the abbey recently sent a book of hours to be bound in Oxford by Henry Stalbroke. With your agreement, I purchased the book. Now, I have a wide clientele for holy books, especially books of the same quality as that book of hours – members of the university, leading burgesses of the town, and the wealthy families for some miles around Oxford. I would like to suggest to you an arrangement between us. If Godstow's scriptorium could produce similar books of a devout nature – books of hours, Psalteries, lives of saints – bound by Henry Stalbroke with his usual skill, then I would be prepared to purchase them. It would provide a steady income for the abbey, in these days when tithes and rents from property have been blighted since the Pestilence.'

I was rather pleased with this final part of my proposal, which had but that moment occurred to me, reminded suddenly of Warden Durant's claims of collegiate poverty.

The abbess laid her hands palm to palm and rested her chin on the tips of long, elegant fingers. Not an act of prayer but a pose of shrewd calculation.

'Master Elyot, our scriptorium is small. Not many of the sisters are lettered, beyond the reading of abbey documents, church services and the words in the choir books. That is, they can read and write for all practical day-to-day needs, but have no skills in the elegant penmanship required for the copying of sacred books. We are more accustomed to augment the abbey's purse by selling our ecclesiastical embroideries to the great monasteries of our brethren.'

'I would not expect you to be able to provide many books,' I reassured her. 'One every few months, as finely written and illuminated as that first book of hours, and I could obtain a good price for you.'

She gave me a knowing look. She understood very well that I was aware Emma Thorgold was responsible for my book of hours.

'I should need to consult our precentrix and librarian, Sister Mildred. She would best be able to say whether we could provide what you wish. We have only three with the skills to create illuminated books, Sister Mildred herself, one of our senior nuns, and one of the novices, who is shortly to take her final vows. Unlike our brothers' monasteries, we do not habitually train our sisters in these skills. Needlework is considered a more suitable occupation.'

'But the copying of *holy* books–' I suggested modestly.

'Indeed, it can be a form of devotion, and turn the mind to thoughts of God. In the case of one of our scribes, it might prove salutary. She is in some turmoil of mind at present. Aye, that might be a useful occupation, to steady her in these last weeks.'

She laid her palms flat on the desk and gave a brisk nod.

'I think we might undertake to provide one book to you, for a start, and then we will decide how to proceed thereafter. I would not wish to enter into a more permanent arrangement until we have had time to consider further. Have you a preference? A life of St Frideswide, perhaps, as patron saint of Oxford?'

This would have very limited appeal, but I smiled encouragingly.

'Such a life would be excellent, but what I know many people desire heartily these days is a book of hours. While a saint's life makes for inspirational reading, a book of hours is a personal means of daily devotion. Even quite simple people long to own one. Such a one as I know you can produce here would be fit for one of our noble families.'

I was not flattering her, I truly meant what I said, and I think she understood that.

'Very well. I will instruct Sister Benedicta at once to make a start on a book of hours. I am sure you are aware that it was she who made the other.'

We both rose. I understood that I was being dismissed.

'If you wish,' I said, 'I can supply you with the parchment and colours.'

'I thank you, but I believe we have sufficient.'

'In that case, I will leave matters in your hands, Reverend Mother. At some point, in a few weeks, perhaps, I should like to view the progress of the work.'

'I expect that can be arranged.'

I knew from her tone that she meant I might see the pages, but not the scribe, though I was sure I would be able to insist on consulting Sister Benedicta.

We had reached the door and she was about to bow me out when I turned, as though I had only just remembered.

'If you are speaking to Sister Benedicta,' I said, 'you might tell her that her aunt will shortly be moving to Oxford, to a house in St Mildred Street, owned by Merton College.'

She shook her head. 'It would be best not to give her any news that might disturb her state of mind any further. Wiser if she forgets about her past kin. Her family now is here amongst her sisters in the Order.'

I reflected on this as I walked slowly across the court toward the gatehouse. It seemed a cruel attitude, to deprive Emma of the knowledge that her aunt would soon be a mere four miles away. If Mistress Farringdon paid a visit to the abbey, would she be banned from seeing her niece? Why was the community at Godstow so bent on keeping Emma here against her will? The Benedictines were generally known for a tolerant and kindly order, and Godstow in particular was famous for welcoming secular guests, which meant that it was more open to the world outside than many a nunnery. It remained a conundrum, and it seemed to me a somewhat distasteful one.

As I neared the gatehouse, a small ball of white fluff burst from the open door and collided with me. Looking down, I found that a small dog, one of those Maltese – as they are called – was sniffing my shoes and hose with some interest.

'That is our dog Rowan you can smell, you ridiculous animal,' I said.

I recognised the white dog which appeared engaged in mischief in some of the pictures which adorned Emma's book of hours.

'I apologise, Master Elyot.'

John Barnes had pursued the dog from the gatehouse. He now picked it up and tucked it under his arm, from which position it eyed me with a friendly but remarkably shrewd expression.

'I am minding Jocosa while her mistress works in the laundry,' he said. 'When she is loose in there she is apt to get underfoot and trip the sisters up.'

'She belongs to one of the nuns?' I fondled the dog's ears. Her hair was very fine and soft, fluffy as lamb's wool. Though she was smaller than our puppy, I judged her to be full grown.

'Nay, one of the novices, Sister Benedicta. Brought the dog with her when she came last year. She told me once that Jocosa is all she has to remind her of home and her late mother.' He made an awkward attempt to cross himself, while still keeping a firm hold of the dog.

'She may have more reminders soon of her home and family.' It occurred to me that if the abbess refused to pass my message to Emma, the good-natured porter might do so. 'Sister Benedicta's aunt, Mistress Farringdon, will be moving to Oxford in a few days' time, so she will soon have kin a short distance away.'

I did not go so far as to defy the abbess and tell Barnes that he should pass the information to Emma. I hoped that it might come out briefly in conversation, for if Emma regularly left her dog with the porter, they must be on good terms with each other.

'You had a successful meeting with the Reverend Mother?' he asked. Like the porters at every college I have ever known, clearly Barnes was a keen collector of news and gossip.

'Indeed I did. As you know, I am a bookseller.' I did not think I had ever told him this, but I was sure that he would have found it out for himself. 'I am by way of doing a little business with her in the matter of making illuminated holy books.'

The porter's curiosity satisfied, I gave the dog a final pat. I saw that she was well fed and cared for, and wore a collar of soft blue leather, which was slightly marred by the ends of brass studs from which bells had been broken off.

'The collar is damaged,' I observed.

He shrugged. 'Sister Mercy said that the little bells created a disturbance in the quiet of the enclave, and had them removed. Not that I ever noticed it myself.'

I made no answer to this. All the time I had been here the enclave had been filled with the sound of hammering and sawing from some building work, out of sight. Bursts of whistling could be heard from the same direction. Twice an abbey servant had trundled a wheelbarrow loaded with vegetables noisily across the cobbles to the kitchen. In the cloisters, someone was tuning a musical instrument, which was persistently off key. There was no great sense of quietness here at present, although compared with the streets of Oxford, it was peaceful indeed.

I could understand how, for some, life in these beautiful surroundings could be very pleasant. The sturdy, comely buildings, surrounding an exquisite little church. The river flowing softly by, bringing that refreshment to the spirit that only moving water can do. The fine old trees about the perimeter, and the rich farmland with its well-grown fields of wheat and barley, the fat cattle in the water meadow. If you sought tranquillity, you would find it here, in this community of kindly women.

Turning away to the gate, I bade John Barnes farewell. He set the little dog on the ground again and leaned his shoulder against the gatepost.

'They gave her a beating, you know,' he said softly.

Startled, I said, 'The little dog?'

'Nay, not the dog. Sister Benedicta. She finished her lesson early and went paddling in the river against the heat of the day. They beat her for it.' He shook his head and withdrew into the gatehouse.

As I unhitched Rufus and swung myself into the saddle, I was too stunned to think. Emma Thorgold had been beaten for paddling in the river? I knew that discipline was firm amongst the nuns, but I had not known that it was violent.

I looked back just once as I rode away. The small white dog was sitting in the middle of the open gate, watching me.

சு∽భ

She saw him, the bookseller from Oxford, who had brought word that her cousin William had been murdered. Nicholas Elyot, a widower, with two small children. Coming out of the laundry, with a basket of wet linen balanced against her hip, she saw him speak to John Barnes, and fondle Jocosa, before leaving through the gate. Something John said to him had startled him.

They had met three times now. That first, terrible day, when all that she had feared for William had been confirmed. He had been kind to her, Master Elyot. Although she was stunned with grief by the confirmation of what she had dreaded, she had found herself warming to him, blurting out her resentment at being confined here. William she had loved as much as she would have loved a brother, had God ever seen fit to give her one. For this man, this barely known bookseller from Oxford, she had felt the stirrings of something else. She wanted to say, 'Rescue me! Take me away from this place where they keep me imprisoned and where I can scarcely breathe. Take me away from pious hypocrites like Ursula and vindictive bullies like Sister Mercy.'

But he was a stranger. She had choked the words back, unspoken. Though when they both noticed their identically ink-stained hands, it seemed almost like an omen. What folly! She shook her head impatiently as she crossed the court.

The second time, they had hardly spoken. His daughter was in danger and she must give him the Psalter to buy the child back. Two children, he said he had, but he was a widower. He looked too young to be a widower, but that was more folly, for the Death had made widows and widowers younger even than he.

And when he came at last to tell her that the child was safe, the book restored, and William's murderers in hold, she had found herself pouring out her own life to him in the few minutes they had alone before Sister Clemence arrived. She blushed now to think of it, as she elbowed open the gate into the garden. What had she been thinking of? That he cared a farthing for her pathetic confidences? That he could somehow rescue her, if he even understood her need to escape? And now that she knew she was bound here by means of the agreement signed by her stepfather, it was useless even to think of him, the bookseller. Surely he would not break the law for her, a stranger?

She set the heavy basket on the ground and began to spread the wet shifts and table linen on the lavender hedge to dry. The load of garments washed that morning would already have dried in the sun. She would take them back to be folded and laid in the press.

He had stroked Jocosa as though he was fond of dogs.

But she must stop thinking of him, this Nicholas Elyot. What had he been doing here? Certainly he had not come to see her. What other business might he have at Godstow?

What she must turn her mind to, now, was her plan of escape. She could look for help nowhere else. There was so little time. And that document the abbess held seemed to secure her here for ever. She knew that if a novice was determined not to take final vows, however persuasive the arguments urging her to profess, it was possible for her to leave. Somehow, that document made things different for her. What was uncertain was her own position in law, given to God as an oblate, though against her will. If only she could consult a man of law! But that was impossible.

At least working in the laundry, exhausting though it was in the summer heat, had given her the opportunity to steal a pair of hose and one of the rough brown cottes provided for the lay servants. These she had hidden in the thickest part of this very hedge. Her sandals were adequate, though not normal wear for a lay person. She would not need a cloak as long as the weather remained fine. Dressed in the cheap cotte, she could pass for a peasant.

What she still required was a covering for her head. Although unmarried peasant girls left their hair uncovered, her own shorn pate would give her away at once as a renegade nun. Either she must find a dull head cloth, brown or grey – anything but her Benedictine black and white – or she must steal a boy's cap. Could she pass for a boy? It might be safer. Yet once she reached Oxford, if she did indeed reach Oxford, she must turn girl again, to find suitable employment. The cotte she had stolen could pass for either man's or woman's wear, though it was somewhat short for a woman.

Once all the wet linen was spread out to dry, she folded the dry morning's washing and laid it in the basket. It was remarkable how much washing the abbey accumulated, for the laundry dealt not only with the household linen and the clothing of both religious and lay sisters, but also the garments of the schoolgirls and all the servants and farm labourers. Emma had never counted them, but there must be at least a hundred people attached to the abbey. Who would miss one unwilling postulant amongst so many? Why keep her here at all?

Back in the linen room next to the laundry, she had laid all the folded washing in the clothes press and was screwing down the head to flatten all and remove any creases, when Sister Ursula arrived, wearing her usual smirk signifying that she knew something to Emma's disadvantage.

'The Reverend Mother has sent for you, Sister Benedicta. Again. Is there to be no end to your sinful behaviour?'

Emma ignored the attempt to goad her into an angry response, but merely carried the empty wicker basket back into the laundry, where two of the lay sisters were draining the water out of the huge stone tubs into the channel which emptied into the river. She knew that she looked flushed and dishevelled after a day working in the laundry, but there was no time to tidy herself if the abbess wanted to see her now. She straightened her wimple and veil as best she could and rolled down her sleeves, which had been drawn up to save them a soaking. Ursula stood in the doorway, blocking it, but Emma pushed past her and made her way across the court to the abbess's lodging.

She knocked quietly but not timidly on the study door, and to the abbess's 'Come', she entered, dipped her head modestly, and stood with her hands clasped before her waist.

'Ah, Sister Benedicta.'

Emma stole a glance through her lowered lashes. Abbess de Streteley was regarding her thoughtfully, with an expression Emma could not read.

'I have had a visitor today,' the abbess said, 'who came with a business proposal which involves you.'

Emma found that her heart was suddenly beating more quickly. Had her stepfather sent someone with word that he withdrew his gift of an oblate? Unlikely. There had been no sign of a visitor to the abbey. Except one. Nicholas Elyot. A business proposal?

'You will remember the . . . gentleman who brought you word of your cousin's death.' It seemed Agnes de Streteley, born of a distinguished Norman family, was not quite sure whether Nicholas was a gentleman or not. 'Master Elyot.' That was better. He had been an Oxford scholar, if not quite a gentleman. 'It seems that he has a shop in Oxford. He sells books.' She sounded as though she did not quite understand this matter of selling, although Emma knew very well that the abbess managed Godstow's finances with consummate skill.

There was a pause, as though something was expected of her.

'I remember Master Elyot, Reverend Mother. He was kind enough to bring me word that my cousin's killers had been captured.'

'Very true. Well, it seems he is interested in selling any illuminated books we might produce here at Godstow, holy works, for his devout clients. It was he who purchased that book of hours you made.'

Now Emma's heart truly leapt, and she was forced to keep her face lowered, so that the abbess might not see her look of joy. My book of hours! She thought. He has seen, he has bought, my book of hours. He will love my creatures playing in the margins, and sometimes escaping into the Bible scenes themselves. I know it! Did he recognise Jocosa? Oh, I hope he studied it before he sold it. He knew that I made it, he told me that, but I did not know he bought it. I never even knew what became of it, after it was sent to the binder.

She had hardly been paying any heed to what the abbess was saying, but now she picked up the thread. Nicholas Elyot wanted her to make another book of hours, which he would sell to the profit of the abbey.

'After that, we shall see,' the abbess said. 'I have not yet agreed to a regular supply of books. Let us see how this first one fares. What work have you been set this week?'

'I have been working in the laundry, Reverend Mother.'

'To the neglect of your lessons?' The abbess's voice was sharp.

'Sister Mercy said that, because the weather held fine, it was important that all the linen should be washed. I have been helping the lay sisters and servants.'

'Show me your hands.'

Emma stepped closer to the desk and held out her hands for inspection. They were red and sore from the coarse soap and from scrubbing at stains with pumice. The abbess frowned.

'You cannot work in the scriptorium with hands like that. I excuse you from all duties in the laundry from now on. See the infirmaress about some kind of soothing lotion or salve to restore your hands. As soon as they are fit, you are to make a start on a new book of hours. Sister Mildred will provide you with parchment and inks.'

'Thank you, Reverend Mother. Am I to attend lessons?'

The abbess considered. 'For the next two days. After that we will hope that you will be sufficiently recovered to start work on the scribing. Now you may go.'

'Thank you, Reverend Mother,' Emma said again. She made her reverence and retreated from the room. Outside in the hallway she permitted herself a moment of pure joy, wrapping her arms around herself, before straightening and assuming a sober face.

In the court, as expected, Sister Ursula had found some excuse to linger. 'Well?' she said, putting on an expression of false sympathy. 'In trouble again, I suppose.'

'Not at all,' Emma said, sweeping past her toward the gatehouse, to fetch Jocosa from John Barnes. 'Indeed, it was altogether the opposite.'

To this Sister Ursula had no answer, but was forced to resume, in silent frustration, whatever duties she had been assigned. As the most favoured of the novices in the eyes of Sister Mercy, she was generally set such onerous tasks as sorting the music in the choir stalls, or supervising the younger schoolgirls at their private studies, an experience not welcomed by the girls, who found Ursula's sharp tongue hardly more bearable than Sister Mercy's.

Emma made her way across the court, only with difficulty restraining herself from breaking into a dancing step.

'You look like the cat who was shut in the dairy all night,' John Barnes said.

He would never have used such language to any of the other novices or the nuns, but he and Emma had established an easy friendship from the time she arrived at Godstow. John found that she reminded him of his favourite younger sister, married these five years and moved far away to Henley.

Emma laughed. Here, in the gatehouse, with no one but John to hear, she could laugh. 'I am excused the laundry from this on, and I am to sit like a scribe in the scriptorium and make a new book of hours, like the one I made at Sister Mildred's request. It seems it has been taken up by that bookseller from Oxford.'

She would not speak his name.

'Ah, so that was what he was about, Master Elyot, meeting with the Reverend Mother. I did wonder.'

'You spoke to him?'

'Aye. He was quite taken with Jocosa, and she with him. Seems she could smell his own dog about his ankles.'

'What manner of dog?'

'I did not ask.'

'There must be good in any man that Jocosa takes a liking to.'

'Aye, indeed. And he had news for you as well.'

'For me?' Emma picked up the little dog and held her close. 'What news?'

'It seems your aunt – that would be Mistress Farringdon, would it not? – she is coming soon to live in Oxford. Mother of that fine young cousin of yours who used to visit.' He looked at her sympathetically. He knew the whole history of William Farringdon.

'My aunt is to live in Oxford?' Emma said. 'That is good news indeed. Not so very far away.'

'Not far at all. She will perhaps come to see you make your vows.'

'Perhaps,' Emma said, and went away, looking thoughtful.

Chapter four

However well one may plan, circumstances can always conspire to defeat those plans. The house in St Mildred Street was as ready as we could make it, clean and fresh, but necessarily bare. Alysoun had gone with Margaret to the town meadows behind St John's Hospital, where they had gathered flowers and woven them into garlands to decorate the house, ready for the Farringdon family, but on the day they were expected, they did not come.

'It takes time to pack up a household and transport it several miles,' Margaret said to reassure Jordain, who was sitting in our kitchen, fretting. 'Something has been forgotten, or required mending, or the farmer found that suddenly he needed his cart for some other purpose. They will come, never fear.'

'I hope you may have the right of it, Margaret,' Jordain said dubiously, 'and that it does not mean there has been some accident, or one of the children has been taken ill.'

I could see that the Farringdons were to become more of his flock, over whom he presided like a watchful shepherd. Celibate by reason of his profession, Jordain nevertheless had the instincts of a *pater familias*.

Two more days passed. Margaret and Alysoun took down their withered garlands and wove fresh ones.

'Why has Mistress Farringdon not come to Oxford, Papa?' Alysoun asked, her mouth drooping with disappointment as she gathered up her discarded garlands to throw away at the end of the garden.

'I do not know, my pet. I'm sure all will be well in the end. Something has delayed them, that is all.'

Halfway through the next morning, I was in the shop, sorting through a pile of tattered books I had bought from students who had finished their studies at the end of the Trinity Term. I had paid what I could for them, knowing how little coin these lads had in their pockets to get them home to their families, even if they walked all the way or were able to beg a lift with some carter. Nevertheless, it was a shabby collection. Several were coming loose from their bindings. They were not worth taking to Henry Stalbroke for repair, but I could stitch them together myself, well enough to serve another generation of students, though they would look far from elegant. One copy of Euclid had lost its last gathering of pages, but we could replace that and bind it in. There were five books with torn pages. It was possible to stitch together torn pages of parchment, if all the pieces were there. I would not buy the paper volumes students had put together for themselves by copying *peciae*. Those were too ragged and fragile, and the pages, once torn, could not be mended.

Jordain arrived as I handed the Euclid over to Roger, together with a complete volume, from which he could make a copy of the missing section.

'I am not sure whether you look relieved or annoyed,' I said to Jordain, who had a letter in his hand.

He waved it at me.

'From Mistress Farringdon. Brought to Hart Hall this morning by a pedlar coming into town to purchase goods. It seems that the cart in which her neighbour was to have brought her belongings to Oxford has lost a wheel – the spokes sprung from the rim, which was somehow twisted driving over a rough patch in the farm track. The local wheelwright is laid low with a summer fever, so her neighbour had to ride to the nearest wright, in Abingdon, six or seven miles away, who is so overwhelmed with work he cannot mend it for a week.'

'A tiresome delay,' I said, 'but not the disaster you were imagining.'

'Perhaps not, but the cart which would have been free to bring them here will now be needed for the hay harvest as soon as the wheel is replaced, so they needs must wait as much as another two or three weeks. She does not say, in so many words, but I sense that she feels they have outstayed their welcome.'

'That is indeed tiresome,' I said sympathetically, thinking of Alysoun and her garlands, prepared with such excitement and love.

'I have another plan,' he said. 'I thought I would hire a cart and fetch them to Oxford myself. Will you come with me, to lend a hand?'

'Where is this neighbour's house?' I asked.

'He holds a tenant farm near Long Wittenham,' he said. 'We would go south from Grandpont, then turn west to Clifton. I discussed it with Mistress Farringdon when they were here. You have to cross the Thames to reach Long Wittenham, but there is a ferry.'

'When do you plan to go?'

'Tomorrow, if I can hire a cart. No need to waste any more time.'

'There is no reason I should not come,' I said slowly. 'Walter and Roger can spend the day repairing these student books, all but the stitching, which I shall do myself. No need for them to hurry, the books will not be needed until the Michaelmas Term.'

I found that the idea of a drive through the countryside behind a slowly ambling cart horse was pleasant indeed. In the heat, the Oxford streets had begun to stink. The country roads would be full of the scent of new-mown hay, the air fresh amid the rich farmlands of Oxfordshire and Berkshire. Within the town it seemed as though the very air was sullen and motionless, as thick as soup.

'Good. I shall go at once and bespeak a cart. The

vintner Edric Crowmer has a cart he will sometimes hire out if he is not using it.'

Jordain was soon back, with word that Edric was willing to hire us the cart on the morrow. I insisted on paying half the charge, and we agreed to start soon after dawn the next morning.

Alysoun and Rafe, on hearing of the expedition into the country, begged to come with us, but regretfully I was obliged to be firm in my denials.

'Impossible, I am afraid,' I said. 'Coming back, there will be three more people and all their household goods, even furniture. It is a fair sized cart, but not big enough for the two of you as well.'

Rafe ran off at once. He had only asked to come because Alysoun had done so, but Alysoun looked rebellious.

'We usually go to Grandmama's in the summer,' she complained. 'And you promised I could practice riding there. And instead we have to stay here in this horrible heat.'

She did indeed look flushed, but I was sure it was due to no more than running about in the sun.

'If you do not like the heat, my pet, stay in the shade, or indoors. Even Rowan has the sense to do that, young as she is.'

We both looked at the puppy, who had chosen to lie on the cool flagstones, as far away from the kitchen hearth as possible.

'We will visit Grandmama at the farm later this summer,' I promised, 'but she has not been well. Best let her recover before the four of us go to visit.'

My widowed mother lived in a cottage on the land my family had held for generations, now farmed by my cousin Edmond Elyot, and it was the usual practice for my sister and me to take the children there for a week or two in the summer, to escape the worse of the summer illnesses due to the bad air rising from the Canditch here in town, and also to give my mother the chance to see something of her grandchildren. I suspected she was often lonely. After my wife died, she had wanted to take the children in and look after them herself, but I would not part with them. I suppose that it was partly guilt that prompted these regular visits in the summer and also – if the weather permitted – in the winter around Christmastide. However, Edmond had sent word two weeks before that she was not well, having suffered a bout of the bloody flux, which had weakened her.

'You may not come with us to Long Wittenham, Alysoun, but we will bring back Juliana Farringdon. You remember that you liked her. And she will be living not far away.'

Alysoun went off, somewhat mollified, for she had admired the older girl and been flattered by her attention.

At dawn I was standing in front of the shop when Jordain drove the cart along the High from Edric Crowmer's wine shop. The horse was strong, but elderly, and I could see that we should need to treat him with care.

I clambered up beside Jordain on to the driver's bench, and stowed a basket of food and a flagon of ale beside our feet.

Jordain grinned. 'I hoped Margaret might provide us with a dinner to take with us.'

'I know that is the only reason you wanted me to come,' I said. 'That and my strong arms for loading furniture.'

'Naturally.' He began to turn the cart, a manoeuvre somewhat hampered by the horse's determination to continue stubbornly in the same direction, which would have taken us to the East Bridge, quite the wrong way. With a sigh I climbed down again and took the horse's head to bring him round to set our course for Carfax.

Once he had realised that I had a stronger will than his, he proceeded placidly up the High to the crossroads and I resumed my seat. As Jordain and I were both country born, we were well used to driving a cart, and would take it turnabout. At Carfax we headed down Fish Street and left the town at the South Gate. The rivers of Oxford meander over much of the land south of the town, so that first we crossed Trill Mill Stream by the single arch of Trill Mill Bow, before driving through the crowded houses of Grandpont.

These houses formed almost a village of their own, outside the town wall, spilling out from Oxford and yet not quite part of it. Until the Pestilence came, this had been a busy community, mostly made up of craftsmen, some of them plying trades driven out of the town by the encroachment of the colleges – skinners and tanners, several blacksmiths and a small brickworks, as well as the usual weavers, fullers, tenters, and dyers, still remaining from the days when Oxford had been important for its production of fine woollen cloth. Grandpont was a kind of island, surrounded on all sides by water – a sharp bend of Trill Mill Stream to north and east, the mill stream that served Blackfriars to the west, and Shire Lake Stream, which joined parts of the Thames and the Cherwell, to the south. Since the deaths visited upon us by the Pestilence, half the houses now stood empty, slowly decaying from neglect. They were too far from the centre of Oxford to interest the colleges, nor were they the kind of profitable manors which would bring in rents. It was a sad place.

We left Grandpont by Denchworth Bow, and here the houses ceased, giving way to water meadows and marsh, and a confusion of small islands in the river, joined by causeway and bridges. At last we were in the true countryside and heading along the road south. One branch led to Abingdon, one to Dorchester and Wallingford. We would take the Dorchester road.

Jordain gave a sigh of pure content. 'It is good to be out of the town sometimes. We forget that a whole world lies out here, no more than a few miles from our colleges and halls and busy streets.'

'And the air is sweet,' I said, filling my lungs. As I had suspected, the air was rich with the delicious scent of freshly mown hay. 'Is there any sweeter smell in the world than hay? No wonder cows have such clean breath, not the foetid smells emitted by so much of humankind.'

'You are very hard on humankind,' he said. 'But I suppose what you say is true. Do you think that, if we lived on a diet of grass, we should never have rotten teeth?'

'Mm, like Nebuchadnezzar?' I was sleepy from the early start and the sun, and had no inclination to pursue the notion any further. 'Do you know where to turn off for Clifton?'

'Aye, I think so. It is some way yet. Look, beyond that rise and then down in the dip there is a clump of trees. Let us stop there a while to rest the horse, and we can explore what Margaret has put in the basket.'

It was still early for dinner, but I too was hungry, having taken no more than a small cup of ale and a piece of bread when I woke. And I think country air sharpens the appetite. We meandered up the low hill, and then down the slope beyond, which proved longer than it had looked. When at last we reached the shade of the trees, the horse seemed as glad to stop as we were.

I climbed down and hung his nosebag from his harness, while Jordain drew off the cloth which covered the basket and explored the contents. He handed it down to me, then joined me on the wayside verge, carrying the ale flagon with care.

'She has provided a feast,' he said, with a smile of delighted greed. Hart Hall's meals were notoriously dull and parsimonious. 'Fresh bread, a pat of butter wrapped in a dock leaf, two large meat pasties, a huge piece of cheese, a pot of onion relish, half a dried apple pie, and a poke of early cherries.'

I could see that his mouth was watering at the prospect of such abundance.

'Best keep some of it for later,' I said. 'We have the return journey to make, and Mistress Farringdon will not be expecting to feed us.' I took two pewter mugs from the basket and poured us each a generous helping of ale. Even under the trees it was hot, and we were both thirsty.

'Aye,' he said regretfully, 'I suppose you are right. I had no time to let Mistress Farringdon know that we were coming. I hope we may not have made things difficult for her.'

'I suppose if they were packed and ready to leave several days ago, it will be quite easy for them to come with us now.'

I was used to Jordain's sudden impulses of generosity, but they sometimes took others by surprise. Even with our unexpected arrival, from all I had heard I guessed that Mistress Farringdon would be glad to make the move, despite any brief inconvenience caused by this last minute change of plan.

We limited ourselves to half the food in the basket, though I fear we drank more than half the ale, then, refreshed, set off again. It seemed that Jordain had but a vague notion of where to turn off the Dorchester road for Clifton, but by asking first at a cottage and then seeking clearer directions from two men repairing a broken hedge, we found the road and headed south west for the village.

'I believe Clifton lies just within Oxfordshire,' Jordain said, 'this side the Thames. Then we cross the river by ferry and find ourselves in Berkshire, where Long Wittenham is the first village on the other side.'

'That fellow said something about the Wittenham Clumps.'

'Aye. A hill or hills, I think, where there was an ancient fort. But we do not go there.'

Clifton proved to be a small but tidy village. Like all villages it was diminished by the Great Pestilence, but not as desolate as many I had seen when riding north of Oxford on the Banbury road. By now I was driving, and I halted the cart so that Jordain could get down and speak to a man digging his vegetable patch, asking the way to the ferry. It was clear from the man's gestures, even where I sat, that we had only to follow this road a little further to the river and we should find the ferry there.

'I hope it may be large enough to take the cart,'

Jordain said as he joined me again.

'Surely,' I said. 'Else how do people get about here, with the river cutting through, dividing village from village, and the villages from Abingdon and Dorchester?'

The ferry proved to be more than ample for horse and cart, a wide shallow vessel, like a much larger version of the punts the watermen of Oxford used to get about, especially amongst the maze of streams to the west of the town. Like those boats, this ferry was poled, not rowed, but it required two strong men, for it was heavy. When the river was running full and fast, it would be difficult, even with two men, but today the water level was low after the weeks of hot weather, never relieved by rain. The river had shrunk in upon itself, leaving shelving banks of mud upon either side of the river.

The ferry was usually boarded easily from the bank or a wooden landing stage, but the shrinkage of the river meant making our way down over the slippery mud, and Edric's horse baulked at the prospect. I could hardly blame him. The treacherous footing of the mud, followed by stepping on to a dipping, swerving platform of planks, was enough to alarm any horse, and I suspected that this fellow had never before been asked to board a boat. He stood with his feet planted firmly on the ground – forefeet on the mud, hind feet on the grass – head down, stubborn as any mule, and would not move.

Usually I have a good hand with horses, but this one did not know me and was being asked to do something both unfamiliar and frightening. I cannot think how long it took us to persuade him on to the ferry, but it must have been at least half an hour, by which time the ferrymen, Jordain, and I were all red-faced, irritable, and sweating, and the horse, standing trembling on the ferry, was wild-eyed and seemed like to overturn the whole boat, and us with it.

The ferrymen set to, poling us across the river as fast as they might, clearly anxious to be rid of us. The bank on the far side, being a little less steep, made it easier to disembark. The horse, seeing the promise of solid ground ahead, lurched forward, setting the ferry pitching and nearly throwing me into the water. Hastily Jordain paid the men, and did not mention that they would be seeing us once more, on our way back.

'All that to do again,' I said, wiping the sweat off my face with my sleeve. 'And with the cart loaded as well.'

'Perhaps the horse will make less of it,' Jordain said hopefully, 'now that he has made the crossing safely once.'

I doubted it. The horse had been truly frightened, but at least he was calmer now.

'Look,' I said, 'there's an inn there, new built and clean, by the look of it. I should be glad of a quiet drink before we drive the last mile or so to Long Wittenham, and it will calm the horse to rest for a few minutes. What do you say?'

'I say I agree, and heartily. It looks a fine place. As you say, new. By all I can tell, no more than a year old.'

I did not even trouble to climb into the cart again, but walked at the horse's head to steady him, until we reached the inn, which was no more than a stone's throw from the ferry landing. The timbers of the framework were still the gold of freshly cut timber, not yet having assumed the soft silver of weathered oak. At the most they had been felled no longer ago than last summer. The thatch of the deep pitched roof was still crisp and fresh, and on a bench beside the door two ancients sat with tankards of ale upon their knees, watching us with interest.

'Aye,' said the innwife, when I asked. 'Us been open just this twelvemonth past.'

'It's a fine spot you have here,' I said, 'next to the ferry. A welcome spot for travellers.'

''Tis so. Be youm going far?'

'Only to Long Wittenham. May I beg a bucket of water for our horse? He took fright at the ferry and is it a fair sweat.'

''Deed you may, my dear.' She dimpled at me. 'Jack, lad,' she called into the kitchen behind her, 'fetch the gen'lman a bucket of water for his horse.'

With the horse unhitched and settled, Jordain and I took our ale outside and joined the two locals on the adjacent bench.

'Had some trouble with the ferry, did youm?' one of them said, ending with a wheezy laugh which set him coughing.

'Aye.' I grinned into my ale. Clearly these two ancients chose their present seat for its advantageous view of the ferry and any misadventures that might befall its passengers.

''Tis a hired horse,' Jordain said earnestly. 'He does not know us, and I fancy he has never been required to step aboard a boat before. We come from Oxford, where all the crossings of the rivers are by bridge.'

The old man nodded sagely. 'Aye, us could be doing with a bridge here, but who's to pay for 'un, that's what I'd like to know? Us poor folk a'nt got the means, and th'old lord be going fast, so they say. Won't see the summer out.'

'Ferrymen'd be out o'work,' his companion said gloomily.

'Aye.'

I pricked up my ears at the mention of a lord. Would this be the Farringdons' overlord who had turned them out of their home? Questioned, however, the old men set me right.

'Ah, Mistress Farringdon, poor woman. Friends of hers, be youm? Her man's holding was further south nor here. She come with the lasses to stay at Hobb's farm, two-three months ago, would it be? Mebbe four. Nay, the big lord hereabouts be Sir Anthony Thorgold, but when he's gone, as he will be soon, who's to say who 'twill be?'

Thorgold? I felt my heart lurch and I looked astonished at Jordain. He opened his mouth as if to speak, but I forestalled him.

'How do you, mean?' I said, trying to sound casual.

''Tis like this, see.' The more garrulous of the old men looked into his empty tankard and coughed again. 'Eh, but my throat be powerful dry.'

I took the hint and signalled through the open door to the innwife to bring more ale. When the old man had soothed his parched throat, smacking his lips in appreciation, he drew a deep breath.

'Sir Anthony and his lady had a fine family, see, two boys and three girls that lived past babes. But the girls all died young, before they could be marrit. Both sons, they was marrit, but the firstborn, Sir Harold, had no children. The younger – that was Sir Stephen – had a daughter, but he died, and his widow wed again.'

At this point I was holding my breath. This must be Emma's family, no question.

'It is a story of sad loss. You say there is doubt who will inherit when Sir Anthony dies,' I prompted. 'Will it not be the elder son?'

'Nay, first he lost his wife to the Pestilence. His father wanted him to marry again and get an heir, but 'tis said he had no heart for it. He was a sickly child, and nobbut a weakling of a man when all's said. He died, spring of last year.'

'Leaving the old lord all alone,' the other man said, with gloomy relish. 'None but hisself in that great manor house. Wife gone. Daughters gone. Sons gone.'

'But you said the younger son had a daughter,' I said casually, avoiding Jordain's eyes, which I knew were fixed on me.

'Oh, aye, but she went for a nun.' The old man dismissed the granddaughter with a shrug. 'So there's no one left. Sir Anthony has no close kin at all.'

The innwife had lingered in the doorway, listening to all of this.

'I did hear tell,' she said, 'as how the man who married Sir Stephen's widow has a mind to claim the manor and all.'

'Nay, how can that be? He's no kin to Sir Anthony.'

'Kin since he's stepfather to the granddaughter.'

'That don't make 'un kin.'

They began to argue about it.

'Where is Sir Anthony's manor?' I interrupted.

The innwife pondered. 'Two miles, about, south of here. You'll pass the turn if youm going to Hobb's farm. A turn on the left, between here and the village. It lies over toward Little Wittenham.'

''Tis time we were on our way,' Jordain said, getting up from the bench. 'We thank you, mistress, for your excellent ale.'

I bowed to the two old men, who were sharing out the last of the flagon of ale.

'A sad story,' I said. 'I hope that somehow it may have a better ending.'

I could barely contain myself until we had the horse hitched to the cart and were on our way. Hobb's farm, we had been told, was just beyond the village, no more than two miles along the road, which followed the river.

'Emma Thorgold,' I said, as soon as we were out of hearing. 'Mistress Farringdon's niece. She must be the granddaughter who has "gone for a nun". Except she hasn't.'

'It does seem probable,' he conceded. 'It isn't a common name, and since the Farringdons come from these parts, it seems likely that Mistress Farringdon's sister–'

'Of course she must be. Emma's mother married the younger son of a landed gentleman. But we did not know of this before, that she is the only one of the family left. She must be the old man's heir.'

'I wonder whether Mistress Farringdon knows of this.'

'It seems to be common gossip hereabouts,' I said.

'It may be that the locals do not gossip to her. She has only recently come into the neighbourhood.'

'Perhaps. So the word is that Emma's stepfather is trying to seize her inheritance. Could he do that?'

'As the old man pointed out, he is not kin,' Jordain said.

'I do not know what the law is. I suppose he became Emma's guardian when her mother died. He would have power over her until she was wed. But if she entered a nunnery, what then?'

'Would the nunnery not take possession of her property?'

I shook my head. 'It is too much for me. We must ask a lawyer. What is the name of this stepfather, do you know?'

Jordain shook his head. 'Mistress Farringdon has never mentioned it.'

A little further on we passed a well made road on our left, which must lead to the Thorgold manor. It soon disappeared amongst trees, and although I held the reins, there would be no chance to turn aside that way today.

A little while afterwards, Jordain pointed ahead, as a cottage came into view. 'Look, this must be Long Wittenham.'

We drove slowly along the single street, lined on both sides by a huddle of cottages. The village stood on a slight rise of ground, but behind the cottages on our right, water meadows sloped down to the river, where sheep were grazing. Just as in every other village I had seen in the last few years, many of the houses stood empty. No smoke rose from their roofs. Doors hung askew. And the thatch on many roofs was ragged and sagging into holes. A few children, half naked in the sun, were playing knuckle-bones in the dust of the street. They watched us go by with lacklustre eyes. Their faces were thin and pinched.

'A poor village,' I said. 'I wonder whether they are villeins of this manor belonging to Sir Anthony Thorgold.'

'Some say that villeins have learned the value of their labour, now that there are so few left to work the land,' Jordain said, 'but the law stops them claiming more for their labour than before the Death, nor does it allow them any easing of their customary obligations, but ties them all the more closely to their lords.'

'Yet it does not stop them running away,' I said.

'Easier for young men to do so. Not so easy for a family like these.'

'Aye, that's true enough. See! There is the track the innwife told us about, leading to Hobb's farm.'

'You'd best drive carefully then,' Jordain said. 'Remember that wheel, shattered on this track. We do not want to find ourselves marooned here for weeks.'

We proceeded along the broken, rutted track with great care, for it was in a dreadful state, so I was near shaking with relief when we reached the house without mishap. Whether we should be able to return undamaged, once the cart was heavily loaded, I was not so sure.

The house was no more than a single storey, with a low attic above, and it was surrounded by a mob of children. A woman who might have been thirty, but looked like fifty, thin and careworn, was scrubbing clothes in a wooden tub standing in the dirt yard, while another woman, with her back to us, whom I recognised as Mistress Farringdon, was scattering scraps for chickens, which ran about amongst the children. As I brought the cart to a standstill before colliding with either chickens or children, the girl Juliana came out of the house with another basket of clothes. Although the unknown woman stared at us blankly, Juliana recognised us at once.

'Master Brinkylsworth and Master Elyot! What do you here?' She dropped the basket beside the wash tub and ran across to us. Laying her hand on the horse's side, she looked up at us, her face radiant.

'Have you come to fetch us to Oxford? Oh, Mama, see who is here!'

Mistress Farringdon turned, and her face too lit up with a welcoming smile.

'No wonder there is little room here,' I murmured to Jordain under my breath. I thought they must all pack in at night like salt fish in a barrel.

It took only a few minutes to explain that we had decided to help them convey their belongings to Oxford, to spare Master Hobb and his cart the necessity of making the journey. The relief on his wife's face was plain to see. She was polite and as gracious as a woman could be, with a gaggle of children pulling at her skirts, falling over with howls, and fighting like puppies around her feet. One of these children, I supposed, must be Mistress Farringdon's granddaughter.

As if she guessed my thoughts, Juliana drew a somewhat grubby child out of the pack, a fair-haired girl with the face of an innocent cherub and the scabbed knees and elbows of an infant fighter.

'This is my niece, Maysant,' she said, 'my brother's child. Make your reverence, Maysant.'

The child bobbed a curtsey and put a dirty thumb in her mouth.

'I fear my man is away at the hay harvest, the other side of Wittenham,' Mistress Hobb said. 'We share our labour here, turn and turn about. It will be our hay next week.'

'Do not concern yourself, mistress,' Jordain said. 'Master Elyot and I will soon have the cart packed up, if Mistress Farringdon will show us what is to be taken.'

After that, we were all hard at work, the women and the older children as well as Jordain and me. First to be loaded were the pieces of furniture – a large table and stools, a dresser, two coffers, the parts of dismantled beds, a smaller table. Once these were in the cart, I wondered whether it would hold any more, but somehow we managed to pack in between these items bundles of clothes and bedding, a few cushions, kitchen pans, some sacks of dried food. To this Mistress Hobb added a basket of eggs and another of food for the journey.

'Now,' I said, 'the only remaining problem is where to fit in the three ladies. Perhaps Maysant had better ride the horse.'

The child did not appreciate my teasing, but simply stared at me in astonishment. Juliana whispered in her ear, whereupon she favoured me with a reluctant smile.

'I think if we moved these stools,' Jordain said, suiting the action to the words, 'we could make a fairly comfortable seat for you, Mistress Farringdon, with these cushions, and your back against the back of the driving bench. If you do not mind facing the way we have come?'

'I will be very comfortable there, Master Brinkylsworth,' she said, 'and Maysant can sit on my lap. I expect she will fall asleep before we reach Oxford.'

''Deed I shall not, G'andma,' the child said, the first words I had heard her utter.

'Juliana is slim enough to sit between us on the driver's bench,' I said.

She looked delighted, so I cautioned her. 'It is a very hard seat. Perhaps you should have a cushion.'

'I have no need of a cushion,' she said firmly, 'I am not one of your grand ladies. Will you let me drive?'

'Er,' Jordain said, looking at me helplessly.

'We shall see,' I said, having more experience than he in dealing with young girls. 'This is a borrowed cart and a borrowed horse, and he has had one fright already today. He did not care for the ferry.'

Once we had the women settled, we made our farewells to Mistress Hobb and the children. Mistress Farringdon leaned over the side of the cart to kiss her friend. There were tears in her eyes.

'I do not know what we should have done without you, my dear, all these weeks. May God bless you and yours, for all your kindness.'

The other woman blushed and patted her hand.

'Send me word when you are settled, Maud. That pedlar will come by next month. You may send by him.'

'I will so.'

Not trusting the cart over the pitted farm track, especially now that it was somewhat top heavy with its load, I decided to walk beside the horse and lead him until we reached the Long Wittenham road. It was a slow, tricky trip along that track, which seemed to take twice as long on the return journey. I hoped this would not be repeated all the way back, or we could not reach Oxford before nightfall, even on this long summer day. However, once we reached the road safely, I joined Jordain and Juliana at the front of the cart, and we made our decorous way back through the village, where the same children were now playing some game which involved kicking an ancient and dented pewter cup between two sticks driven upright in the tired grass of the verge.

As we reached the turn to the Thorgold manor, I twisted round to speak to Mistress Farringdon, who was sitting behind, back to back with me.

'The innwife told us that Sir Anthony Thorgold lives down there,' I said. 'Would that be your niece Emma's grandfather?'

'It is,' she said, without turning her head, for she was holding the child Maysant steady, who had indeed fallen asleep.'

'He is very old.' Juliana clearly felt her mother had not said enough. 'And he is very ill. Dying, probably.' She said it respectfully, with a hint of something in her tone that I could not quite place. 'We went to see him last year, when William was still alive. Sir Anthony did not like it that Mama's sister had married again. That was before she died in childbirth, and Emma was staying with us, so she went with us. I think Emma had not seen her grandfather for some time.'

I decided not to say more on the subject now, but it occurred to me for the first time that if Sir Anthony was as wealthy as he probably was, why had he not helped these relatives of his deceased daughter-in-law, in their time of need?

Ahead of us the inn by the ferry came in sight. This gable end of the building, I now saw, was constructed of a magnificent pair of lofty cruck beams, which explained the height of the steep roof. There was a window at this end of the gable. That upper room must be very large indeed, though low near the eaves on either side.

'This is where we had problems before,' Jordain said. 'The horse was frightened by the ferry, so I think it will be safest if you climb down from the cart, lest he panic and overturn it.'

I jumped down and helped Juliana to the ground.

'Pass me the child,' I said to Mistress Farringdon, 'and Juliana, help your mother. Look, there is the ferry coming over from Clifton now.'

The two ferrymen were propelling the boat swiftly across the river, with only three people aboard – two women with baskets of vegetables, and a youth leading a nanny goat. They disembarked easily, then the ferrymen looked across and saw us approaching. I did not hear them groan, but the expression on their faces made their feelings clear.

The horse was easier to manage this time, though still nervous. The Farringdons waited until horse and cart were safely aboard the ferry, then joined us in the bow, well away from the horse's heels. Mistress Farringdon and Juliana had used the ferry before, but it was strange to Maysant, who kept tight hold of Juliana's hand until we reached the safety of the further bank of the river.

Once on the Clifton side of the Thames, the horse seemed to regain his courage, and moved along at a brisk pace. It was a heavy load for him now, but he was strong, despite his age, and accustomed to hauling Edric Crowmer's barrels of wine. Whenever we reached a rising slope of the road, either Jordain or I would get down and walk, and Juliana joined us, to ease the burden for the horse.

Back on the wider road leading from Dorchester to Oxford, we began to make better time, but stopped once to rest the horse and to eat the food we had brought with us. I wished I had thought to refill our flagon with ale at the inn by the ferry, but we were so occupied in persuading the horse aboard that it went quite out of my head, so by the time the cottages of Grandpont came into sight, we were all thirsty and eager to reach Oxford.

As I hoped, Margaret welcomed the tired women with a good supper at our house, while Jordain and I drove the cart to St Mildred Street and unloaded their belongings.

'We can but guess where everything should go,'

Jordain said, 'but at least it will seem less bare.'

'Table and stools and coffers and cushions here in the main room,' I said. 'The smaller table in the kitchen, I would think, together with all the cooking gear and the food. Beds and bedding upstairs.'

It took us some time, especially as we had to puzzle over how the beds fitted together, but at last we were done, locked the door, and returned cart and horse to Edric.

After Jordain and I had hastily eaten the food Margaret had kept hot for us, our whole party processed solemnly to St Mildred Street. I carried Maysant, who had fallen asleep again, at which Alysoun flashed me a jealous look, but Juliana took her by the hand and chattered to her all the way. At the door of the house, Jordain handed the key to Mistress Farringdon.

'I am afraid the front is very patchy,' he said anxiously. 'It is the new plaster. It has not dried out yet.'

Mistress Farringdon was not listening to him. I think she was holding her breath, and her cheeks had grown quite pink. She unlocked the door, then stood aside, as if waiting for someone else to lead the way.

Margaret touched her gently on the shoulder. 'This is your home, my dear. It is for you to welcome us, not t'other way about.'

Mistress Farringdon stepped over the threshold and the rest of us followed. There were brier roses in the garlands Alysoun and Margaret had made, and their scent drifted softly over us. Jordain and I had done our best, and although the room did not look fully lived in, it promised comfort and safety. For a long moment Mistress Farringdon simply looked about her, then she sank down on one of the stools and began to weep. Juliana knelt down and put her arms around her mother.

'Please, Mama, do not weep. Why do you weep? We have a home now.'

'I do not weep for sadness, child,' she said. 'I weep for joy.'

❧❦

Emma and Sister Mildred were sorting through the abbey's supply of parchment, so that Emma might make a start on the new book of hours the following day. The little book room – which Sister Mildred liked to call a library – opened off the carrel in the cloister that was used as a scriptorium whenever the weather permitted. It faced south and made the most of the daylight, essential for judging colours correctly, as well as easing the tasks of ruling lines for the script and copying with precision and care.

Emma felt more at ease with Sister Mildred than with any of the other nuns. It said something of the precentrix's character, she felt, that she had kept her secular birth name, instead of changing it upon taking her vows. And yet she too had been an oblate, given to God when she was eight years old, and professed at twelve.

'I think this will be enough,' Sister Mildred said, tapping together the pile of parchment they had chosen from the cupboard of writing supplies, all the sheets matching in size, colour, and texture. 'And here is a good supply of black ink for the lettering. You will not need the colours yet awhile.'

'Do we have plenty of the carmine and the lapis blue?' Emma said. 'I was running short as I finished the other book. I should not like to skimp on the illustrations, when the book has been specially commissioned.'

Sister Mildred lifted down the glass bottles from the high shelf where the colours were kept for safety's sake.

'You have the right of it, Sister Benedicta. I will order more at once from Oxford. They should be with us before you need them. There is enough here to make a start.'

'And the gold leaf?'

'Ah, now that I think is almost finished. When I was copying out the new anthem I used almost the last of it, for the capitals on each page. I will order that as well.'

They put the parchment and the black ink on one of the open shelves, ready for Emma to make a start in the morning. Next to them she laid her straight edge and the thin metal stylus she used for drawing lines for the text, and she selected a dozen uncut quills from the general supply, while Sister Mildred locked the expensive coloured inks away again in the cupboard.

If I had only to deal with Sister Mildred, Emma thought, and could spend my time making beautiful books, I should not be so unhappy here. But I must also be able to come and go as I please, to go forth from within these prison walls, out into the world.

'Sister Mildred,' she said hesitantly, not wanting to look the older woman in the eye. 'Have you never regretted being given to God when you were a young child? You never had a chance to know the world outside, to decide whether that was the life you would have preferred.'

Sister Mildred turned from the cupboard and hooked the key on to her belt, with the others she carried. She stepped round until she could look Emma fully in the face.

'Child, I have never regretted it, not for one moment. How could I? Oh, I am not so unworldly that I do not know I might have had husband and children in the life outside. By now, perhaps grandchildren, too! But the joys of my life have been books and music, and where else could I have filled my days with them more fully than here in this beautiful place, amid the quiet buildings, the peace of the countryside, and the murmur of the river? As the lady of a manor, I should have been too much occupied with daily tasks ever to have spent one tenth of my time with them. And to devote one's life to God and holy works, here in Godstow, how could I not be content?'

She reached out and touched Emma's cheek lightly.

'But you, I know, are not content. Perhaps you have already spent too long in that world outside to give yourself, body and soul, to this life.'

Emma choked back tears. 'Do you remember,' she said, 'the skylark that Sister Clemence kept in a cage?'

'I do. Poor little thing, it died within the week. I fear she did not know how best to feed it.'

'I do not think it starved. Did not starve of food, in any case. It died because it starved of freedom. Have you never watched a skylark, Sister Mildred, and heard it sing? They nest in the meadow beyond the abbey gardens, and they fly there, soaring up and up until you can hardly see them against the dazzle of the heavens. And then they sing. Oh, how they sing! Such music from such a tiny creature! Is that not a worship of God, one of His tiniest creatures filling the air with music?'

She caught her breath.

'It died because it was imprisoned and could no longer sing. I am like that skylark, Sister Mildred, and like that skylark, I think I shall die here.'

Chapter Five

Lady Amilia turned over the pages of the book of hours thoughtfully and with apparent care, but nevertheless I watched her anxiously. Her nails were somewhat long – a privilege of the aristocracy, spared any manual work – so when she ran her fingers over the illuminations I held my breath, for fear she might score the rich colours or rip the gold leaf. I had intended only to hold it up for her to see, not meaning her to finger it, but she had simply taken it out of my hands without a by-your-leave. One does not remonstrate with a member of the noble classes. At any rate, not if you wish to make a sale.

'My husband sent for the bookbinder – what is his name? – to discuss the repair of some volumes which had belonged to his grandfather, and mentioned that I wished to purchase a finer book of hours than the one I use at present. The fellow said that you had one for sale here in Oxford, so I felt I must come and examine it.'

'I very much regret, my lady, that this particular volume is not for sale.'

She had reached the final pages, so I removed it firmly but tactfully from her hands.

She looked affronted. 'But surely not. That was not what the fellow said. The bookbinder.'

I did not like the way she spoke of Henry Stalbroke as if he were some worthless churl, bound to service on her husband's lands, but I kept my tone deferential and polite.

'I am afraid it is already bespoken, my lady.' I did not explain that it was I who had bespoken it for myself. 'However, the same artist has just begun work on another book of hours which will be just as fine as this. Possibly finer. If you wish, I will reserve it for you, and let no one else even see it.'

She pulled a face. She was young, rich, pretty, and spoiled, her husband's third wife, and accustomed to getting her own way.

'And if you wish,' I added persuasively, 'I can make a note of any particular features you would like to see included. A perpetual calendar? A table of saints' days? Your favourite prayers? And we can specify whatever binding you desire. Perhaps another colour of the leather? A deep purple?'

She was wearing a gown of deep purple, a particularly expensive dye, only permitted to the highest ranks in society. I knew she would relish the same colour in her book of hours. She would carry it ostentatiously, another adjunct to her wealth.

When she left at last, after much discussion, I returned Emma's book of hours to its safe high shelf, and flung myself down on the stool behind my desk. Walter and Roger both gave me knowing looks.

'I feel like a prostitute,' I said in disgust. 'That woman would no more value a priceless book than, than . . . a pig! But we shopkeepers must bow and scrape to the nobility.' I glared at them. 'And there is no use your looking at me like that. I must earn enough to pay your wages.'

'It does seem a shame, though,' Walter said. 'If the new book is to be as fine as the first. It should go to someone who will value it at its true worth.'

I sighed. 'I know. I agree.' Then I brightened. 'Perhaps I can persuade Em . . . er . . . Sister Benedicta to insert a few mischievous jokes into her illuminations. Something too subtle for Lady Amilia to understand. That would be some consolation.'

'Best not get the novice into trouble,' Walter said.

Of course, he was right.

'In any case, I shall need to see her, Sister Benedicta, to explain all these things her ladyship wants.' The thought cheered me. 'I shall ride out to Godstow in the next day or two and consult with her.'

There was, however, a good deal to do before I could make the journey. With all the work on the house in St Mildred Street, and the trip to Long Wittenham, I had been neglecting the children's lessons. In the hot weather I did not expect them to spend as much time as usual at their books, but they could not be neglected altogether. Alysoun had pointed out that the students of the university had a long break from their studies.

'All summer long, Papa, from the end of Trinity Term to the start of Michaelmas. Should we not have a break from our lessons too?'

She was making but a token protest, for I knew she enjoyed her lessons.

'Ah,' I said, 'but the students are set work they must complete even during their break from university lectures. Great volumes they must read, translations from Greek or Hebrew they must prepare, the many philosophers they must peruse and summarise. I remember when I was a student I seemed to study all summer long, except when I was needed to help with the hay-making and harvest.'

The fact that I had enjoyed those times of quiet reading up in my garret room of our old farmhouse was not something I wished to bring into the argument. Of course I had also loved the warm summer days swinging a sickle in the hay meadows, or stooking corn to dry before threshing. Sometimes in this town life I missed the countryside. If we were able to visit my mother during this summer, I would lend a hand to cousin Edmond with the harvest, though this year we would have missed hay-making.

Alysoun and I came to a compromise. We would hold our lessons on Saturdays only, outside in the garden, and I would find some more entertaining Latin for her to read.

'I am sure Master Caesar was a very important soldier,' she said primly, 'but, Papa, I have had quite enough of all those soldiers marching about in France and having battles and sieges.'

She was right. Although the Gallic Wars were excellent reading for a young scholar, being written in a clear, straightforward style, they were hardly likely to interest a lively six-year-old girl. There were some funny animal fables we could study, not in the purest Latin, but a better choice for summer reading.

As for Rafe, he was still reading in English, and practising his writing. Less argumentative than Alysoun, he accepted that lessons were as much a part of life as meals and bedtime.

Work in the shop also occupied much time, now that our labours at the house in St Mildred Street were finished. Although I am no professional bookbinder, when I first began to work for Humphrey Hadley in the shop which was now mine, he insisted that I should learn at least the basic skills required for the making of a book. I spent a rather unpleasant, smelly month working for Dafydd Hewlyn, learning the many stages in the preparation of parchment. Afterwards, the two months in Henry Stalbroke's workshop were a joy. I found I had a natural aptitude for assembling and stitching the pages of a book, then creating a cover from boards and leather, tooling and embossing the leather before putting the whole volume together, tinting or gilding the edges of the pages, and for some books, attaching clasps to hold a sometimes bulky volume together.

Of course I would never pass muster as a master bookbinder, or even as a journeyman, but I enjoyed exercising my modest skills from time to time in repairing the cheap student texts, like the ones I had just bought.

As a boy, I was sent by my father to be taught to read and write by our parish priest, who had himself attended Oxford. He was a patient man, but he demanded high standards of penmanship, so that by the time I myself became a student at the age of fourteen I had a true scribe's hand. Indeed, had I not married Master Hadley's daughter, he would have employed me as one of his scriveners, along with Walter, who already worked for him then. And although I could draw a simple decorative initial, or the border for a page composed of flowing vines and small flowers, I had not the skill to portray people or animals, while my buildings always looked as though they were about to topple over, a fault I could never see how to correct. I was therefore all the more in awe of Emma Thorgold's artistic talent.

Stitching and rebinding the broken student books, and catching up with the children's lessons, kept me busy for the best part of a week after Lady Amilia's visit to the shop. If I was to consult with Emma – *Sister Benedicta* – about the new book of hours, I must needs ride out to Godstow soon, before it had progressed too far.

'Not today,' Margaret said, when I broached the subject one morning. 'I need your help today.'

'Of course,' I said. 'In what way?'

'I have looked out some spare dishes and kitchen pots that we do not need, and I have a salted side of bacon and a crock of dried peas. It is too much for me to carry by myself to St Mildred Street.'

I nodded. I had noticed that most days Margaret managed to visit the Farringdons and always took something with her, either to furnish the house or to augment their sparse supplies of food.

'I am coming too, Papa,' Alysoun said. She was packing ends of cloth into a basket. 'Juliana is going to show me how to piece squares together to make a pretty coverlet.'

I opened my mouth to point out that her aunt had offered to teach her, no more than three months before, and was refused with scorn. Margaret raised her finger to her lips and shook her head. I suppressed a smile. It was a matter of some contention between my sister and me, for she thought Alysoun did not need lessons in Latin and mathematics, while I had no wish for her to be brought up with only housewifely skills. On the whole, Alysoun favoured my view, although she enjoyed cooking with Margaret, especially if there were something sweet to nibble. I did not mind if Alysoun spent time sewing with Juliana today. The older girl was intelligent and well lettered. A little needlework could do no harm.

'Is Rafe coming?' I asked.

'Nay,' Alysoun said. 'He is taking Rowan over to Jonathan Baker's.'

'Then let us be off,' I said. 'Where is this side of bacon, Margaret?'

I had not been inside the house in St Mildred Street since the day we had moved the Farringdons in, and I was surprised to see how much like a home it already seemed. The new plaster on the street frontage had dried out in the summer heat, despite the fact that the street was narrow and shaded. Merton must have sent one of their servants to lime wash the whole front of the building early that very morning, for it was still drying out, the wet patches shining, while the dry areas were dull and chalky white.

Inside, Mistress Farringdon had hung a single painted cloth on one wall. It was quite small, but added colour, since the rest of the walls were the same chalk white as the outside of the house. There was also a bright home-woven rug on the floor, which I recognised from Margaret's bedchamber. With cushions piled up on the stools and coffers, and a posy of pink cranesbills on the table, the room was pretty and welcoming.

When I carried the crock of peas and the side of bacon through to the kitchen, I found Mistress Farringdon taking a batch of pastries out of the bread oven beside the hearth. Like Margaret, she would have baked her bread first, then used the residual heat for any other baking. With her cheeks rosy from the heat, she had lost the drawn and fearful look she had worn before.

'Where shall I put these, mistress?' I said.

'Oh, Master Elyot,' she cried, 'you and Margaret have done so much for us, too much. You cannot give away all your store of food!'

'I am sure we have more than enough,' I said. 'I see there's a hook on that beam. I'll hang the bacon there.'

'Aye, thank you. And the crock will fit on the shelf by the window.'

As I was hanging up the bacon, Juliana and Alysoun ran past to the stairs, followed by little Maysant, who seemed determined not to be left out. Beyond them, the door to the garden stood open, to disperse the heat from the cooking, although the air outside was not much cooler. I went to look out of the door.

'Someone has made a start on the garden,' I said.

'Aye,' Mistress Farringdon said. 'Master Brinkylsworth and one of his students have been scything it.'

'Jordain had best take care he does not sever his foot,' Margaret said dryly, as she unloaded her own basket of kitchen goods on to the table. 'He is apt to go off into a dream and forget what he is doing.'

'Oh, come, Margaret,' I said, 'Jordain grew up on a farm, just as we did. He knows how to wield a scythe.'

I stepped out into the wilderness behind the house. As well as the path cleared to the well, there was now a another leading toward the far end of the garden, but so far only reaching about halfway. The scythe had been left propped against the back wall of the house, so I took off my cotte, rolled up the sleeves of my shirt, and set to. I could at least clear a few more feet while I waited for Margaret and Alysoun.

I came back into the house perhaps an hour later, hot, tired, and wringing with sweat, to find food laid out on the table, which Mistress Farringdon insisted that we must share. After we had eaten, Alysoun begged to stay sewing with Juliana, while Margaret, Mistress Farringdon, and I walked down to the High Street.

'I am taking Maud to meet Mary Coomber,' Margaret said. 'Mary may have work for her, making cheeses in the dairy.'

I frowned. 'But Mistress Farringdon,' I said, 'you are a gentlewoman. You should not labour in a dairy.'

She laughed. 'Oh, Master Elyot, although my sister married into the gentry, I am but a yeoman farmer's wife. I know very well how to make cheese. It is pleasant work. All the more pleasant to be in a cool dairy on such hot days as these! And, if you would be so kind, please call me Maud, as your sister does.'

I bowed my acknowledgement of this. 'And I am Nicholas, if you please, mistress.'

She smiled. 'Nicholas, then.'

We had reached the corner where St Mildred Street met the High, with All Saints church on our left and the Mitre on our right. As the women turned left, I hesitated.

'I think it is not too late to ride out to Godstow today,' I said. 'I shall bespeak a horse at the Mitre. I shall be home for supper, Margaret.'

She nodded. 'You had best change your shirt before you go,' she said. 'It is stained from the garden.'

I looked down and saw that she was right. It would not do to address the abbess in a shirt besmirched with green stains from carrying bundles of nettles and thistles to the heap Jordain had started. My hands, too, were far from clean.

'I shall not disgrace you,' I said lightly. 'I shall make myself respectable.'

Indeed it took me the best part of an hour, I should judge, to wash thoroughly after my strenuous labour in the heat, and then to don not only a clean shirt but also clean hose (the ones I had been wearing were likewise stained, and one knee previously darned). I was reluctant to wear a cotte, having carried mine home with me slung over my shoulder, but I decided that to appear before the holy sisters in shirt and hose might be considered tantamount to undress. I found the thinnest cotte I possessed, made of a fine linsey-woolsey, cooler than pure wool.

As the afternoon was wearing on, I urged Rufus along St Giles and the Woodstock road more swiftly than on our previous visit to the abbey, so that we were both glad when we reached the shady tunnel through the trees on the trackway to Wolvercote. I saw that the inn perched on the nearside bank of the river was busy dispensing ale to a large group of villeins, reddened from the sun. Haymaking must be finished.

At Godstow, John Barnes greeted me cheerfully.

'Dost wish to see the Reverend Mother again, Master Elyot?' he said as I tethered Rufus to the same ring as before. 'I do believe she is working with Sister Clemence over the monthly accounts.' He winked at me. 'Not the best time to visit. Short tempers all round, when the figures do not add up right.'

'Oh.' My face fell. 'I have really come about the new book of hours which is being made for me. It is to be for Lady Amilia Stanhope, and she has certain special requirements. I was hoping to pass these on before the book has progressed too far.'

'I'll tell you what will be best, sir,' he said. ''Tis Sister Mildred the precentrix who looks after everything to do with books. You wait here and I will see whether she is in the scriptorium or the library.'

This was better than I had hoped. If I could bypass the abbess and Sister Clemence, I might even be able to see Emma Thorgold herself. I sat down on the porter's stool, placed outside in the shade of the gatehouse and waited impatiently. It seemed a long while before he returned, but perhaps he had not found the precentrix at once.

'If you will follow me, Master Elyot,' he said, 'Sister Mildred is in the scriptorium with the novice who is making the book. You will know her, of course, Sister Benedicta, whose cousin was murdered.'

I nodded and sprang to my feet. So I would be able to speak to Emma, if the two women were together. The porter led me across the wide outer court of the enclave, past the guest house where I had met Emma before, and into the cloisters.

The scriptorium lay at one end of the south facing

cloister, occupying two adjacent carrels, so that two nuns might work at copying and illuminating, but it was clear than only one was in use at the moment, where one black clad figure was bowed over the desk, and another, standing behind her, was examining the work.

'Sister Mildred,' Barnes said, 'here is Master Elyot, to see you about the new book.'

I made my reverence to the nun, who must have been about sixty. She had a tranquil face, marked only with creases about the eyes and mouth, betokening a lifetime of smiling. If this was the nun who supervised Emma's work, she was indeed fortunate. I tried to keep my eyes averted from the girl herself, whose head was bent in concentration over her work, but I noticed that the hand holding the quill had begun to tremble. She laid down the quill in a groove at the back of the desk, for fear – I suspected – of spoiling the page.

Barnes leaned over to examine it.

'Very pretty, Sister Benedicta. Is that Daniel with the lions, there in the capital?'

I was surprised that he spoke so freely to the sisters, but they did not appear to mind. It seemed the porter had an assured place here, at least amongst the more tolerant nuns. Perhaps he would be more deferential to the abbess and Sister Clemence. Which of the nuns, I wondered, had carried out the beating of Emma that Barnes had mentioned on my previous visit? Not this Sister Mildred, I was certain. And it must have been authorised by the abbess, though I would not have thought her a cruel woman.

'Aye, John,' Emma said quietly. 'It will be Daniel. But of course at the moment I have only outlined it. It will be better when I have applied the colours.'

'A rich tawny gold for the lions,' Sister Mildred said. 'We may need to make it up specially.'

'I believe I may have the very colour you need,' I said. 'I can bring you a bottle.'

All this time, Emma had kept her back to me, but I sensed that she was very aware of my presence just behind her.

John Barnes returned to his gatehouse and Sister Mildred smiled at me.

'I understand that you have some particular instructions for this book, Master Elyot, is that right?'

'It is,' I said. 'Lady Amilia Stanhope wishes to purchase it, and has requested certain special features to be included, if I might explain them to your scribe?'

'Certainly. I will leave you to discuss them with Sister Benedicta. I shall be in the library if you should need me.'

She withdrew through the door into the adjacent room, which I saw contained shelves for a collection of books and scrolls. Quite a respectable collection for a nunnery, but Godstow was long established and wealthy. She left the door open between us, so that we were in a sense chaperoned, but only mildly. I sat down on the scribe's bench, but took care to keep to the far end, so that I did not touch even the edge of Emma's habit.

'How are you?' I asked softly. 'John Barnes told me you were beaten.'

For the first time she looked at me. I thought she seemed tired and drawn.

'The injuries are healing,' she said dully. 'A friend – one of the schoolgirls – salved them for me, else they might have festered.'

I felt myself flushing with anger. 'That is monstrous!' I said. I wanted to shout it, but managed to keep my voice down.

She shrugged. 'I was disobedient. I took off my sandals and waded in the river, out by the meadow, where we are not permitted to go. The punishment was justified. But the pleasure Sister Mercy took in it was not.'

'Sister Mercy?'

'The mistress of the novices. You had best tell me what Lady Amilia requires. We will not have long.'

'I have it all written here.' I drew a folded paper from the breast of my shirt. It was warm from contact with my chest. 'I could have sent it with one of my scriveners, I suppose, but I wanted to see you.'

I had not meant to say that, but the words were out of my mouth before I could stop them. In confusion, I laid the paper on the desk, and our hands touched briefly. She flinched, or so I thought, until she turned her head and looked me full in the face. I caught my breath. She was flushed and her eyes were full of appeal.

'Can you help me?' she whispered. 'My stepfather has handed me over as a gift to the abbey, an oblate, but I cannot, I *will not*, take the vows. I must escape.'

'When?' I too was whispering now, though I cast a sidelong glance at the open door to the library. 'When are you to take your vows?'

'Less than two weeks from today.'

'Did you know that your aunt is now in Oxford? My friend Jordain and I have been helping her settle, with the two girls.'

'John Barnes told me she was coming, but he did not know where she would be living.'

'I have been there this morning,' I said. 'It is a small house, but pleasant, two doors south of St Mildred's Church, in St Mildred Street. Do you know Oxford?'

She shook her head. 'Nay, I do not. And I cannot be a burden to my aunt, she has nothing. If I can escape this place, I must find work, but how to escape is my greatest worry.'

I opened my mouth to tell her what I had learned about her grandfather, then closed it again. No need to confuse matters now.

'Have you any plan?' I said. 'I do not know how strictly you are confined within the enclave.'

'Very strictly,' she said, with a wry smile. 'I may not set foot outside the walls.'

'So little time. Otherwise I might have found you a lawyer, but you could not take your case to court within the next two weeks.'

'I should not know how to go about it.'

'Nor I,' I admitted. 'I believe such a case would be heard in the Court of Chancery, in London, although that might be disputed by the Church. They might claim that it is an ecclesiastical matter.'

We looked at each other helplessly.

'I can hardly kidnap you,' I said ruefully.

'If I came to Oxford, could I become a scrivener?'

I hated to disappoint her, but I must be honest. 'Women are never employed as scriveners. Not in the world outside. Only within a nunnery.'

She sighed. 'It does not matter. I will do anything. I can cook, a little, do laundry. We learn many useful skills here, besides singing and praying.' Her tone was ironic. Then she spoke more earnestly. 'I should be happy to be a servant in some decent family's house, if only I can be free!'

I thought she did not understand how little freedom a servant maid would have, but such matters could be decided later.

'My sister Margaret could probably help you. She is trying to find work for your aunt.'

'You have a sister?'

'An older sister, widowed. She keeps house for me.'

'You are fortunate. My parents are dead and I have neither sister nor brother.'

I realised I could not linger here much longer, or it would arouse suspicions. 'When do you think you will complete the book? I would then have reason to collect it, to take it to the binder. Perhaps we could contrive some means for you to go with me.'

She shook her head. 'It cannot be finished. Not before the time appointed for Sister Ursula and me to take our vows. I can only work on it when the light is good and I am not required to attend services. Even though I have been excused lessons, it cannot be finished in time.'

She was right, of course. Work as fine as hers took time. She would not rush it. I was beginning to realise that Lady Amilia's book might never be completed.

I was thinking frantically. I had come hoping merely to see her again, and yet I knew that at the back of my mind had always been the thought: What if she could avoid taking her vows?

'There can be no hope of taking your plea to court before then, but I will speak to a lawyer – Oxford is well provided with lawyers! I am sure I can find someone to act as your man of law. It might be possible to delay your admission as a nun until the matter had been settled in court. I think that is your best hope. That way all may be resolved without offense to the abbey. Surely they have no wish to have a forced nun living amongst them?'

She shrugged again, and I saw that I had disappointed her. 'Whatever you wish.' She picked up her quill. 'Do you need to explain the wishes of the lady about her book?'

She was dismissing me. I rose to my feet. As I did so, the little dog Jocosa peeped out from beneath the bench, where she had been hidden by the skirts of Emma's habit.

'They are all set out clearly in the paper.' I felt ashamed that I could not offer more positive action, but to carry her off from the abbey could bring us both nothing but grave danger. It was surely best to use the weapon of the law.

'I will bring you the tawny gold ink,' I said, in a voice loud enough to be heard by Sister Mildred in the library. 'Probably in two days' time.' I lowered my voice and added. 'By then, I shall have spoken to a lawyer. Be of good courage.'

I stepped through the door to the library and bade farewell to the precentrix, then made my way out of the cloisters and across the enclave to the gatehouse.

'Very talented artist, isn't she?' John Barnes said, as I unhitched Rufus and prepared to mount. 'Not happy here, though.'

I paused, with my left foot in the stirrup. 'I am sure you are a good friend to her.'

He smiled. 'Not much help a lay servant can be to one of the ladies, Master Elyot. Nor you neither.'

He was no fool, John Barnes.

I swung my right leg over the horse's back and gathered up the reins. 'I shall be back in a few days, with the ink for the lions,' I said.

'Aye,' he said, and winked.

҈

Emma turned her head cautiously and watched him stride away across the cloister garth. It was unreasonable to have expected him to help her. If he should be caught trying to smuggle her out of the abbey, he might be accused of any number of serious crimes. Abduction of a nun – even if she was only a novice – probably carried the death penalty. They would accuse him of rape, and no matter how violently she claimed that it was at her own instigation, she would be ignored, being a mere woman, and unfit to give evidence in such a case.

For a moment it had seemed possible. An ally, a man from outside the abbey, who had already shown her kindness over the matter of William's death. And who seemed, unless she was imagining it, to care more for her than merely as a well-disposed stranger. She shivered. Her own feelings were confused. But she must keep her head clear. Nothing mattered now but escape from the abbey. Afterwards – if there should be an afterwards – in the world outside, then she would let herself think about Nicholas Elyot. As for now, she was alone, and she must take action alone and for herself.

She bent over her work again, but her hand was too unsteady to form the letters with the meticulous care she demanded of herself. Instead she picked up the paper Nicholas had left and unfolded it. It was ridiculous that her heart beat a little faster as she did so. When he had laid it on the desk, their hands had touched, and the paper had been warm. Now it was merely a sheet of paper, containing a list of the additions the Lady Amilia wished to have included in her book of hours.

So he had written this. It was excellent penmanship. She smiled. He could even earn his living as a scrivener, if he wished. Although she, being a mere woman, could not. She would have enjoyed completing this book of hours, even with all the unnecessary additions, but she knew that she could not. What she had told Nicholas Elyot was true. It would be impossible to finish it before the date set for her admission as a professed nun, therefore she must leave the work incomplete. She felt a pang of regret at the thought that someone else would finish the book, for it would have been some of her best work. Sister Mildred had a beautiful hand, but her drawings were tentative, as though she was shy of allowing herself too much freedom in a holy book. Sister Aegytha, the only other sister who sometimes worked in the scriptorium, mainly copying service books, was competent but dull.

After reading through the list of additions, she folded the paper again and tucked it into the breast of her habit, where it gave her a sudden spasm of delight. Then she bent to her task again. Her hand was steady now. She must make the best of the light.

Nicholas Elyot had said he would return in two days, and would speak to a lawyer before then, to discover whether it would be possible to delay her vows until the case might be taken to court, but Emma herself held out little hope of such an outcome. She was sure that she understood better than any outsider just how powerful the Church was in controlling its members, particularly the women. They would be unlikely to allow the secular authority, even a royal court, to interfere with its internal affairs. Abbess Agnes de Streteley came of a great aristocratic family. She was accustomed to exercising power and would not be intimidated by the intervention of some provincial lawyer from Oxford.

Before Nicholas's visit Emma had known she had less than two weeks to effect her escape. Now she knew she must leave before the two days were up. For if Nicholas and his lawyer arrived with his proposal of delay, she would be watched all the more carefully. Why had she not told him that he should not come? She had not been thinking clearly. She must think clearly and carefully now.

The cotte and hose remained concealed under the lavender hedge. Fortunately there had been no rain. But she still lacked some kind of covering for her head. And it would be wise to carry food with her, for she had no idea how long it would take to reach Oxford on foot, nor was she clear about the route, although she knew that the river led to the city. If she followed the river it might not be the shortest way, but it must bring her there in the end.

All these thoughts swarmed in her head like bees while her hand continued automatically to copy the prayers for Ash Wednesday. A day of lamentation. Appropriate for one who was about to defy Holy Church. Abandoning her place as a novice in this quiet abbey was a kind of defiance, a rejection of God Himself. For a moment she caught her breath and her hand froze on the page. *Jesu, forgive me, that is not my intention.* She closed her eyes and breathed in and out slowly. The thought was terrifying. Was she condemning herself to eternal hellfire for her sins?

When she opened her eyes again, she saw that a drop of ink was about to fall from her quill and ruin the nearly completed page. Carefully she wiped the tip of the quill on the lip of the ink well. It was fortunate that Sister Mildred was still busy in the library and had noticed nothing.

It would be necessary to make her escape at night, for there would be no opportunity by day, when the whole enclave was full of people, religious and secular, about their daily business. And there were only two ways out, for she could not climb over the wall. Standing as it did on an island, Godstow was nearly as impregnable as a fortified manor, and as difficult to leave as to enter. The usual entrances and exits were through the gatehouse, which would be locked at night, when John Barnes retired to bed in his rooms in its upper storey.

There was another possible way. The meadow beyond the abbey gardens lay in a loop of one of the branches of the river which encircled the abbey. Normally the river was as formidable a barrier as the walls, but the continual hot dry weather had caused it to shrink. Emma had no way of knowing how deep it might be. The day she had walked into the river and been beaten for it, the river had been flowing fast, but, when she had waded perhaps a quarter of the way across, the water had only reached a little above her knees. It was certain to be deeper in the middle and she could not swim. Did she dare venture that way? She might risk drowning.

She had thought of trying to hide in one of the carts or boats which brought supplies to the abbey, but rejected the idea. As they returned empty, she would have nowhere to hide. She had offered to run errands for the chambress to the home farm, which lay across the bridge, on land near the village of Wolvercote, but had been refused. It was as though Sister Piety suspected that her intentions were not without some hidden purpose. Or else all the sisters had been instructed not to allow her outside the walls. This was not the case with all the novices. Sister Ursula frequently went to the farm, and had once accompanied Sister Piety to Oxford to order supplies. It was clear Ursula was hoping that, once she had taken her vows, she might find a place as assistant to one of the obedientiaries, the first step on a remorseless climb up the abbey hierarchy.

Emma realised that she had been copying the prayer and had even begun a new page without being aware of what she was doing. She stopped writing and read what she had written, but there seemed to be no mistakes.

It must needs be tonight. Despite the continued heat, clouds were gathering. If she was any judge, they threatened a heavy storm and that meant the river would rise. The way across the river was the only possibility, and she could not risk any delay. If it should prove that the river was too deep to wade across, she might drown, but she no longer cared. Better a quick death now than the long slow death of a lifetime imprisoned here against her will.

'The light is beginning to fade, Sister Benedicta.' The

precentrix had emerged from the library and was looking down at Emma's work. 'You have done well today. These additions that the lady requires, will they be difficult?'

'Nay, sister,' Emma said. She wiped her quill clean on a rag, and flexed her fingers. 'They are quite simple, really, although I am not sure about the perpetual calendar.'

'There is one in the library. Come, I will show you.'

They went together into the library, Emma carrying with her the half finished sheets of her book of hours. Sister Mildred lifted down a large volume and opened it on the slope of the reading desk.

'This is a most useful work, though somewhat disorganised. You must read it when you have time. Maps, terrestrial and celestial, a copy of the Reverend Bede's *History*, explanations of how the date of Easter is to be calculated, and even some advice on the use of medicinal herbs. All put together some hundred years ago and given to the abbey, but a little haphazardly. Ah, here we are. The perpetual calendar.'

It was a kind of grid of letters and numbers, with notes below it on how it was to be used, the whole ornamented with suns and moons, and some lively cherubs blowing winds from each corner.

Emma frowned. 'It looks very complicated. Do you suppose the Lady Amilia will understand how to use it?'

Sister Mildred chuckled. 'That need not worry you, child. I do not suppose she will attempt it. I suspect she asked Master Elyot to include it because she had heard of such a thing, and thought it would add to the importance of the book and its owner.'

Emma smiled. Sister Mildred might have lived all her life in the abbey, but that had not prevented her from becoming a shrewd judge of human nature.

'I will leave the book open here for you,' the precentrix said. 'Then you will know where to find it when you need it.'

Emma felt herself flush with guilt, for she knew she would never use it, and regretted that she must deceive one of her few friends here at Godstow.

'Come, it is nearly time for Vespers,' Sister Mildred said.

They left the library together, the precentrix heading toward the church to ensure that all was ready for the service, one of the duties of her post, while Emma took Jocosa up to the dortoir, to wait there while she herself attended Vespers. It was only when she reached her cubicle that she realised she was still carrying the sheaf of parchment. What should she do? There would be no chance to return it to the library this evening, with all that she must do. She needs must leave it on her bed when she left. In the meantime she slipped the pages under her mattress.

It seemed that Fortune, or perhaps some kindly saint, had laid a protective hand over her that evening. When she went to fetch food for Jocosa from the kitchen before supper, she was able to slip half a loaf and a piece of cheese into the wide sleeve of her habit. On the way out, she noticed some oiled cloths stacked up in one of the pantries. These were used for wrapping certain food stuffs to keep them from developing mould, and were fairly waterproof. She had been worried about setting off with her clothes soaking from the river, but if she made the crossing in her habit, she could wrap the stolen garments in one of these cloths. It would keep them fairly dry, and she could change into them once she was safely on the far bank. Glancing quickly behind her, she made sure that all the kitchen servants were occupied, then grabbed the largest of the oiled cloths and slipped it down the front of her habit. It made a noticeable bulge, but she hurried across the enclave to the dortoir, and hoped no one would notice.

During supper she closed her ears to the passage from the testament of Matthew being read aloud for the nuns' improvement while they ate, and concentrated on what she must do. It would be necessary to leave during the hours of darkness, but she could not do so before the midnight services of Matins and Lauds, or her absence would be noticed at once. She must wait until everyone had returned to the dortoir to sleep, then creep out once it was safe to do so. That would give her until the service of Prime at dawn. It was unfortunate that dawn was early in midsummer, but she would have been on her way for a few hours by then.

If only she had something to cover her shorn head! She could not wear her monastic headgear. All through the meal she fretted about this. When the final grace was said and the nuns dismissed for their brief leisure time before Compline, she made up her mind to run a necessary risk.

Leaving the frater after supper, she collected Jocosa, then walked confidently to the gatehouse. There was nothing unusual in this, for John Barnes often looked after Jocosa, and everyone was accustomed to seeing her at the gatehouse with the dog. As she had hoped, he was sitting outside, enjoying the cool of the evening, the plate that had contained his supper – brought to him by one of the scullions – on the ground beside him.

'Evening, Sister Benedicta,' he said cheerfully. 'You'll not be needing me to mind the dog this late in the day?'

'Nay, but she needed a walk.' Emma drew a deep breath. 'John, I have a favour to ask of you. Will you lend me a cap? Nay, will you give me a cap? Like the one you are wearing?'

He stared at her, puzzled, and touched the cap of coarse brown cloth atop his thick head of wiry dark curls. 'A cap like this, Sister? Why would you want an ugly old thing like this? Is it for one of your drawings?'

'Best you don't know, John.'

He gave her another sharp look, then got to his feet. 'Wait you a moment.'

He went into the gatehouse and returned a few minutes later with a rather better cap, of blue woollen cloth. 'Would this suit?'

'That is your best.'

'Only the best for you, Sister Benedicta.' He held it out and she took it, hesitated a moment, then folded it and slipped it into her pocket.

'I'll not ask,' he reassured her.

'I thank you, John, for this and for . . . for everything. You never gave me a cap, if you don't mind.'

'What cap?'

She smiled. 'Good night, John.'

'Good night.' As she turned away, he whispered, 'Fare you well, my maid, and may God go with you.'

'And with you, John,' she murmured, without turning round.

The nuns were supposed to sleep between Compline and Matins, but once Emma could hear soft breathing around her, she made her preparations as quietly as she could. Before Compline she had fetched the stolen clothes, which she now wrapped, along with the cap and the food, in the oiled cloth from the kitchen. At the last minute, she added the manuscript pages to the bundle, for she realised that leaving them openly on the bed would simply advertise that she had gone. She hoped that at first they would search the enclave, which would give her a little more time, before they sought her further afield. Taking the manuscript was stealing, she supposed, but a trivial crime compared with the greater one she was committing.

When she came to cross the river, she would tie the bundle to her waist with her rope girdle, for she would need both hands to hold on to Jocosa. She was not at all sure how the little dog would react to being carried across the river. She might be quite unmoved, or she might panic and struggle. When all her preparations were done, she lay down on her hard bed with Jocosa curled up beside her. The nuns did not sleep on bare boards, but the straw mattresses were so thin that the bed was never comfortable, so Emma was sure that she would have no difficulty in staying awake after the midnight services.

There was always a curious quality about the services of Matins and Lauds, the second following immediately upon the heels of the other. Nuns and novices descended the night stairs into the church by the light of a single candle, leaving the schoolgirls at the far end of the dortoir to their sleep. The church was a cave of mysterious shadows, even the great east window nothing but darkness, except where, here and there, the glass caught a reflected gleam from the altar candles. The women filed into the choir stalls in silence but for the shuffling of sandals on stone. Some seemed hardly to wake, but to move and sing in their sleep. They sang without choir books, and without candles, the simple plainsong of the night services. The abbess stood remote at the altar, the prioress beside her partly concealing one of the great altar candles, seen from where Emma stood, so that she seemed to wear an areole of lambent light, yet melted into dark nothingness herself.

This is the last time I shall sing here, Emma thought, raising her voice in praise and glory to God. I wish I might have been at one with these women, many of whom are good and admirable. Perhaps, had I not been forced . . .

The slow procession mounted the night stairs again to the dortoir and in silence each moved to her own cubicle. The ritual was engrained, so accustomed that most slept at once, bodies relaxed into the few hours of sleep before the dawn service.

Emma lay rigid, suddenly afraid that the slumberous air would betray her into sleep. If she slept, her bundle would be discovered in the morning, and all would be lost. Someone coughed, further along the dortoir. It was the elderly Sister Aegytha. She had been coughing earlier, during Compline, and now it had begun again. It would keep her awake, and she lay between Emma and the outside stairs.

Gingerly, willing the straw of her mattress not to rustle, Emma swung her legs round to the floor and sat up on the edge of the bed. Jocosa was immediately alert. Emma stroked her. If the dog made a noise now, she was lost. She groped under the bed for her bundle, and picked up her sandals with her other hand. Going barefoot, she could move more silently.

Sister Aegytha coughed again.

Emma felt sweat break out around her neck and back. What if the old nun never fell asleep, but lay awake and coughing all night? Time crawled by. She heard the creak of the bed as the nun turned over, then she was silent. Still silent. She would have to risk it. She lifted Jocosa and tucked her under the arm holding the sandals, for she dared not let the dog run across the floor, her claws were so noisy on the bare boards.

She had almost reached the head of the stairs, when Sister Aegytha coughed again. Then she murmured sleepily, 'Sister?'

Emma did not wait, but hurried on. Blessedly the door at the top of the outside stairs was left open on these hot nights, for the hinges squealed loudly.

Down the stairs, struggling to hold Jocosa, who was wriggling delightedly at this unexpected walk. Nearly, Emma dropped her. The foot of the stairs now, and the open court, a woven pattern of greys and black, under an almost moonless sky. It was something she had forgotten to allow for, just how dark it would be.

She set Jocosa down and began to feel her way toward the gate into the abbey garden. There were sharp stones underfoot, but she dared not stop to put on her sandals.

The garden, being more open, seemed less dark, or perhaps her eyes were becoming accustomed to the night. Jocosa ran joyfully ahead, untroubled by the dark and heading for the meadow. Once through the gate into the meadow, Emma stopped. Her heart was pounding in her throat, and she felt sick, but she must remember just what she needed to do. Sitting on the ground, she put on her sandals and untied her rope girdle. It was quite long, normally hanging nearly to the ground, but even so there was only just enough to tie round her bundle and then around her waist. She tugged at it. It seemed firm enough.

Suddenly there was a yelp and an indignant bleat from a goat. Emma sprang to her feet. For once Jocosa must have ventured near the goats and the encounter had not been pleasant. Would anyone have heard, inside the abbey? A furry shape pressed itself against her legs, and she scooped the dog up, hiding her face against the soft fur.

'Foolish dog,' she whispered. 'I hope you are not hurt. Now we must both be brave.'

She felt her way across the meadow to the large willow where she had stepped into the river before. On that occasion she had noticed a bank of shingle part way across, so it looked like a possible way to ford the river. But that had been in the daylight. Now, although she had gained some night vision, she was not at all sure that she could find it again.

Here was the river's edge, and this must be the little cove she had found before. She stepped into the water, which was surprisingly cold. She had decided to wear her sandals, for it would have been difficult to carry them as well as the dog, and besides they would be some protection against sharp stones on the river bed.

The water was lower than it had been before. Nearly halfway across and the water had risen barely to her knees, soaking her habit, which dragged at her legs. She should have kilted it up, but could do nothing now, with the dog in one arm and steadying the awkward bundle with her other hand as it banged against her side.

Here was the patch of shingle. She climbed on to it thankfully, and paused to draw breath. Jocosa, who had been quiet until now, either because the goat had frightened her or because she was puzzled by Emma's behaviour, now began to squirm, demanding to be put down.

Emma gripped her more firmly and stepped into the river again. She could make out the loom of the further bank now, only a few yards away, but the water on this side of the shingle was deeper, as though the river had scooped out a hollow here. She slid one foot carefully in front of the other. The water was up to her thighs now and her sodden habit clung to her legs like clutching arms.

Then her foot reached out and found nothing. The river bed fell away and Emma pitched forward. Jocosa leapt from her arms with a squeal. Then the river caught her up and bore her away.

Chapter Six

All the way back to Oxford, I cursed myself for my weakness. The girl was desperate in her appeal for help, and I had nothing to offer her but the vague promise of a lawyer, so far unknown, and a bottle of tawny gold ink. Fool! Coward! Cautious as an old maid afraid to cross the road without help! I despised myself. An old grandfather would have ventured more for her sake.

That put me in mind of her own grandfather, lying sick and alone on his manor away to the south of the county. And her unscrupulous stepfather living – where? – somewhere nearby? I must ask Mistress Farringdon. Could the fellow really have forced Emma into the nunnery, given her as an oblate, as part of a plan to seize her inheritance? Not only would such an action be a crime against the girl herself. It was an insult to God, to use His Church as an instrument in perpetrating a devious scheme to gain worldly wealth. The man would be punished for such a sin in the life hereafter, but I must find a way to ensure that he was foiled in the life here and now.

This resolution did something, though not a great deal, to assuage my guilt. In one aspect I was sure that I was right. The matter of whether Emma could be forced to take her final vows must be decided in court, so that there could be no question about her status as laity in the future. Supposing, perhaps, that she might wish to marry.

I jerked my mind away from that notion.

We were nearing the North Gate of Oxford, and I had

hardly realised that I had been riding down St Giles. It was fortunate that Rufus knew his own way home, for I was certainly not guiding him. For once Northgate Street was relatively quiet, so I soon turned into the High and returned Rufus to the Mitre. I considered walking round the corner to St Mildred Street to ask Maud Farringdon where Emma's stepfather lived, but decided against it. At present, I had no real need to know. Later, when it was a matter of taking Emma's case to Chancery, it would be necessary.

As I continued down the High, I ran over in my mind such lawyers as I knew in Oxford. Most, if not all, were scholars of jurisprudence, not practising lawyers, but surely they would know how the law stood in the case of a woman forced into a nunnery. There must have been other such cases. Jordain knew more law than I did, but his interests lay in the field of theory, the ethics and moral basis of law. There was John Wycliffe, of course, a brilliant man, but he was contentious, more likely to stir up trouble than to give a calm appraisal of Emma's rights under the law. He would go galloping away on one of his wild theories about the Church. Nay, Wycliffe would not be the best man to approach.

Just as I reached my shop, already closed and shuttered by Walter, another name occurred to me. I stopped. Philip Olney. Although Olney was now *librarius* of Merton College and jealous custodian of its valuable collection of books, he also lectured in the law. His own advanced studies had lain in that field. It was his bibliographical passion which had prompted him to persuade Merton to put him in charge of their books, and I knew he was arguing that a dedicated building should be erected in the college grounds to house the ever growing collection. However, he had continued to lecture in both Canon and Common Law, for there was a great demand in England for more trained lawyers to be turned out by the universities, especially since King Edward had taken the organisation of the country in hand. Every county of England needed lawyers for the administration of local justice, and the reorganisation of England's central government and the major law courts in London demanded even more trained men. Many a boy coming to Oxford from a quite humble background could – with talent and hard work – rise high through a career in law.

It would be an hour or more before Margaret would expect me for supper. There was time to go in search of Philip Olney.

I retraced my steps a short way and headed down Magpie Lane, reaching Merton, as I realised too late, just at the hour the Fellows would be sitting down to their evening meal.

'Master Olney?' the porter said. 'Nay, Master Elyot, he went out some time ago and he'll not be back now to eat in Hall. When he goes out of an evening he is often not back till the morning.'

His face was bland and the tone of his voice gave nothing away, but the absence of a Fellow overnight from his college tended to mean only one thing amongst the well informed college porters – a visit to a whore house. There was one nearby in Magpie Lane, a street which had another, more unsavoury name, but a visit there was unlikely to involve an overnight stay.

I wondered whether the porter knew, as I did, where Philip Olney was in truth likely to be found. Like others of his profession, Merton's porter was probably privy to most of the Fellows' secrets, but I knew that Olney had gone to a good deal of trouble to keep this particular secret well hidden from his college, for fear of the consequences.

'No matter,' I said. 'The affair is not urgent. I will speak to him tomorrow.'

Fired up with my eagerness to consult a lawyer, however, I had no intention of waiting until the morrow, but walked east along the High, past my shop, past the turn to Hammer Hall Lane and out through the East Gate.

Between the gate and the Hospital of St John, which lay on my left just before the bridge over the Cherwell, there was a row of pleasant small houses, mostly, from their appearance, occupied by craftsmen and small traders. The third cottage was particularly neat and pretty, the area before the front door laid out in symmetrical beds with medicinal and culinary herbs and such flowers as lavender and marigolds which are both ornamental and useful. The door gleamed with fresh paint and the windows (unlike most of the other houses in the row) were glazed. Although the cheap glass was lumpy and irregular, it would allow light into the house when its neighbours must either remain dark with their shutters closed or freeze with them open in winter weather.

On the other side of the road, but further on and opposite the front of the hospital, there was another row of cottages, altogether more shabby and neglected than these. I hesitated in front of the third house on the left. Although I was certain that this was where I should find Philip Olney, I was suddenly conscious that I had no right to intrude on him here, although he was aware that I knew of the house and what – or rather who – it contained.

While I was still standing there, debating with myself and occasionally being jostled by passersby heading for the East Bridge, the door opened and a woman stepped out. She was younger than Olney by perhaps ten years, near my own age, and very pretty, a fresh country beauty I would have thought, and not the sort to have been found in Magpie Lane. I had seen her once before, at a distance. Seen closer, she was even prettier. I thought she had come out to gather herbs from the garden, but instead she approached me smiling.

'Master Elyot? Were you looking for Philip?'

I was taken aback at her words, in the first place because she knew my name, and in the second because she was aware that I knew of her connection with Olney. It could only mean that he had told her. I found myself unaccountably blushing.

'Indeed I was, mistress. Is he here?'

'He is. Will you step inside?'

I walked up the path between bushy hedges of

lavender, whose full summer blooms cast up their sweet and spicy scent as I brushed against them, and found myself being ushered directly into the main room of the cottage, which was not unlike the Farringdons' house, but much more comfortably furnished and full of the signs of family life: several bright rugs, a drop spindle wound with wool, a basket of darning, on the table three pewter plates scattered with crumbs, a fine shawl thrown over a coffer, and several books. Books? Was she literate? Beside the plates there were a few sheets of rough paper and a child's horn book. On the far side of the table Philip Olney was sitting on a stool and appeared to be mending a small shoe with cobbler's twine.

For a moment I was lost for words.

'Please to sit down, Master Elyot.' The woman cleared a stool of a small pair of hose she must have been darning. She had been sitting with her back to the window, so it had been Olney who had seen me out in the street.

He looked at me, half smiling but nervous, as I sat down. The woman brought a flagon of ale and poured for both of us, but took none herself.

'Good evening, Philip,' I said, raising the pewter cup. 'I thank you, mistress.'

'My dear,' he said, 'may I present Master Nicholas Elyot, bookseller and sometime scholar of this university? Nicholas, this is Beatrice Metford.'

I rose and bowed. Colouring, she dropped a curtsey, then sat down and took up her mending. I was pleased that Olney had presented me to her first, rather than the other way about, just as he would have done for a woman of higher rank. Yet it was difficult to discern exactly to what rank she belonged. I knew that she was Olney's mistress, but she was certainly no whore.

'You are not making a very good job of that,' I said, gesturing at the shoe, where the twine had now become entangled in several knots. 'Let me look at it. This cannot be so very different from bookbinding.'

He handed me the shoe, needle, and twine with some

eagerness. The upper of the shoe had become detached from the sole, and all it needed was some simple stitching. I borrowed Beatrice's scissors and cut away his poor effort. When I had threaded the needle and begun to sew the two parts of the shoe together, Olney gave me a wry smile.

'Is there no end to your talents, Nicholas? I did not have you down as a cobbler.'

'My father-in-law obliged me to learn a little about book binding. I enjoy working with leather. There, it is finished.' I bit off my thread. 'It is your son's shoe, mistress?'

'Aye.' She looked startled, but then relaxed, perhaps realising that if Olney had told me about her, he might well have mentioned the boy. 'He is abed now. Philip carried him up. He finds the stairs difficult.'

She nodded towards a sturdy staircase which led up from the back of the room, much better than the stairs in the Farringdons' kitchen.

'My son is lame, Master Elyot, and drags his foot. His shoe springs apart.'

I nodded my understanding. I had seen the boy in the spring, walking with crutches. He was the very image of his father.

'What is his name?'

'We call him Stephen,' she said, then blushed again, for by saying 'we', she made clear Olney's relationship to the child.

'You are teaching him, Philip?' I indicated the horn book and the papers, on which I could see childish writing.

'I am. It would not be easy for him to attend school, although he is a bright child, and also has a pure singing voice. However, I do not think one of the choir schools would take him.'

Once again I nodded my understanding. The Church is prejudiced against those whose bodies are not perfectly formed.

'It is about a Church matter that I wished to consult you.'

He looked astonished. 'I thought you were about to offer me some wonderful new book for our collection.'

I laughed. 'Not this time. Nay, it is a matter of law that I thought you might be able to explain.'

I saw that Mistress Metford was listening with interest, but now she rose. 'You will not want me here.'

'Please do not go,' I said. 'There is nothing secret about this. Philip may know the point of law which I need to understand.'

She sat down again and I turned to Olney.

'This is the case. A young woman of seventeen was forced by her stepfather to enter a nunnery as a novice, against her wish, her mother being dead. She has no vocation for the religious life and abhors the thought of taking vows. Now, a year later, she has been told that her stepfather signed papers handing her over as an oblate, given irrevocably to God, and she *must* take her final vows. She wishes to leave the nunnery and resume a secular life. Do you know what her position would be, in law? Would it make a difference that she was not given as an infant or young child?'

Olney drummed on the table with his fingers.

'Difficult. It is an area somewhere between Common Law and Canon Law.'

'That is what I feared.'

'The Church would argue that once the girl became a novice, she was entirely under their jurisdiction and the matter must be settled under Canon Law.'

'And they would insist that she must remain a nun?'

'Almost certainly. No doubt the stepfather provided an ample nun's dowry to buy her a place in the nunnery. They would be eager to retain that. Even more eager to stamp out any examples of backsliding amongst its nuns, lest such disobedience should spread.' His tone was sour. He had good reasons to deplore certain aspects of the Church's laws for men like himself.

'What would be the view of secular law?'

'Difficult to say with certainty. If any force was used

against the girl, it might support her wish to leave. On the other hand, in some cases a woman is regarded in law as a child. She cannot make such decisions for herself. You say she was seventeen when she entered? And under the care of a stepfather? Even if he was not kin, he would probably be regarded as her legal guardian and so free to dispose of her as he wished, as surely as if she *were* a young child.'

I thought of the capable women in my family, my sister Margaret, my wife Elizabeth, even Alysoun, who at six had more intelligence and strength of will than many a grown man. 'It seems unjust,' I said slowly. 'I wonder whether that is another ill practice that John Wycliffe opposes.'

'Do not pin your hopes of reform on Wycliffe's wild fancies.' Olney grinned. 'We must deal with the law as it exists.'

'Very true.' I sipped my ale, thinking. It was excellent and I wondered whether Mistress Metford had brewed it herself. Many women bought their household ale from vintners like Edric Crowmer or professional ale-wives, but those who took pride in their housekeeping brewed their own.

'The girl in question does have one male kinsman,' I said. 'Her grandfather, the father of her father. He disapproved of her widowed mother marrying again, so I do not know what may be his relationship with his granddaughter. He is said to be in his final illness.'

'Hmm.' Olney drummed his fingers on the table again. 'In that case, if the grandfather was prepared to sign a document asserting that it was his wish that the girl should be released from her vows, it would probably count for more than the stepfather's actions.' He gave a wry smile. 'Even more so if he waived his right to the return of the dowry. Is he a man of some standing?'

'Aye, a knight. And, I believe, a man of property. The girl is his only heir.'

'Aha! Do I smell a rat?'

'Probably.'

'Well, well, Nicholas, it seems you have nosed out a pretty plot once more.' He rubbed his hands together. 'One which – it is to be hoped – will not put you and your family in danger again. I have reason to be grateful to you for your–' He searched for the right word.

'Interference? Nosiness into the affairs of others?'

'I was going to say your championship of those less fortunate than yourself.'

He glanced across at Beatrice Metford. I guessed from her expression that she was well aware of the history between us.

'May I know the name of this unfortunate novice?' he asked.

I hesitated. I had wished to consult him merely on the point of law, but it seemed I might need his help in pursuing the matter further, certainly in drawing up a legally valid document for Emma's grandfather to sign, if Sir Anthony could be persuaded to do so. Or was not so ill that he could not write his name.

'Her name is Emma Thorgold, or Sister Benedicta, novice at Godstow Abbey.' I paused. 'She is the cousin of the late William Farringdon.'

Olney went quite white, and I saw that his hands, loosely clasped before him on the edge of the table, began to tremble, so that he clenched them together until the joints stood out white against the skin. Although unintentionally, Olney was not altogether without blame in the matter of William's murder by his colleague at Merton, the equally late, but unlamented, Allard Basset.

He let out his breath in a long sigh.

'So that is how you know her.'

'That is how I know her. I took her word when her cousin was killed. And it was she who had your Irish Psalter hidden away for safety.'

'I see. In that case, I will do all I can to help her, but I think I would have done so in any case. Such a forcing into the religious life is distasteful.'

All this while, Beatrice Metford had continued with

her sewing in silence, only looking up from time to time to glance from one to the other of us. Now she spoke for the first time.

'Of course you will help her, Philip. A woman has as much right to justice and to choose her own life as a man. We are not children.'

I saw a look flash between them and realised that what she said held more significance than the mere words themselves, but this was a matter into which I had no intention of prying.

'I am grateful, Philip,' I said, 'for although I studied as much of the law as was necessary to graduate as a Master, I barely dipped below the surface. If you could draw up a suitable document for the grandfather to sign, I will try to discover whether it will be possible for me to visit him. Mistress Farringdon may know. Emma's aunt.'

He nodded. 'I will do it tomorrow. With the students away I am not much occupied.'

'I ride out to Godstow in two days' time,' I said. 'My excuse – to take a bottle of tawny gold for the illuminated book of hours Emma is making. Why do you not come with me? That way you can ask her any questions that might be necessary.'

'Do you think we would be admitted? Two men, not kin, allowed to visit a novice?'

'In the ordinary way of things, perhaps not, but I have already arranged with the librarian, who is in charge of Emma's work, that I will bring the ink. You can be presented as her man of law.'

'That may well put a cat amongst these holy doves. Still, if you think we may bring it off, I will come. Perhaps I should wait to draw up the document until I have spoken to her.'

'One other point,' I said. 'You mentioned it might count in her favour if force was used. I am not sure about force, but I do know that her stepfather sent her surrounded by an armed escort, rather more than would be necessary for quite a short journey.'

He nodded. 'In such a situation it would have been difficult for her to resist. It will help to strengthen our case.'

I was pleased that he said 'our'. It seemed he was committed to Emma's defence. I felt more optimistic than I had done since leaving the abbey, for from what Olney said it seemed that there would be a good case in law to support Emma's determination to leave the cloister. At least a court should be prepared to hear the case, which was the essential first step.

'Tomorrow I will see whether I can find any precedents,' Olney said. 'I am sure there have been other cases of women enclosed against their will, who were able to secure their release.'

I stood up. 'I am grateful to you, Philip. If you can make a case, perhaps we can help the girl. There is not much time. She told me that she is expected to make her final vows in less than two weeks' time.'

'So soon?' He looked worried. 'There is no chance of a hearing by then, but we can argue for a delay, especially if we have the grandfather's support. I have not heard that the abbess is an unreasonable woman.' He stood up also.

'Not unreasonable, I should say, but a woman of great strength of will, accustomed to being obeyed. And one who would not endure any slight upon her abbey, which this will likely seem.'

'We shall move with great courtesy,' he said. 'Stay, will you not sup with us?'

I smiled. 'I think you have supped already, Philip. Nay, I thank you, but my sister expects me, I gave her my word.'

I turned to Mistress Metford. 'I am sorry to have intruded upon your evening, mistress.'

'You have not intruded, Master Elyot. I am grateful to have met you.' She rolled up her mending and laid it on the table. 'I truly hope you are able, between you, to help this girl. It seems to me she has been monstrously ill used.'

'She has,' I said. 'But I hope, with Philip's help, we

may be able to set her free.'

As I stepped outside and turned back toward home, I felt the first tentative drops of rain. They did nothing to dampen my sense that I was on my way to atoning for my previous cowardice.

∾∾

She could not breathe. There was darkness all around her, a swirling darkness, and she was being tossed round and round like an empty sack, except that she was not empty. Nay, her body was not empty but heavy, encased in clinging, tangled cloth. Her chest was bursting as though it would explode at any moment, yet it felt as though an iron band was tightening around it, holding it closed. That band and her exploding lungs fought each other. She had once watched a wheelwright fit the iron rim round a wooden wheel, and as it cooled it grew tighter and tighter, until it held all the separate parts of the wheel together in its relentless grip.

Why was she thinking of wheels? She was become a wheel. A wheel, turning and turning.

At first she did not know what had happened or where she was, but then she realised. She was in the river and she was going to drown. The dog had leapt from her arms. Such a small dog. A small dog would have no chance in this river, a river which was bearing her inexorably along. She opened her mouth to cry, 'Jocosa!' and swallowed water. She began to choke. Then she rolled over and for a moment her head was out of the water and she gasped for air, then she went down again. Her thick habit, sodden and heavy, was dragging her deeper.

It would not be long now, before the end.

Holy Mary, Mother of God. The words went through her head, but what could the Blessed Mary do for her now, a self-condemned renegade novice? The pain in her chest was almost unbearable. Soon she would grow unconscious, and then it would be over.

Something struck her hard on the head. Something caught hold of her and held her fast, as it fought against the flow of the current. Why had she ever thought the river was low and quiet, easy to cross? It was a wild beast, determined to devour her, in despite of whatever this was, that was holding her back.

With the last of her strength she reached up to feel what had hit her. Her hand met wood. Wet. A thick branch, fallen out over the river, with many small branches sprouting from it? Nay, that felt wrong. She struggled to get her arm around it, in case it decided to abandon the battle with the river and let her drift away. With almost the last of her strength she hauled her head and shoulders out of the water and lay across the branch, spitting and retching.

A fallen branch, and at any moment it might part company with the bank and float away down the river.

Desperately she scrabbled at the thing until she could get a better hold, then began to inch her way painfully sideways toward the bank.

It wasn't a branch, it was a root. The root of one of the riverside willows, projecting out into the river. A blessed root, firmly joined to the trunk of the tree. She lay on her stomach across it, half laughing, half crying. Unlike a fallen branch, it would not part company with the trunk of the tree. If she could just drag herself a few more feet she could scramble on to land.

She was so weak by now that she almost gave up, but some tiny flame of courage or determination drove her on until she rolled over on the hardened mud of the bank and lay too exhausted to sit up. The hateful bundle was still attached to her waist and had probably helped to drag her down. But Jocosa was gone. She began to weep. It was all her own fault. She should have left the little dog behind, safe in the abbey. John Barnes would have cared for her. Now Jocosa was drowned and no one to blame but herself and her selfish folly.

How long she lay there, she could not say. Away down river there was a rumble of thunder. Earlier, as they had processed into the church for Vespers, there had been a brief shower, but it was soon over. Now she heard the whisper of a few first drops of rain on the leaves of the willow. The storm, if that was what the thunder presaged, was coming nearer, throwing down the first threatening handfuls of rain. Suddenly aware of how cold and wet she was, Emma shivered. Her wimple had vanished, along with her veil, snatched away by the river, and her habit clung to her in sodden folds.

Somehow she managed to drag herself to her feet and peer around at the place where she had fetched up. The dark was still too intense to make out much of her surroundings, although the racing storm clouds overhead occasionally opened enough to permit a little starlight to filter through. There were more willows here, and an undergrowth of low bushes, too indistinct to make out clearly. She was standing on a small patch of rough grass, almost entirely enclosed by these trees and bushes, though she thought she could just see the traces of a riverside path where she had dragged herself ashore.

She shivered again. If the clothes in her bundle had remained at least partly dry, she should change into them now, for her teeth were beginning to chatter and she was cold, cold to the very bone. How she wished she had stolen a cloak as well. The prolonged hot weather had deceived her into thinking she had no need of one, but she longed for something warm to wrap round her shaking body now.

The water had swollen the cord around the bundle, so that the knots seemed to have fused together and she broke two nails struggling to prise them apart, but at last the awkward thing fell open. One bit of the hose had worked its way out of the oiled wrapping and was wet, but everything else had remained dry. She squeezed the wet portion to rid it of as much of the water as possible, then struggled out of her soaking habit. She was in two minds what to do with the linen nightshift she had worn underneath. It had been her intention to wear it under the cotte, as she had no shirt, but it was now as sodden as the habit, clinging unpleasantly to her skin. She peeled it off and stood naked and shivering as she unfolded the cotte and hose. Her hands were shaking so much, she had difficulty in dressing, but at last she was clothed again, though the rough fabric rubbed her back painfully, where the scabs left by the beating were not yet healed. The shift she wrung out to rid it of as much of the river as possible, and realised she must take it with her, wet as it was, for the change in the weather meant that later she would need the warmth of an extra layer.

John Barnes's cap was a little too large on her shorn head, but it was marvellously comforting, bringing warmth and the memory of one good friend. Her habit she rolled up tightly and pushed under the thickest of the bushes that she could just make out in the intermittent starlight. Then she wrapped up the rest of her bundle, spreading out the shift on one of the bushes to dry, if it might. If the rain held off, yet a while.

As long as it remained so dark, it seemed foolish to try to continue on her way. She had no idea how far the river had carried her, and while it remained so dark she might stumble into the river again, or twist an ankle feeling her way through the undergrowth. She would wait here until the sky began to lighten a little and she could make out the best way to go.

There was a sort of hollow cave amongst the bushes – bushes of broom, *planta genista*, that occasional badge of the royal house of England. Was it fanciful to suppose that was a good omen? Pushing her bundle before her, Emma crawled into the hollow under the broom. If the rain started up again, it would afford some protection. She was shivering a little less now. If only her habit were dry, she could have wrapped it around her for extra warmth.

She curled up on her side, as much to fight the insidious cold as to rest. It would be unwise to sleep, for when the dawn came she might find that this place was near some cottage or farm, and she must not be taken unawares. Now there was no sound to betray human habitation, no barking of a dog, no noise from beasts of the field. Only the relentless rushing of the river, and the whisper of the leaves overhead. The wind was getting up.

When she jerked fully awake, she knew she must have slept after all, or half slept, but not for long, since it was as dark as before. What had disturbed her? Then it came again, a rush of wind through the heavy summer foliage, and the hammer of rain like pebbles on the earth, dried hard after weeks of hot weather. She crawled out of the hollow and retrieved her shift. Left lying on the bush, it would only get even wetter. Back under the arching broom, she laid the shift to one side of the place she had flattened here, like a hare's form. The shift was as wet as before.

If the rain truly set in, not only the shift would be soaking. Soon everything she was wearing would be sodden as well. How foolish she had been, not to procure a cloak. Even if she had taken another of the oiled cloths, she could have draped it around her shoulders for some protection, but she could not spare the one she had. Were she to eat the food, she still needed it to protect the pages of her unfinished book. It had somehow become important to her to keep them intact.

Resigned, she decided that she might as well try to sleep. Few people would be about in the morning if the rain continued, and surely she could avoid them. She needed rest. The half drowning had left her exhausted. Yet it was not easy to sleep, now that she had woken once. The ground was very dry and hard, riddled with roots and punctuated with sharp stones, so firmly embedded in the earth that she broke another nail trying to remove one that was digging painfully into her hip.

Despite the discomfort, eventually sleep overcame her, though her dreams were haunted by frightening images, as if the wall painting of the Last Judgement, which adorned one wall of the abbey church, had come to life. The demons who dragged the sinful down to Hell had burst from the painted image and chased after her in her dream. The entrance to Hell was the gaping mouth of some huge monster, spiked teeth dripping with blood, and the

Devil's imps towed the helpless dead through it and down, down, to flaming fires and bubbling cauldrons of thick oil. The painting had always terrified Emma and now it was come to life in her dreams.

Suddenly something pushed against her and she woke with a shriek.

She lay very still, her heart pounding.

This side of the river, seen from the abbey, appeared mostly uncultivated and wild. So she had assumed there would not be many people about. John Barnes had told her that there used to be a few scattered farms here, but the people had all been wiped out by the Great Pestilence.

In land abandoned by men, the beasts of the forest would return. Wild boar and wolves, the most fearsome amongst such beasts. Even a fox could have a dangerous bite. And dogs whose owners had perished had turned wild and vicious. She had even encountered one at home, before she had come to Godstow. One of her uncle Farringdon's men had shot it with an arrow as it was wreaking havoc amongst the chickens.

With great care she drew herself up into a sitting position. She thought she had once been told that wolves on the whole did not attack people, except the very young or frail. Boar, however, were another matter. One slash of a male boar's tusks could rip a man's belly open.

The creature, whatever it was, pressed against her leg, and whimpered.

It could not be. Could it?

Nervously she reached her hand down and found herself touching matted hair, soaking wet – but familiar.

'Jocosa?' she whispered. 'Oh, Jocosa!'

She gathered up the little dog in her arms and clutched her tightly. The dog licked her chin apologetically, as if to show that she had not intended to abandon her mistress.

'How did you escape that terrible river, little one? Oh, I thought I had lost you forever!'

Jocosa, certain now that she was not going to be

scolded, wriggled into a more comfortable position, thereby managing to transfer much of the wet from her fur to the front of Emma's cotte.

'I suppose dogs know how to swim by instinct,' Emma said. 'Somehow you must have contrived to scramble ashore, but I do not know how you managed it, out of that terrible current.'

Then she remembered that the flow of the water was erratic, some places fast and fierce, in others, small coves hollowed out of the bank, almost tranquil. As Jocosa had leapt from her arms, she had been heading for the bank and must have landed in one of these quieter spots. Afterwards, she must have known by some inexplicable canine sense, that Emma had been borne away down river, and had followed her along the bank.

'Well, little one, I shall keep most of this food for later, but I think you deserve some sustenance after tracing me all this way.'

Burrowing into the now much smaller bundle, she tore off some chunks of bread and fed them to the dog, who gobbled them down eagerly and looked hopefully at the corner of cheese which was poking out. Emma wrapped it again securely in the end of the oiled cloth, keeping it well away from the manuscript, on which it would leave greasy marks.

'Later,' she chided Jocosa. 'We do not know when we may find another meal.'

Despite the fact that her cotte was now wet all across the chest, Emma felt warmer. She eased herself down on to the least uncomfortable part of the ground and put her arms around the dog. Somehow the appearance of Jocosa, small as she was, had banished the fear and despair she had been feeling before. She was not entirely alone in the world. And the survival of the dog as well as her own escape from the river, seemed like a blessing on her plan, if only she could survive long enough to reach Oxford.

She would go to her aunt first, but would explain that she intended to find work and earn her own keep. Any work. And she had the pages of the unfinished book of hours. It was, perhaps, a kind of theft, for the parchment was the property of the abbey, although she considered that the copying and illumination were hers, as the product of her own labours. Once she had work, she would buy parchment to replace what she had taken – what she had stolen – and send it to Sister Mildred. She would hand over the pages to Nicholas Elyot. One of his scriveners could finish the book.

So she argued to herself as her eyes grew heavy with sleep and Jocosa squirmed into a more comfortable position. What she would not articulate to herself, though the thought lurked behind these conscious thoughts, was the hope that Nicholas would allow her to finish the book. No one need know how much had been completed before she left the abbey.

No woman is permitted to be a scrivener, except in a nunnery.

If she completed the book, it would be her last one.

As sleep began to steal over her, she began to pray again, not a desperate appeal for help, but a prayer of thanks. Thanks that Jocosa had survived. Thanks that she herself had not drowned in the river. Thanks that, so far at least, she had escaped the cloistered life.

Holy Mary, Mother of God . . .

Chapter Seven

The storm broke in earnest during the night. A roof of thatch has a number of advantages – it is cheap to replace, even though it provides a refuge for birds and mice and is at risk of fire – but one advantage less commonly realised is its ability to absorb noise. As the downpour hammered on our slate roof for most of the night, I found it difficult to sleep, even when I pulled the feather bed over my head, then threw it aside again, stifled. I suppose it was not entirely the noise which kept me awake.

Ever since I had seen Emma at the abbey I had been acting impetuously, allowing my heart to rule my head. The affairs of the Thorgold and Farringdon families were in truth no affair of mine. What did I think I was about, planning to seek out the dying Sir Anthony Thorgold with a request to sign a legal document, releasing his granddaughter from a religious life to which her legal guardian had promised her? Assuming, that is, that he was her legal guardian, this unknown stepfather. Why should I think ill of him? He might be a most worthy gentleman, who wished only the best for the girl. I knew that Mistress Farringdon did not like him, but that might arise from the fact that her sister had died of his child. Perhaps Emma's mother had wanted the baby. Perhaps we were all maligning the man.

Emma's frantic desire to leave the nunnery might be no more than a young girl's panic after being chastised. Beaten for disobedience. Though she herself had said it was justified. Yet I could not ignore the memory of my first meeting with her, back in the spring. She had been calm, apart from her understandable distress at her cousin's death, but even then she had declared her determination not to take her final vows. This was not a new notion. And young as she was, she was intelligent and clearly had no vocation for the religious life. How many of the women who entered the monastic orders did have such a vocation? I suspected many chose it as a peaceful and safe alternative to being bought and sold in the marriage market, useful commodities with inherited estates attached. For most nuns came of good families. I had heard that the conditions for entering a nunnery were sometimes abused, a substantial price being demanded for the privilege. Few women of lower rank ever became nuns.

How much had the stepfather paid Godstow to take Emma off his hands?

What was he called, the stepfather? Mistress Farringdon had mentioned his name. Falkes Malaliver, that was it. An ugly name. Perhaps it was his name alone which made him loom large as a villain.

And now I was committed to action, having drawn Philip Olney in. I had sought him out meaning merely to clarify a point of law, but somehow it had all got out of hand. Now we were planning an assault upon the abbey, demanding a delay to the service of making Emma a nun, proposing a visit to a dying gentleman who would probably have me thrown out by his servants, and anticipating both the removal of a novice from the jealous arms of the Church, and the presentation of a case at law to the Court of Chancery.

Had I gone mad? I found I was sweating, and threw off the feather bed altogether. The fact was – I could admit it to myself here, alone in the dark – I was more interested in Emma Thorgold than I would care to admit to Philip Olney or anyone else. Elizabeth had been dead for more than four years now, and she still haunted my thoughts, especially when I looked at Alysoun, who grew more like her every day. Yet Emma stirred something in me which was not merely compassion for an unhappy girl. Philip regarded her as some unfortunate to be championed, but if I was honest with myself, I knew that I was being drawn to her for quite other reasons.

As if to emphasise my self-confession, the thunder, which had been drawing gradually nearer, suddenly crashed, so it seemed, directly overhead and the flash of lightning which accompanied it shot slabs of light through the gaps around the shutters of my window. There was a cry from the children's room, then the patter of bare feet on the floor boards. Rafe burst through my door.

'Papa, I don't like it!' he wailed, hurling himself across the room. 'Jonathan says lightning can strike you dead!'

I put my arms around him and drew him into my bed.

'But see,' I said. 'You are quite alive. The lightning did not strike you dead.'

'But it hasn't stopped.' He flinched as another simultaneous flash of lightning and crack of thunder burst seemingly over our very roof. He buried his head against my shoulder.

'Jonathan says, even if the lightning doesn't get you,' he mumbled into my night shift, 'it will hit a tree, and that will fall on you.'

'But lightning always strikes the highest point,' I reassured him. 'None of our trees, and none of our neighbours' trees, are tall enough. Here in Oxford, the tallest things are the churches. I am quite sure we are safely guarded by St Peter's on one side and St Mary's on the other.'

'But God would not let the lightning strike a *church*!' he said in a shocked voice.

'It is not for us to guess what may be God's purpose,' I said. It was a lame answer, but he seemed to accept it.

'Can I stay here with you, Papa?'

'Is Alysoun awake as well?' I could see myself abandoning all hope of sleep as my bed was taken over.

'Not her,' he said dismissively. 'She is snoring like a pig.'

'Rafe, Alysoun does not snore.'

'Well, perhaps not. But sometimes she talks in her sleep.'

'Does she?' This was new to me. I wondered what she said. Such an infringement of one's private thoughts, I have always felt. I hoped I did not do so.

'Very well, you may stay.' I sighed. Rafe is an uncomfortable bed fellow. 'But you must be quiet now. No more talking.'

'I promise.' He wriggled down and sideways, until he was occupying at least two thirds of my bed. 'Goodnight, Papa.'

'Goodnight, my little man.'

I retrieved the feather bed from the floor and made myself as comfortable as possible on what was left to me of the bed. Rafe fell asleep at once, but not before he had pulled most of the feather bed over him.

By the morning I was totally deprived of covering and I had woken with the first cock crow. As I lay there, watching my son's peaceful sleep, I realised that the thunder had passed, but there was still a heavy downpour hitting the roof. Sometime during the night I had decided that I would tell Jordain the outcome of my visit to the abbey and also my discussion with Philip Olney. I need not mention that I had sought Philip out at his mistress's house. I was somewhat ashamed of that, for it was a private part of Philip's life which he needed to keep hidden. A woman with whom he had lived for at least eight years could be counted as a common law wife, which meant he was in danger of losing his fellowship and any future within the university. To hold his position as a Fellow of Merton, he must remain unmarried.

Walter and Roger arrived soon after we had broken our fast, cursing the rain and hanging up dripping cloaks on pegs beside the door. We were unlikely to see much trade today. Business always diminished during the university summer vacation, when most of the students returned to their homes, except for a few (like Jordain's pair), who must undergo their disputations again at the beginning of the Michaelmas term. Some of the Masters left Oxford as well, either to visit family or to travel to one of the other great universities. The current war with France meant it unlikely any would venture to Paris, but there were others where they might meet scholars with similar interests – Padua, Salamanca, Bologna. Some might even venture as far as Prague. Our few customers amongst the townsfolk were mainly merchants' wives, who had the coin to buy books and the leisure to read them, but these ladies would certainly not venture out on such a day.

I donned a stout pair of boots that I wore normally in winter, and my thickest hooded cloak, not for warmth but as some protection against the rain, and set out for Hart Hall. Catte Street was awash, the central kennel running like a stream, with here and there puddles too wide to be jumped over. At Hart Hall I found Jordain and the two students sitting glumly over their books by the light of a smelly tallow candle, for the heavy cloud still lowering over the town cast a gloom over everything. As usual the place reeked of old boiled cabbage.

'I had not expected to see you out in this weather,' Jordain said. 'A wise man stays withindoors.'

'There is a matter I wish to discuss with you,' I said. Now that I was here, I was not quite certain why I had come, although I have always found that Jordain talks good sense, and I was not sure that my own recent actions reflected much of that estimable quality.

Jordain glanced at the two boys, who had abandoned their studies and were regarding my dripping form with interest. I gave them a friendly nod.

'Why do you not let them have a day free of study?' I suggested. 'This weather is gloomy enough. Even with their disputations looming at Michaelmas, I am sure a little leisure will not come amiss.'

The boys exchanged hopeful grins.

'And I am sure they will return to work all the more readily afterwards,' I added, seeing Jordain's doubtful expression.

He shrugged. 'Very well,' he said. 'It is hard work trying to read in this poor light. You shall have the day free from study. But mark what Master Elyot says. I shall expect all the greater effort tomorrow.'

The students gave me a grateful glance and hurried away before Jordain could change his mind. We heard the clatter of their shoes on the stairs as they made for their rooms. Jordain sighed.

'It will be dice or cards,' he said.

'Oh come, it is not so very long since we were their age,' I said. 'I remember that you were not averse to a game or two yourself then.'

'I do not suppose it will do them any harm.' He crossed the room and closed the door which they had left open. 'Ale?'

'Nay, I've not long broken my fast.'

'So why are you here? You did not come out in this foul wet for no reason.'

'Sit down, and I will tell you.'

We sat on opposite sides of the battered trestle table which served Hart Hall for both dining and study, and I gave Jordain a full account of my visit to Godstow, the plea of Emma Thorgold, my determination to discover the legal position, and my discussion with Philip Olney.

To begin with he said nothing, only rubbing his chin with a rasping sound. He cannot have shaved for two or three days.

'Olney is very sound on the law. Practical law,' he said. 'He can be a prissy fellow at times, but there is no faulting him on his knowledge.'

I thought of Philip Olney in that welcoming little house, trying to mend his son's shoe, with the horn book and the written exercises lying amongst the supper plates.

'He's not such a bad fellow when you know him

better,' I said. 'He has offered to draw up a document for Emma's grandfather to sign. He is going to search for legal precedents today.'

'From what those old men at the inn said, over by the ferry, Sir Anthony is very ill. I wonder whether he is capable of signing such a document. Or, provided he is not too ill to understand it, whether he would be willing.'

I shrugged. 'That we cannot know, but I thought I would seek Mistress Farringdon's advice. I am certain she would do anything she can to help Emma.'

'That I am sure she would. But why have you taken this upon yourself, Nicholas? It is no affair of yours.'

He had put his finger on it. 'She appealed to me for help,' I said. 'They keep her very close and I think she knows no one else outside the abbey. Her cousin used to visit her, but since his death, she has no one.'

'Her aunt is now living here in Oxford.'

'Forgive me, Jordain, but I do not think Mistress Farringdon is capable of taking on the might of the Church, however much she might wish to.'

'And you are?'

'With the assistance of Philip Olney, I think I am. He will come with me to Godstow tomorrow.' I avoided his eyes.

Jordain sighed, leaned his elbows on the table and his chin on his fists.

'There is more to this than the girl simply asking for help, is there not?'

Jordain had known me since we were boys. My sister might think him a dreamer, but I knew better. When he put his mind to it, he was very shrewd.

'I don't know.' I prevaricated. 'She is so helpless, so afraid she will be forced. It seems unjust.'

'Nicholas, tell me the truth. Have you fallen in love with the girl?'

'I am still in love with Elizabeth,' I said sharply.

He reached out and laid his hand over mine.

'Elizabeth has been dead these four years and more,

Nicholas. She brought you joy. She brought joy to everyone who knew her. And she would not want you to spend the rest of your life in mourning. You are still young. Why should you not love again? Marry again? Give your children a mother?'

I shook my head. 'Rafe might accept it, but I do not think Alysoun would. And they have Margaret.'

'Alysoun cannot remember her mother, she was but two years old.'

'She thinks she does.'

Jordain shook his head. 'That is perhaps some comfort to her, but I think she is imagining it.'

'And there is Margaret.'

'Margaret is a good woman and sensible. I do not think she would want you to remain alone for her sake.'

Jordain's arguments were persuasive, but he lived a celibate bachelor life as Warden to a student hall. He could not understand the complexities of my domestic situation. Nor could he understand how caring for my children had helped Margaret to cope in part with the loss of her own.

'I do not know, Jordain,' I said. 'I find the girl moves me deeply – but is it love, or merely pity? She is very young, seven years younger than I. Elizabeth and I were of an age and knew each other when we were barely more than children. I do not understand my own feelings. And why should I suppose that she could feel anything for me? A widowed shopkeeper with two children?'

He gave me a long, penetrating look. 'As one who has had to put aside all thoughts of marriage, I suppose I am not the one to judge how you are feeling, or what she might feel. However, at the moment she is pledged to the celibate life as much as I am. If your plan to free her from her vows succeeds, then that is the time to think of these things more carefully. Not now.'

I nodded. 'Of course you have the right of it.'

I had said more than I had intended to say, but it had somehow made me feel a little better to have said it. On impulse I said, 'Why do you not ride out to Godstow with

Philip and me tomorrow? Then you may see Emma for yourself. Perhaps you might judge of her feelings more clearly than I can do myself, in my confusion.'

'Very well,' he said, 'I will come with you.'

I left Hart Hall soon afterwards and ploughed through the streets to the Farringdons' house. The heavy rain through the night had turned the hard packed earth of the minor lanes to sticky mud, for Oxford stands on clay. Although the principal streets were cobbled, the town authorities regarded a dirt surface quite sufficient for the lesser ones. As the colleges began to encroach on these minor streets, a few areas of cobble had been laid. However, those on foot had tracked mud across the cobbles as well, so that they were treacherously slippery and I was hard put to it to stay on my feet.

'Come you in, Nicholas!' Maud Farringdon exclaimed. 'It was too much to hope the fine weather would last, though the crops have needed rain. I hope the hay is all cut safely.'

I smiled. You may rely on a country woman to think of the crops first and personal discomfort last.

'And I hope the corn may not be beaten down,' I said. 'It was fierce last night.'

'Aye, 'twas indeed. And why are you about in this downpour? I am working in Mistress Coomber's dairy this afternoon, for your sister has found me a place there at the cheese making. I hope the rain may slacken a little by then.'

'It is not far to the dairy, and the rain is not so heavy now,' I said. 'I have come to ask your advice, Maud, in the matter of your niece Emma.'

Emma's cousin Juliana was sitting at the table fashioning a poppet out of scraps of cloth for little Maysant, but she stopped at the mention of Emma and looked at me intently.

'You have seen Emma, Master Elyot?'

'I have, and she is as determined as ever not to take her final vows.'

I turned to Mistress Farringdon. 'I have spoken to a friend who is a lawyer. He thinks that if Emma's grandfather supports her wish to leave the nunnery it will override any action by her stepfather. Did you know that he had given her to Godstow as an oblate?'

'Nay, I did not!' She pressed her hands to her throat and sat down suddenly. 'He had no right to do such a thing. She was seventeen, a young woman of marriageable age, not an infant! Surely that must be contrary to the law?'

'On that point I am not sure, but it is certainly contrary to the spirit of giving young children to the Church, not grown women. However, the thing has been done, and for Emma's sake we must contrive how to set her free.'

I realised that I was speaking a little too passionately. I sat down and resumed in a more practical tone.

'My friend believes that if Emma's grandfather is willing to sign a document which he will draw up, then it will be possible to delay her final vows until the case may be heard in the Court of Chancery. There are precedents, he is certain.'

'Would the court decide in her favour?'

'That we cannot know, but this is the way to proceed, step by step, using the due processes of the law.' I thought I sounded like some ancient greybeard, but let my words stand.

'And why do you wish to consult me? I am more than glad for you to go ahead with this plan.'

'I need your advice on how to approach Sir Anthony Thorgold,' I said. 'When Jordain and I came to fetch you from Long Wittenham, we heard from some local men that Sir Anthony is in his final illness. Can you tell me any more of this? I would need to take the document for him to sign, but would I be permitted to see him? Is he likely to be too ill either to receive me or to sign such a document? For that matter, do you suppose he would even be willing to support his granddaughter's wish to leave the abbey?'

She folded her hands in her lap and did not speak at

once.

'I have not seen Sir Anthony since the spring of last year,' she said at last. 'Just after Eastertide, it was.' She sighed. 'My husband and William were still alive then, and my sister too. How everything has changed in so short a time. Emma had come to us over Easter and was to return to her stepfather's house in time for her mother's lying in. It is close by Sir Anthony's manor, in fact the lands touch. So we decided to pay a visit to Sir Anthony on the way, before delivering Emma home. I was anxious, too, about my sister. She was older than I, and lost three children, stillborn, before Emma. I feared the birth might be dangerous for her, and I was proved right.'

Juliana got up quietly and brought a cup of ale for her mother, then stood beside her, resting her hand on Maud's shoulder. Little Maysant was playing with the poppet Juliana had made, and paid us no heed.

'How was Sir Anthony with his granddaughter?' I said. 'Was he – is he – fond of her?'

'Indeed he was. At that time, at least. They were very close while his son, Emma's father, was alive. Emma and her parents lived there, on the manor. Even after my sister remarried, Emma managed to visit her grandfather from time to time. When we saw him last year they were very happy together. Indeed we all were. Do you remember, Juliana?'

'I do, Mama. It was a beautiful day and the bluebells just coming into flower in the woods. We ate our dinner outdoors in the garden. It was the first day warm enough.'

'So we did.' Her mother smiled wanly. 'I had forgot. It was to be last day of such happiness. I thought Sir Anthony looked a little frail at the time, but he walked us around the formal gardens, pointing out the changes he had made. Then we left for Falkes Malaliver's house, only to find my poor sister already abed and in terrible pain. Now she is dead, and my husband, and William, but Sir Anthony lives still.'

She sighed bitterly.

'But to answer your question, Nicholas, I do not know how ill he may be. He is most courteous and I am sure he will receive you if he can. Whether he will support Emma's wishes, I do not know. I do know that he was angered at the news she was to become a nun. She is all the family he has left. I suppose she would have been his heir.'

I kept my thoughts to myself on that subject and on the question of whether Falkes Malaliver might benefit if Emma were to be shut away from the world. Was it significant that the two estates were neighbours? And if Emma were to come into her inheritance *before* she took her final vows, what difference would that make? I must ask Philip. I thought it might mean that the abbey would have some claim on the estate when she did profess.

'I think I will send word ahead of my visit to Sir Anthony,' I said. 'I would not wish to cause him the disturbance of an unannounced appearance. Will you permit me to mention your name in my letter? For Sir Anthony will otherwise wonder what my place is in all of this.'

'Of course you must mention me,' she said, recovering a little of her animation. 'Better still, I will write a note to him myself, for you to enclose with yours. He has always taken an interest in our family. I shall tell him that Juliana, Maysant, and I are now settled in Oxford through your kind offices, and that Emma has approached you for help. Then he will understand that you are no stranger to us all.'

'That would be excellent,' I said. I had not liked to ask, but a letter from his granddaughter's aunt would surely open doors for me, if Sir Anthony received visitors at all.

'Tomorrow Jordain and I, and our lawyer friend, Philip Olney, will be going to Godstow to seek an audience with the abbess, with a request to see Emma. I am already expected there. After that Philip Olney will draw up the document for Sir Anthony and I will take it to Long Wittenham. The estate is near there, I understand?'

'About two miles. I will write my letter tomorrow

and you may collect it when you come back from Godstow. You will carry our greetings to Emma? And tell her that there will be a home here for her if she leaves the abbey?'

'I will so.'

Juliana left her mother's side and walked to the window. 'I believe the rain is stopping, Mama. You will not have a wet walk to the dairy after all.'

'Wear some stout shoes,' I advised. 'There is mud everywhere.'

As I walked home through the diminishing rain, I pondered one question I had not liked to ask Maud Farringdon. When she and her family had been in such dire straits after her husband's death and the loss of his pension from the royal coffers, why had Sir Anthony not come to their aid? Although they were only kin by marriage, it seemed the families were on close and friendly terms with each other. Had he helped them at the time, William would never have undertaken work for Allard Basset and would be alive today.

Still, it was possible Sir Anthony was already ill at the time, for William's father had died shortly after Christmas, not very long ago. Perhaps Sir Anthony knew nothing of the family's difficulties, and I was sure both Maud Farringdon and her son would have be too proud to appeal to him for help.

The rain did stop altogether by the afternoon, and I spent the rest of the day busy about the shop. If I was to be occupied in this affair of Emma Thorgold and the law, riding about the countryside and possibly even to the courts in London, then I needs must get ahead of myself here. The student texts were all but complete. By the end of the day I had finished my stitching of the loose covers and Roger handed me the copy he had made of the missing gathering from the Euclid. After he and Walter left I sat on in the shop until that too was stitched together, and all the student books stored away on a shelf, ready for the beginning of term in October.

Just as I was about to lock the door of the shop and go through to the house, there was a hesitant knock, followed by a head round the edge of the door.

'Master Elyot? You are not closed?

It was Juliana Farringdon.

'Just on the point of closing. What can I do for you, Juliana?'

'Oh, nothing for me. When she came home from the dairy, Mama sat down at once and wrote to Sir Anthony. She asked me to bring the letter to you now, so that you need not be troubled with calling tomorrow. She is to work in the dairy all day.'

She held out the folded paper to me. It was sealed with wax, but the wax was not impressed with the sender's mark.

'She thought it best to seal it,' Juliana explained, 'but I have memorised what she wrote, so I can tell you what it says.'

'No need,' I said, touched by this scrupulous consideration. 'I am sure she has said just what was necessary and proper. Will you come through to see the family?'

She shook her head. 'I must go back. Mama was cooking supper when I left.' She hesitated, clearly wanting to say more.

'Alysoun tells me you are teaching her Latin.'

'Aye, Latin and mathematics. She wants to learn Greek.'

The girl's face lit up. 'Oh, I should dearly like to learn Greek! They use different letters, do they not?'

'They do, but they are quite easy to learn. Some are almost like our English letters.' I studied her eager expression. Here was another girl anxious for learning. 'But I think you have studied Latin already.'

'When we were younger, I shared William's lessons with our parish priest. He did not want to teach me at first, but William said he would not study unless I came too. Later, when he was a student here, he used to read with me when he came home. I have read some of Vergil's *Georgics* and some Tully. And some of the Church Fathers.'

'I would suggest that you join Alysoun's lessons, but you would be much too advanced for her.'

'Perhaps,' she paused, looking around the shop. 'Perhaps you could lend me a book? I would be very careful.'

I can recognise a true hunger for books when I see it. William had been a gifted young scholar. It seemed his sister might be another. I ran my finger along a shelf of Latin volumes and took down one, a small book in a dark brown binding, modestly embossed on the cover.

'Perhaps you would like to read this. It is the complete *Aeneid*. If you have already met Vergil, you should certainly read his most important work.'

She took it from me and ran her hand caressingly over the spine, her eyes glowing. 'Oh, I thank you, Master Elyot! I have always wanted to read it, but William did not have a copy of his own. I will be very, very careful with it.'

I smiled down at her. 'I am sure you will. Now, if your mother is waiting, you'd best hurry.'

I watched her run up the High Street, the book clutched to her chest and her hair in a heavy plait, flying out behind her. Perhaps I should start a school?

Over supper we chatted of the storm, and Alysoun boasted that she had not been afraid of the thunder and lightning, while Rafe assured her that we were quite safe anyway, under the protection of the two churches, St-Peter-in-the-East and St-Mary-the-Virgin.

'But especially St Peter's,' he said. 'Isn't that right, Papa? Because St Peter's is our own church.'

He spoke as if it belonged to him personally.

'Aye, it is our church,' I agreed, 'and Rector Bokeland will be glad to hear you say so.'

Despite any arguments over who had been afraid of the storm or not, they both ate heartily. I wondered what supper Juliana had gone home to. I hoped that Maud

Farringdon's work in the dairy might provide a few extras in the form of cheese, butter, and milk, and perhaps some of the eggs from Yardley's farm. Mary Coomber was a kindly woman. She could probably not afford to pay Maud much, but might make it up in food.

When the children were saying their prayers before sleeping, Rafe assured me that he was giving special thanks for being protected from death by lightning. I was smiling as I joined Margaret in the kitchen again.

'You must have made quite an impression,' she said. 'With your explanation of where lightning will strike.'

'As long as it helps him to overcome his fear.'

'You used to be frightened when you were small.'

'I know. I was always sure that big oak tree would be struck. I used to run as far away from it as I could.'

'And when did you stop being afraid?'

I looked at her thoughtfully. 'You know, I cannot remember. I think the fear just gradually faded away.'

'We outgrow some fears,' she said, 'only to be beset by others.'

'Aye.' I wanted to say, *fear for our children*, but could not. Margaret's own worst fears had been realised when her two boys died untimely in the Pestilence.

'I must tell you what plan we have afoot amongst us,' I said. 'Jordain and I. And – although I expect you will hardly credit it – Philip Olney.'

She turned from clearing the dishes off the table.

'Philip Olney?' She raised her eyebrows. 'I did not know he was a friend of yours.'

'He is not so bad a fellow.' I found myself apologising for him a second time that day. 'He is a good lawyer, and I needed a man of the law.'

I told her all that I had been doing during the last two days, in the matter of Emma Thorgold, and our plan to visit Godstow on the morrow.

'And you will go to see this gentleman, Sir Anthony Thorgold?'

'As soon as Philip has the document prepared. If Sir

Anthony is willing to support his granddaughter, I think we will have a good case in law.'

'Well, I hope the girl understands all the trouble she is causing,' Margaret said, somewhat brusquely.

'That is unlike you,' I said, stung. 'The girl has been grossly ill-used. Would you have her submit to a future which is entirely against her nature?'

She sat down with a sigh. 'I only wish you to have a care, Nicholas. Nay, I know I spoke unkindly. I do not think the girl should be enclosed against her will, but I hope you will not run yourself into danger again. It is but weeks since you were badly hurt and Alysoun was in terrible danger.'

'I know,' I said soberly. 'I shall not endanger my family again. But you need not worry. This is nothing but a matter of law. The greatest excitement will be lawyers arguing in Westminster Hall.'

She laughed. 'Let us hope so.'

'That is, if we are able to take our case there,' I added. 'This is all unfamiliar to me, but I shall do my best for the girl. It seems to me that the whole affair is somehow unfinished business, left after the murder of her cousin. William's sister came just before I closed the shop, bringing Mistress Farringdon's letter to Sir Anthony. It seems that there is another girl whose future has been blighted by this affair. She is clever, and had William lived, he would have cared for her, seen to it that she made a good marriage. She has no male relatives left.'

'Since the Pestilence,' Margaret said, 'many are in a like case.'

The next morning I rose early. I had already been lying awake some time, composing in my head the letter I would write to Sir Anthony Thorgold, and I wanted to commit it to paper before I forgot. I was grateful that I could enclose Maud Farringdon's letter, for my own would not then seem impertinent or interfering. Before the rest of the family had risen, I had written my letter, enclosed the other, and sealed both, stamping the wax with my business seal, which showed an open book with a quill pen laid across it.

'Are you coming to breakfast, Nicholas?' Margaret called from the door at the back of the shop.

'Do not wait for me,' I said. 'I am just going to send this on its way.'

As I hurried up the High Street, I hoped I would be in time. There was a carter who left the Mitre every other day to fetch and carry goods to Wallingford, Dorchester, and back again. He would deliver letters if they did not take him too far out of his way, and the sender paid for the extra time.

Just as I reached the Mitre I saw the man leading his horse out of the stable yard. His cart was barely half full, so I hoped that meant he would be glad of a letter to carry and a little extra money with it.

'Two miles from Long Wittenham?' he said. 'That will mean taking the ferry.'

'Aye,' I said, 'I will pay the cost of the ferry, both ways.'

He rubbed the side of his nose with the handle of his whip.

'Very well, master,' he said. 'I will take it. Will there be an answer to bring back?'

I had not thought of that.

'If you are offered an answer without too long a wait, then aye, bring me the answer. It should be no more than a simple "aye" or "nay".'

'Right you are, master.' He took the letter and tucked it into the band that ran around his cap. 'That way I won't fergit it, see? Every time I turns me head, it rustles.'

He demonstrated.

'Good plan,' I said, handing over the requisite money, plus a little extra for his good will.

He climbed up and chirruped to his horse, who plodded off, at the steady but untiring pace of all cart horses, in the direction of Carfax. After arranging to hire Rufus again for the day, I headed back home. I was making so much use of the horse with the constant expense, I might as well buy him. I turned over the idea in my mind, but I had no stabling, and a horse must be fed, whether it is working or not. And my need for a horse in recent months was unusual. He was a reliable beast, though, should I ever change my mind.

Back at home I ate hastily, for Jordain was already there, a borrowed horse hitched outside the shop, and Philip arrived, with one of the Merton horses, before I had finished. Once I had collected Rufus, we set off at a leisurely pace up Northgate Street. It was still early, the only people about in the town being tradesmen's apprentices. Out of term, members of the university rise late, making up for the five o'clock lectures during the winter and spring.

In St Giles the trees which had looked so tired and lacklustre only days before under the heat already seemed fresher, their leaves washed clean of the dust thrown up from the road during the past weeks. The rain had also laid the dust along the roadway and there had been little traffic to churn it into mud before it drained away, so the surface was firm and good for riding. St Giles is wide enough to ride three abreast, and I found I was enjoying the short journey as if it were a holiday.

If I let my thoughts turn to what we might encounter when we arrived at the abbey, I felt somewhat less cheerful. What we were about was audacious in the extreme, and the abbess might very well have us turned away unceremoniously. I fingered the bottle of tawny gold in the pocket of my cotte. I had nearly forgotten it. At the last moment Alysoun had thrust it into my hand, with a matronly clicking of her tongue, that sound all women make at the incompetence and forgetfulness of all men. It was as well she had remembered, for it was the only – and very slim – excuse for our visit to Godstow.

'I have written to Sir Anthony,' I told the other two, 'requesting a brief visit. I said little more, save that it concerned his granddaughter's desire to leave the monastic life. Mistress Farringdon had also written him a letter, which I enclosed, explaining my connection with the family.'

'Excellent,' Jordain said. 'I am sure her good word will gain you admittance, if nothing else will.'

'If Sir Anthony is not too ill,' I cautioned. I turned to Philip, who proved to be a surprisingly good horseman. Jordain rode like a ploughman.

'Were you able to discover any precedents yesterday?' I asked. 'Any cases at all like that of Emma Thorgold?'

'Aye, that I have. There was a case nearly two hundred years ago where a nun was forced by her guardian to take the veil at Ankerwyke. It was fifteen years later that she fled from the nunnery, returned to the secular life, and claimed her inheritance from her father's estate. I have not yet been able to trace the outcome, but it seems that the guardian's motive was to seize her inheritance. She was, however, excommunicated. It may be that if the court did find in her favour the excommunication would have been lifted.'

'She was a professed nun, not a novice?' I asked.

He nodded. 'A professed nun.'

'Let us hope Emma Thorgold does not run the risk of excommunication,' Jordain said, crossing himself.

'Any other cases?' I said.

'One much nearer our own time,' Philip said, 'just fifty years ago. A girl who was forced by her stepfather into Haverholme. That's a daughter house of Sempringham. He too wished to deprive her of her inheritance, and he seems to have persuaded the nuns of Sempringham to claim that she entered the nunnery willingly, but when it came to the point, they would not swear to the truth of their assertions on oath. It seems the girl won her right to leave. I have also come across some instances of oblates entered at early childhood, who declared that it was against their will and were able to escape final vows.'

'That is very encouraging,' Jordain said, smiling at

Philip.

I felt vindicated. I had been certain that a skilled lawyer would be able to ferret out precedents that would serve us well in court.

'Will you cite these cases to the abbess, Philip?'

'If it seems useful at this point. Perhaps I should merely say that there are legal precedents that make it wise to delay Sister Benedicta's final vows until a court has examined the arguments on both sides. It would be far less embarrassing for the abbey if a novice were to be allowed to leave quietly than if one of their professed nuns were to bring a case against her stepfather in Chancery, in which the abbey's complicity would be a matter of public debate.'

'Argued like a true lawyer.' I grinned at him. 'I think Emma's man of law should be able to persuade the abbess by such arguments. Best for everyone that the matter is conducted with quiet dignity.'

'Best also,' Jordain pointed out, 'that you should stop referring to the girl as Emma Thorgold. Within the walls of the abbey she is known as Sister Benedicta, and it would be discourteous to speak of her in any other way.'

'I stand corrected,' I said. 'Sister Benedicta it shall be.'

When we reached the branch off St Giles to Woodstock it became necessary to ride in single file, so it was too difficult to continue our conversation. We rode on in silence but briskly, and it was only as we neared the village of Wolvercote that we realised that something was amiss. Instead of being occupied about their trades or their farm work, the villagers were moving in twos and threes along the edges of the fields or making their way into the patches of woodland, some calling, some poking into the undergrowth with sticks. A few farm dogs bustled about, not seeming to be of much use and getting in everyone's way.

Crossing the bridge, I saw that the wide gates of the abbey stood open instead of the usual narrow wicket. John Barnes stood just inside, talking in agitation to Sister

Clemence, who – if such could be said of a holy nun – appeared on the point of slapping him. John stood with his feet wide apart and a belligerent look on his face.

'What's afoot?' Jordain murmured to me.

On the wider ground before the gate we had drawn up our horses side by side.

'I have visited the abbey four times now,' I muttered, 'and it has always been tranquil. It seems we come at an inopportune time.'

I vaulted from my horse and hastily secured him to the hitching ring where I had left him before. Sister Clemence, who had her back to us and took no note of our arrival, shook her fist at John before striding off across the enclave towards the cloister garth with that curious angular stride of hers. To my surprise, John did not appear chastened. He was smiling to himself as he came back toward the gate and caught sight of the three of us.

'Master Elyot,' he cried, 'I had forgot that you were to come today. And these gentlemen?'

'Master Jordain Brinkylsworth, Warden of Hart Hall in Oxford, and Master Philip Olney, Fellow of Merton College.' I did not, for the moment, describe Philip as Sister Benedicta's man of law. And in truth I had not given thought to how I was to account for Jordain's presence. I suppose I could introduce him as her cousin William's tutor and a friend of the family. And of course William was to have become a Junior Fellow of Philip's college. In some ways the two of them had more right here than I had.

'But John,' I said, 'what's to-do here? As we came through Wolvercote, folk were beating the woods.'

John drew nearer, looking from me to the other two, who had now dismounted and joined me. The he glanced over his shoulder and lowered his voice.

''Tis Sister Benedicta, Master Elyot. She has disappeared.'

Although the dense bushes of broom kept off some of the rain, it fell so heavily during the night that Emma slept little. The thunder and lightning, although mostly further south, was frightening, out here on the river bank, with so little protection. Jocosa too was frightened, whining and pressing herself up against her mistress in distress. By the morning both girl and dog were even more exhausted and wet than they had been the night before.

As the overcast dawn brought a lightening of the sky, the rain slackened a little, and the storm appeared to be moving further south, but it seemed they must either stay in the poor shelter afforded by the bushes, or set out in the wake of the storm and make their way further south along the river.

Emma shared a little of the bread and cheese with Jocosa, but kept back most of it, for fear it might be a long while before she could find anything else to eat. She wished now that she had stolen more from the kitchen. No cloak and little food. She was ill prepared for her escape, but she had intended to take more care over it, not rush away in haste like this, fearing the greater vigilance of the abbey once Nicholas Elyot set afoot his enquiries into the law.

As she crawled out from under the bushes, however, she saw that the river had already risen considerably higher than the day before, and with all the streams feeding it from the Cotswold hills, it would almost certainly swell even more. The Thames was known for flooding the lower land along its course. She sat cross-legged on the bank and watched the water swirling past, brown with churned up mud. Had she delayed longer, as she had planned, she could never have crossed it, so despite her near drowning, she had been luckier than she might have been. Luckier, perhaps, than she deserved.

'Well, Jocosa,' she said, 'I think there is little use in our remaining here. We shall be soaked whether we go or stay, so we'd best be on our way. If we keep following the river downstream, sooner or later we shall reach Oxford. Or so I believe.' She realised she sounded doubtful, but surely if the boats bringing supplies came up river from Oxford, walking in the opposite direction *must* bring her eventually to the town.

Jocosa watched her closely, almost as if she understood. After the night time alarms of the thunderstorm, she looked confident and brave, as if surviving such terrors meant that she was ready for anything her mistress might undertake.

Emma secured her bundle carefully, making sure that the manuscript pages were still dry and intact. This time, instead of tying it to her waist for security, she made the cord into a loop that she could sling over her shoulder, which made it much less awkward to carry. She tucked the still damp shift through this carrying loop, in the hope that it might dry as she walked. These few preparations completed, she looked about her. One fold of her habit projected from its hiding place, something which she had not noticed in the dark, so she thrust it further in. Otherwise there was nothing to show that she and the dog had spent the night here, apart from the flattened grass under the bushes, which might have been made by some animal taking shelter from the storm.

They set off. As Emma had half discerned in the night, there were the traces of a path following the bank of the river, although it did not look as though anyone had used it recently. Perhaps when there had been small farms on this side of the river, as John had told her, the path had been used as the way between them, but with the people gone for the last four years it had become overgrown. Still, it was easy enough to follow, even if it meant skirting clumps of nettles and seedling bushes which had sprung up here and there. She found that she moved much more easily in cotte and hose, freed from the heavy skirts of her habit, but her sandals were poor footgear for walking in, and they soon began to chafe her feet. She would have blisters later.

The walk seemed interminable. On this side of the river there was nothing but the desolate remains of abandoned farms. Here and there a ruined cottage showed where there had once been a family, tilling the land and herding cattle and sheep. There was nothing to show whether these had been villeins' holdings, tied to some manor, or the homes of free yeomen, renting their land from an overlord. The thatched roofs of the cottages and barns had already begun to blacken with rot and fall in. Broken doors stood ajar to wind and wild weather, no doubt providing shelter to those very animals she had feared in the night.

About mid day she was surprised to see a small herd of cattle grazing not far from the path. Perhaps not all the farms were deserted as John had supposed. She stood and debated with herself whether she should approach the house, which was partly hidden behind a copse. She might beg a little food, ask where this was. The thought of food brought consciousness of a growing ache in her stomach. Tentatively she took a few steps toward the house, moving sideways so that she might see it better.

With a shock she realised that this house too had been abandoned. Why, then, were the cattle here? Jocosa began to whine and retreated back to the path. Wondering what had troubled the dog, Emma swung round and saw that the hedge which had once enclosed the field where the cattle were grazing was broken down on this nearer side, and a bull was heading slowly toward it. At the moment he did not look threatening, merely curious. Suddenly she realised from the unkempt look of the cattle, the deserted house, the broken hedge, that the beasts had been left when their owners, like so many, had perished. They must have remained here, gone wild, fending for themselves. The grass in their field was thick and plentiful. They must have found enough to eat. In winter no doubt the weaker ones had died, but the strong had survived.

I suppose the ancestors of all cattle must once have been wild, she thought, so there is no reason why the survivors should not learn to fend for themselves. Her head was filled with a desolating picture of a world in which all men had perished of the plague. All the animals had reverted to their wild natures. Trees had sprung up between the broken cobbles of towns and weeds grew in roofless churches. If the Pestilence returned, it could happen.

Slowly she backed away, not letting her eyes rest on the bull. As she reached the path she saw from a sideways glance that he had lost interest in her and returned to grazing. Turning her face southwards, she hurried on.

All that day she walked, following the river, but the blisters on her feet grew larger, and burst, until she could only hobble painfully. Once or twice she stopped to dip her bare feet in the river, which gave her temporary relief, but made it even more painful to put her sandals on again.

She realised that she was walking more and more slowly, and taking more frequent rests, until she reached a thick clump of willows on the bank as the sun was westering. There was some undergrowth under the trees which would provide a little shelter for the night, for there was no sign of the storm returning. By now her shift was dry, so she removed her cotte, donned the shift, and pulled the cotte on again. It was little enough, but it provided some more warmth. After walking all day, she realised she would feel the cold with the coming of the night. Something else she should have brought was flint and tinder, although she would have been hard put to it to find any dry wood to make a fire. The day had remained overcast and everything about her was still sodden from the storm.

Amongst the bushes again she hollowed out a sleeping place, like one of those same animals returned to the wild, and she broke the remaining bread and cheese in half. One half she set aside for the next day, the other she shared with Jocosa. It was little enough, and her stomach ached. Scooping up water from the river to drink, she hoped it would help to fill the hollows. Jocosa had already settled in the cleared space, so Emma lay down beside her, hugging the dog close for warmth.

She thought that by now she would have seen the first houses of Oxford on the other side of the river, yet there was nothing but water meadows. And somehow she would need to cross the river again to reach the town. As on the previous night the ground was hard and uncomfortable, but tonight she was so tired she hardly noticed. In a very few minutes she was asleep.

Chapter Eight

I stared at John Barnes, gaping. 'What do you mean, she has disappeared? How could she disappear within the enclave of Godstow? She must be here somewhere.' I lowered my voice, for I had begun to shout. 'Or is she perhaps hiding, for fear of another beating?'

The porter gave me a troubled glance.

'She took the beating without complaint, Master Elyot, and the sisters do not hand out beatings as a regular punishment. More likely half a dozen paternosters on their knees in the church. Indeed, I've heard some whispers that the other ladies were unhappy at the punishment inflicted by the mistress of the novices.'

'Rather too late to be effective,' I said dryly, trying to control my anger. 'But has the enclave been thoroughly searched? When did she go missing?'

'She was not present at Prime yesterday, it seems, and it was thought at first that she had simply overslept. Afterwards there was no sign of her in the dortoir. When she did not appear either to break her fast or to work in the scriptorium, that was when the search began.'

'And you have searched everywhere?'

Jordain and Philip left the questioning to me, but I saw them exchange a glance. Perhaps they felt that I presumed too much.

'Everywhere,' John said, 'from hayloft to side chapel, and from the attics of the guest house to the shed where the chaplain keeps his garden tools. Never a sign. Then one of the schoolgirls, the oldest one, Madlen, who is away to be wed soon – she told me she thought Sister Benedicta must be gone quite away, for the dog Jocosa was missing as well. She was a friend of Sister Benedicta. When it was known the dog was gone, the abbey servants and the folk on the home farm were set to searching as well. That was just before Vespers yesterday.'

'And why was Sister Clemence angry with you just now, John?' I asked. 'I saw her shake her fist at you.'

He looked away, embarrassed, and shuffled his feet.

'If it might have a bearing on what has happened, you needs must tell me,' I said. I took him by the elbow and drew him outside the wall.

He looked nervously over his shoulder and lowered his voice. 'Sister Clemence was angry because the gate was unbolted the night before last.'

'The night Emma may have disappeared?' I no longer bothered to call her Sister Benedicta.

'Aye.'

'Now, how could that be? I have seen that it is a heavy great bar, difficult for a young girl to move.'

He did not answer, merely shifted uncomfortably again.

'I think,' I said slowly, 'that you did not bolt the gate that night, John, and Sister Clemence thinks the same. Have I guessed right?'

He shrugged.

'Now, I wonder why that would be. A conscientious fellow like you. Not wanting to risk a good position as porter to the abbey, with comfortable lodgings, and I daresay your meals provided.'

He gave me a desperate look, then sighed. 'It is the only safe way out of the abbey, and I knew she was going to attempt an escape that night.'

'You *knew*! How could that be?'

'She borrowed a cap from me.'

I was perplexed. 'What has that to do with her leaving?'

'She couldn't go about the world in a nun's wimple and veil, could she? Nor go bare headed either, for all to see her shaved scalp. She needed something to cover her head.'

I rocked back on my heels. 'But her habit would give her away at once.'

He grinned, beginning to relax. 'Oh, I reckon she had made provision for that. She's been working in the laundry of late. Not too difficult to make off with some simple servant's clothing. She's no fool, the maid.'

Nor was he, as I had realised before.

'You were her friend, so you left the gate unbolted a-purpose.'

'I am still her friend. And this is the only safe way out of the enclave.'

Jordain, having kept silence all this time, stepped forward now. 'What do you mean, the only *safe* way?'

John looked at him soberly. 'There is no barrier 'tother side of the meadow but the river. I do not think the maid can swim. I hoped she would not attempt that way. When I was a young lad, working here in the kitchen, there was one of the servants stole some silver plate from the church and tried to flee by the river. He drowned.'

I swallowed. Surely Emma would not attempt the river. I was suddenly angry again.

'The fool girl! I promised to bring her the help of a lawyer, and here he is!' I gestured at Philip. John bowed and Philip inclined his head. 'She had only to wait a few days. You know that she did not want to take her final vows.'

'I know,' John said.

'We think we have sufficient case to delay the rite, or will have when I have seen her grandfather. There was no cause for her to run.'

'Mayhap she saw it differently,' he said.

Inwardly I was cursing not Emma, but myself. I should have told her more clearly to stay quietly in the abbey, until I could bring her legal help. Instead I had been too hesitant. She had not believed there would be anything further to hope for from me, and now she was out there, alone in the world, without help. And where?

'We saw the villagers out searching as we came through Wolvercote,' Jordain said.

'Aye, everyone is searching – the villeins from the home farm, the tenants, the villagers. We cannot know which way she will go. Perhaps to Oxford, for she knows her aunt is now there, but she might fear to be sought there and turn the other way, to Woodstock.'

'If she has been gone more than a day,' I said, 'she's likely well away by now. Villagers on foot will never find her.'

'Aye,' John said, 'but they are helping of their own will. They do not like to think of a maid wandering alone. They may come across some trace of whichever way she headed. 'Tis likely, we think, that she left during the dark, betwixt Lauds and Prime, when all would have been asleep. Blundering about in the darkness, she may have broken bushes, left a trail. As well,' he added, 'the Reverend Mother sent the bailiff to tell Sister Benedicta's stepfather what's afoot. He left last evening. If he reached Master Malaliver before nightfall, they should be here shortly.'

I looked at Philip and pulled a face. The presence of Falkes Malaliver was something we would not welcome.

'Best not to tell the gentleman why we are here,' I said. 'He will not be pleased, should he discover that we might overturn his intentions for his stepdaughter.'

John nodded. 'I'll keep my tongue behind my teeth, Master Elyot, you may be sure of that. I only want to help the maid.'

Over his shoulder, I saw one of the nuns hurrying toward the gatehouse. As she drew nearer, I realised that it was Sister Mildred, the precentrix and librarian. John ducked his head to her and slipped back within the gate.

'Master Elyot,' she said, 'I thought it was you.' She glanced at Jordain and Philip, but did not wait for me to present them. 'You have been told our worrying news?

Sister Benedicta gone, quite gone, it seems, from the enclave.'

She dabbed her eyes with the edge of her sleeve and I realised her eyes were red with weeping. 'Have you heard or seen anything of her?'

'I? Nay.' I shook my head. 'Why should I have done so?'

She straightened her shoulders and gave me a shrewd look. 'She seemed very friendly with you. And moreover,' she hesitated. 'Moreover, the pages from the new book of hours Sister Benedicta was working on . . . they are also missing. I thought she might have brought them to you.'

'Nay, that she has not,' I said, astonished that she should even think it. 'Are you quite sure they are missing?'

'Quite. The last time I saw them, she had them in her hand as we looked at a book together in the library. I think she must have taken them away without thinking. But now I wonder whether her intention was to bring them to you.'

'I think not,' I said firmly. 'There would be no reason to bring me an unfinished book. They will be somewhere hereabouts, I suspect. Is everyone looking for them as well as the girl?'

She coloured slightly. 'I have not mentioned it yet to anyone.'

I considered. 'Perhaps wait a while, then,' I said. 'I will let you know at once if she comes to my shop.'

I did not say *If she comes to me*, although I felt a small spurt of hope.

'You have the right of it.' She nodded her head. 'Some might say she had stolen the property of the abbey, although I am sure it would never seem so to her.'

'A moot point,' Philip said, speaking for the first time. 'The parchment is certainly the property of the abbey, but the work of copying and illumination might be regarded in law as the property of the scribe. If the scribe were a full nun, the work of her hands properly belongs to the abbey. A novice whose presence here may be called in doubt, her work might be judged to belong to her.'

'This is Master Philip Olney,' I said to Sister Mildred. 'Sister Benedicta's man at law.'

She gave me a startled look.

Jordain was momentarily distracted from the matter in hand. 'How could you separate the two, parchment and writing?'

'A judgement of Solomon,' Philip said, with a wry smile.

'Let us not embark on theoretical scholastic arguments,' I said sharply. 'The girl is missing now for more than a day and a night. She must have gone during that severe thunderstorm. She is almost certainly wet, hungry, and lost. I believe she would make for Oxford, to her aunt, even though she has said she does not wish to be a burden to her. Yet we saw no sign of her as we rode here from the town. Therefore the search should be widened, to the country on either side of the road leading to Oxford.'

I turned to Sister Mildred. 'My friends and I will gladly join in the search, and I am sure we can find others in Oxford to help. It cannot all be left to the ladies of the abbey and your servants.'

'I thank you, Master Elyot. And I am sure that Sister Benedicta's stepfather will send men to help as well.' She looked as Philip. 'Master . . . I am sorry, I did not catch your name.'

'Olney, my lady,' he said, bowing.

'Master Olney, what did you mean by saying Sister Benedicta's presence here might be called into question?'

Philip was spared the need to answer by the clatter of many horses crossing the bridge behind us. We all swung round to face them.

They were led by a large, red faced man perhaps in his late fifties, who had driven his horse so hard that its coat was dark with sweat and foam dripped from its jaws, despite the fact that it was a tall destrier, as heavily built as its rider. Behind him followed a company of at least thirty men, most of them armed, though others wore the garb of huntsmen. The company was completed at a little distance by sumpter ponies, carrying large wicker baskets, from some of which came the whining of dogs.

The leader leapt from his horse and threw the reins to Philip, although it was evident from his academic dress that he was no servant.

'Well?' The man said, striding over to Sister Mildred and thrusting his face too close to hers. 'What have you done with my ward, you milk faced ninnies? I ordered you to keep her straitly here, and now I am told that she has escaped, gone who knows where. Well?'

So furious was he that spittle flew from his mouth and Sister Mildred backed away in alarm. So this was Falkes Malaliver. I stepped between them.

'That is no way to speak to one of the holy sisters,' I said, trying to keep my voice calm, though the man looked as though he might draw his sword in order to force his way past me.

'What affair is it of yours?' he said, barely glancing at me as he pushed past into the enclave. 'Be quick and unload those dogs,' he shouted over his shoulder, as he strode off in the direction of the abbess's house.

John came cautiously forward and took the horse's reins from Philip. A whistle brought a groom running, who led it away, while other men dismounted. They shoved their way past Sister Mildred as roughly as their master, shouting for grooms to stable their horses and servants to bring them food and drink. It seemed that they were quite prepared to treat the nunnery as if it were a common roadside inn.

The huntsmen remained outside the gate. Ignoring us, they began unloading the dogs, who were ill tempered with the narrow confines of the baskets and spilled out, some yelping, some silent, and began milling about, raising their legs and liberally watering the trees and the gateposts. Sister Mildred averted her eyes.

There were three sorts of dogs, all of them trained hunting beasts. The large, silent hounds were lymers, the best animals for tracking, who would follow the scent of a quarry, so swift and noiseless that they gave no warning. There were also two kennets, also used for tracking, not as silent as the lymers but small, useful for penetrating narrow spaces.

The noisy dogs were alaunts. I looked at Jordain in alarm, and saw my own fear reflected in his face. Alaunts were used against large game. Big, heavy animals, they would tackle a wild, tusked boar or a wolf without fear, and bring it down, as often as not. They were brave, but also unreliable, and had been known to turn on their handlers, occasionally killing them. The use of lymers to follow Emma's trail I could understand, but why had Malaliver brought alaunts? If he set them loose after the lymers had found her, they would kill her for sure.

'I do not like the look of this,' Jordain said.

The words almost choked me, but I whispered, 'The alaunts will kill her. Is that his purpose?'

Sister Mildred overheard and raised a frightened face to me.

'What do you mean, Master Elyot?'

'Those big dogs,' I said. 'The ones that are making all the noise. They are called alaunts and they are trained to kill game.'

'But surely not a person!' she cried.

I grimaced. 'If the lymers track down their quarry and the alaunts are released, I do not think they would distinguish one type of quarry from another.'

'My lady,' Philip said, 'I think you must speak at once to the Reverend Mother. Tell her to forbid the use of the dogs. Or at any rate, the use of the alaunts. If Master Malaliver objects, she should tell him that we have ridden to inform the sheriff. Hunting dogs may be used legitimately against a lord's escaped villein, but not, certainly *not*, against a lady, even one who has left an abbey without leave.'

She hurried away, heading for the abbess's house. John, who must have heard all that passed, came out from the gate. He looked grim.

'She may try,' he said, 'but Master Malaliver has been here before. I do not think he will take orders even from the Reverend Mother.'

He walked over to the group of huntsmen, who were attempting to disentangle the leads of the group of overexcited dogs.

'Come away within,' he said, smiling at the man who seemed to be in charge. 'I will take you to our kennels, where you can feed the dogs and shut them away to rest after their journey.'

The man laughed. 'Why do you think we carried them in baskets, fellow? They could have run with us, but our lord wanted them fresh for the hunt. And we do not feed then before a hunt. We want them keen and hungry.'

'But this is a young girl you are hunting,' John objected, 'not some fierce boar or ravening wolf. She is to be found. Safe. Not harmed.'

The man shrugged. 'That's for our lord to decide. The woman belongs to him. 'Tis for him to decide what's to be done with her.'

John came back to us, his face pale and worried, but I was already unhitching Rufus from the ring in the wall.

'We will ride back to Oxford at once,' I said. 'The sheriff often has business elsewhere in the shire, but if he is not there, his deputy, Cedric Walden, is more than capable of putting a stop to this. Has the abbey's bailiff not returned with Malaliver? He should be able to stand up to the man.'

'There is no sign of him, as far as I can see,' John said. 'But these men have clearly ridden hard. Master Oakwood has already ridden the distance in one direction. I suppose he would go at an easier pace coming back, having fetched Sister Benedicta's stepfather. I'll keep a watch for him and warn him of what's afoot as soon as he comes.'

I nodded. 'Good. We will fetch one of the sheriffs as soon as we can.'

I swung myself up into the saddle. Jordain and Philip were already mounted. We turned as one and skirted round the huntsmen and their dogs before crossing the bridge and heading along the winding trackway leading to the Woodstock Road.

'Shall we be in time, do you think?' Jordain said. 'That man is a vicious and dangerous brute.'

'Would he really turn those killer dogs on the girl?' Philip turned a look of appalled pity toward me.

'Whether we shall be in time, I cannot tell.' I could barely control the fury in my voice. 'Let us hope Emma is well away by now. If she has followed this road to Oxford, they will soon be on our heels.'

The track widened a little here and I gathered the reins to urge Rufus to a gallop.

'Do you not see, Philip? If the dogs kill Emma – oh, quite by accident – then it clears the way for Falkes Malaliver to claim her estate.'

Philip opened his mouth to answer, but I was not prepared to listen to legal arguments. I lowered my head, kicked Rufus into a gallop, and rode away from them.

కిం∞ఇ

Emma woke, aware of pain and stiffness. She had slept deeply, exhausted from her long walk of the day before, and so had slept unmoving. Now, as she straightened, her back and legs were locked, aching from lying too long in one position. And her feet were afire. She sat up cautiously, waking Jocosa as she did so, and studied her feet. The burst blisters had bled, some oozing yellow pus between ugly clumps of scab. She wondered with a stab of fear how much longer she would be able to go on walking.

Barely able to hobble, she staggered to the edge of the bank, where she sat down and prised off her sandals, breaking some of the scabs as she did so. Involuntarily, she gave a gasp of pain. Jocosa, beside her, anxiously licked her hand. Gingerly, she lowered her feet into the river, then with a gasp at the shock of the cold water, drew them out again. The second time, she was prepared. The pain of the cold overrode the pain of the burst blisters. After a while, it almost became pleasant. In the end, however, she had to draw her feet out of the river. As she rested her heels on the grass, she contemplated them. If only she had some of the salve Madlen had used on her back! And if only her wimple and veil had not been snatched away by the river, she could have used them to bind her feet, to protect them a little from the chafing of the hard leather straps of her sandals.

Jocosa crawled nearer and laid her head on Emma's lap.

'It grows a little worrying,' Emma said, running her fingers, like a comb, the wrong way through Jocosa's coat. It was tangled with the sticky seeds of cleavers. She began to pick them out and toss them in the river. 'We cannot stay here, without food or shelter, but I am not sure how much further I can walk.'

Jocosa turned her head and whined. That was one of the little dog's most appealing characteristics: she would join in a conversation.

'Also,' Emma added, 'I am confused by this river. I thought it flowed south to Oxford, but by the angle of the rising sun, which is now behind my left shoulder, it almost seems to be flowing west, or at any rate, southwest.'

The previous day had been heavily overcast, so that she had been unaware of the position of the sun, but now it was clear that the river – although not flowing in entirely the wrong direction – was certainly not flowing due south. How could that be?

'I think I have heard,' she said, 'that the Thames has many branches and keeps changing its position, but surely it *must* eventually reach Oxford, even though I must be on the wrong side. What do you think, Jocosa?'

The dog raised her head, ears alert, and thumped her tail, as though she agreed.

There was nothing for it but to carry on, however the enigma might eventually be solved. Emma started to put on her right sandal, but the touch of the leather, hardened even more after its immersion in the river, made her flinch and take it off again. With nothing else to hand, Emma tore a strip off the bottom of her shift. Ripping it in half, she wound each foot in the cloth before easing her sandals carefully on to her feet again. It would still be painful to walk, but at least her skin would be protected from contact with the leather. It was a small improvement on the day before.

She set off again, Jocosa trotting happily after her. She would make herself walk until mid day, and then they would eat the last of the food. Worryingly, the river began to veer even more to the west. The countryside which stretched away to her right still lay abandoned and uncultivated, though from the tumbled remains of houses and barns it had once been fertile farmland. Although Emma knew all too well how many had died in the Great Pestilence, she had never before seen so much of the land laid waste for want of men to farm it. It was frightening, as if she were walking through a dead land and would never again meet another living soul.

Yet in spite of the human desolation, the country was full of birdsong. All the common birds flocked about her – blackbirds and thrushes, sparrows and blue tits, squabbling starlings and softly cooing turtledoves. From the evidence of their busy activity, it seemed that many pairs were preparing to rear a second brood. The fine weather this summer, which had lasted until two days ago, must have encouraged them, and the passing storm, violent as it was, had not deterred them.

Young rabbits were gambolling on the open patches of turf, though they scattered in haste to their burrows when a vixen on soft feet padded past, ignoring Emma as if she were invisible. When she stopped to share the last of the food with Jocosa, she saw a water vole sitting placidly on a tiny promontory beside its burrow, washing its whiskers with fastidious care. Jocosa peered over the edge of the river bank, keen to make friendly overtures, but the water vole whisked away into the safety of its home.

Peaceful as the scene was, Emma knew that she would soon be in serious need. With the last of her food gone, her feet in danger of infection, and no sign of habitation, she realised that she might die here, in this lonely place. For the first time the abbey seemed a refuge and sanctuary, her escape the height of folly. She could have survived at Godstow. She could have learned to endure the sense of being imprisoned, could have learned to evade the innate cruelty of Sister Mercy. She had friends there – Sister Mildred, Sister Grace the infirmaress, the cook Edith, John Barnes, Madlen (until she left to be married).

She had been given a home of sorts, clothing, food, shelter, and in return had merely been required to keep the Rule. Godstow, standing tranquil on its Thames island, was a beautiful place. Perhaps her unhappiness was nothing but her own fault, her arrogance and discontent. Would life at Godstow have been any worse, in the end, than being married off to some political ally of her stepfather? A man she might never have met?

With a deep sigh at what she was beginning to recognise as her seriously mistaken actions, Emma got to her feet, whistled to Jocosa, who was investigating a rabbit hole, and set off again. It was soon after they had started again on their way alongside the increasingly baffling and winding river, that Emma detected the first hint of other human beings. Some distance ahead, and possibly also near the river, a thread of smoke rose, gauzy as a lady's veil, and so quickly dispersed that she thought at first she had imagined it by some trick of a hopeful eye.

Then the smoke thickened and darkened a little, and she was sure. Despite the pain of the blisters, she quickened her pace. If there was a cottage ahead, inhabited by people who had lit a cooking fire, then she might be able to beg some food and discover at last why she had missed the way to Oxford.

When at last the source of the smoke came in sight, she was disconcerted. What lay before her was not a cottage but a long wheeled cart, twice the length of any carrier's cart she had ever seen, drawn by three horses harnessed one behind the other. It was neither open like a common farm cart, nor covered by a flat canvas cover like the ones used by those carters who worked the regular routes between towns. Along the wooden sides a series of tall hoops held up a painted cloth to form a curved roof, high enough for a man of fair height to stand inside. The ends were closed by flaps of the same cloth, and fixed wooden steps led up the back and front of the cart, for easy access to the interior.

The smoke she had seen emanated from a fire cheerfully burning within a circle of stones beyond the back of the cart, where a woman in a dark blue cotte was just hanging a large iron cookpot over the flames from a tripod of supports. There were several men busy about the horses and cart, and a boy of perhaps twelve or thirteen carrying a bow and a dead rabbit.

Some kind of travellers, then. Emma hesitated. She needed help, but approaching such people, possibly vagabonds or renegade villeins, might be worse than remaining alone. Yet they were respectably dressed and there was nothing furtive about their appearance. The cart, moreover, had stopped beside what was clearly a road, toward which her riverside path was leading.

As she hesitated, the woman looked across at her and smiled. It was a simple, friendly smile, in no way sly or threatening, and it made up her mind for her. After all, she had nothing about her worth stealing. Even the manuscript pages would have little value to such people as these. Drawing nearer, with Jocosa following cautiously at her heels, she saw that the cart was clean and well-kept, and – by all the signs – recently repainted.

Travelling mountebanks, she knew, might use such a covered cart, going from fair to fair. She had seen such people before she had entered the nunnery, at Abingdon and Wallingford fairs, but their carts were generally decorated with symbols of their profession – the painted figures of jugglers and acrobats, perhaps a performing dog or dancing bear. The cloth covering this cart was decorated mostly with a simple pattern of four-petal flowers and trailing vines, cruder but not unlike the borders she herself painted on the pages of manuscripts. Here and there amongst the flowers there was the image of a lantern or a candle, and, in the very centre of the side facing her, a large sun, enhanced with a smiling face.

'Mornin' to 'ee,' the woman said, immediately identifiable as a native of Oxfordshire. Not travellers from distant parts, then.

'Good morning,' Emma said, smiling somewhat tentatively. She did not want to seem like a hungry beggar, but the smell rising from the cookpot nearly caused her to faint from hunger. 'I seem to have lost my way. I thought I could follow the river south to Oxford, but it is taking me ever further west. Can you set me on my road?'

The woman eyed her speculatively, and Emma realised that her own educated voice did not square with her rough clothes, yet she was loathe to assume a false accent. It felt dishonest.

'We be goin' Oxford way, my dear, though not straight way. Osney first, then Oxford.'

'Osney Abbey?'

'Aye.'

Not mountebanks then, for such would not be going to the abbey.

The woman laughed at Emma's puzzled look. 'We'm candle-makers, my dear, off to make the monks their year's supply.'

So that was it! Travelling candle-makers. A group had come to Godstow last autumn, but not these people. Each group would have their regular customers and work their way around a local district throughout the year, living in their cart, although this was an exceptionally large one. This band must be doing well. The ones who had come to the nunnery were from Woodstock and possessed a much more modest cart, although their work had been skilled.

'I see,' Emma said, and smiled her relief. Candle-makers were respectable craftsmen. It would do no harm to ask for their help.

The boy with the rabbit had joined the woman and was looking at Emma with unabashed curiosity. Jocosa sidled over and began to sniff the rabbit, which he had laid on the ground near the woman. Emma whistled her away.

The woman was still eying her kindly. 'Eaten anythin' today, have 'ee?'

Emma gave a rueful shrug. 'The last of some stale bread and cheese. I confess, my dog and I are very hungry. I had hoped to be in Oxford by this.' Then, 'Jocosa, come here!'

Jocosa was considering taking the matter of the rabbit into her own hands – or paws – though in her comfortable life she had never before been faced with meat contained in a covering of fur.

'Ye'll join us then,' the woman said firmly. 'Rabbit pottage. Jak here is a fine shot at a rabbit.' She turned to the boy. 'What are you about, leavin' that on the ground to torment the poor dog? Go hang it up.'

The boy Jak grinned, but obediently carried the rabbit over to the cart and hung it from a hook projecting from one of the sides.

'I thank you, mistress,' Emma said, then feeling that some return of courtesy was due, 'my name is Emma.'

'And mine be Aelwith,' the woman said. 'And here are the rest on us,' she pointed to the three men who had unharnessed the horses and hobbled them so they could graze. 'My father, Edwin, my man Thomas, and my brother Edgar.'

Emma smiled and nodded to the men, who inclined their heads – politely but not servilely. 'Jak is your son?'

'Nay, he be Edgar's son. His woman died in the plague, like my two girls.'

Her voice was colourless as she said this, but from too much experience in the last years, Emma understood how much grief lay behind the simple words.

'Is the lad coming with us?' The man Thomas said, turning to his wife.

She laughed. ''Tis no lad, surely, ye gummock! However she dresses, 'tis a maid.'

Emma felt herself colouring. So much for her hope of passing herself off as a boy.

Thomas frowned and opened his mouth to say something, then shut it again. It was clear that he disapproved of a woman daring to dress as a man, but Aelwith had given him a warning look.

'I thought 'twas safer,' Emma said, apologetically, 'to dress as a boy, travelling alone.' She had no need to explain herself to these people, but she had warmed to the woman, who seemed a likely ally.

'Aye, and a wise thing, my dear. Now come 'ee by and take some bread and ale while the pottage cooks.'

The older man, Edwin, carried out five rough stools from the cart, and they seated themselves around the fire, the boy cross-legged on the ground, for – Emma suspected – she had been given his stool. Aelwith poured ale into wooden cups and passed out rounds of flatbread, the kind that can be cooked on the hot stones of a fire, for certainly she would have no bread oven in the cart. The bread was chewy, but fresh, with a good nutty flavour. Emma started to tear pieces off hers to feed Jocosa, but Aelwith laid a hand on her arm and shook her head.

'There be plenty.' She gave Jocosa a whole bread of her own and the little dog devoured it in a few bites.

'I am afraid she has eaten very little these last days,' Emma said apologetically, for Jocosa had sidled up the Aelwith in the hope of more.

The woman laughed, and gave the dog another round. Then she gestured toward Emma's feet.

'Ye'll be havin' blisters, I'm thinkin',' she said.

'Aye.' Emma looked down at her feet, where blood and pus had soaked through the dirty bandages. 'My sandals rub.'

'Poor shoes for walkin' in,' Edgar said, speaking for

the first time.

'Ye shall ride with us,' Aelwith said decisively. 'A few days off those feet and that will heal. We'm goin' your way. And I'll salve them for 'ee, like my fool brother's hand.'

Edgar grinned, somewhat shamefaced. Emma had noticed a bandage on his right hand, and the fact that he used his left to lift his cup and eat his bread.

'You have hurt your hand?' she said.

He flicked a glance at his sister.

'Burnt his hand at our last stop, makin' candles for the manor at Swinbrook,' Aelwith said scornfully. 'Great gummock! Five and twenty, bin makin' candles since he was six, and ought to know better.'

'I expect it is very painful,' Emma said.

'Aye, that it be.' Edgar seemed grateful for any sympathy in the face of his sister's scorn.

'Is it difficult to make candles?' she asked.

'A child can do it,' Aelwith said. 'A child with any sense and not an addle-pate. Fetch the bowls, Father. The pottage should be done.'

That night Emma slept in more comfort than she had known for more than a year. The well-filled straw palliasse she was given was probably Jak's, but he had chosen to sleep outside, under the cart, with an elderly hound who had emerged from the cart while they were eating the pottage. He had sniffed Jocosa, decided she was no threat, and subsequently ignored her. The weather was still cool in the aftermath of the storm, so that Emma was glad of the rough blanket she was given. Aelwith had gently smeared her own salve over the festering blisters on Emma's feet, and ordered her to keep them open to the air and avoid walking as much as possible. It had become clear by now that Aelwith, who barely reached her husband's shoulder, was the undisputed leader of the candle-makers.

The interior of the cart was roomy, and ferociously neat, with partitioned sections for sleeping, and for cooking when it could not be done out of doors. The front portion contained the candle-making equipment, which, Edwin explained, would be unloaded and set up for a few days at each stop, either in a yard or an outbuilding.

'Not safe in the cart,' he explained, when Emma asked. 'A fire for meltin' the wax, and the vats of hot molten wax. One spill and the whole cart would burn to ashes.'

'But you have a brazier for cooking.'

'Hardly ever use it. Only when 'tis rainin' or snowin' so hard 'twould put the fire out.'

This gave Emma pause for thought. This travelling about during the summer in the comfortable cart seemed pleasant enough, but it would be a hard life in winter.

After they had eaten that first day, they had travelled on in the direction of Osney, intending to reach the abbey on the following day. Sitting on the driver's bench beside Edwin the next morning, obediently keeping her feet open to the air, Emma asked how she had managed to go so far astray in trying to reach Oxford.

'Ah, 'tis the river, see,' the older man explained. 'That old Thames, he's a tricky bastard, always changin' course and splittin' and joinin', till ye'd go wild, tryin' to make out where un'd go next. Ye wasn't followin' the main stream, see, but one o' them branches. It joins up later, but it wanders about first.'

Emma nodded. The boats that came up to Godstow from Oxford must follow the main stream of the river, but when she was swept away, she must have been carried into one of the side branches. Already they had crossed one rickety wooden bridge, over what was probably the branch she had been following. It seemed there were more ahead.

When they were drawing near the abbey as evening began to set in, Emma made her way to the back of the cart, where Aelwith sat spinning. There never seemed to be a moment when her hands were idle.

'You have been so kind to me,' Emma said, 'is there nothing I can do to help?'

Aelwith looked at her and pursed her lips, though her fingers continued to twist the yarn.

'Edgar is no use to us until his hand mends. Ye could learn to make simple dipped candles. It might save us a day here, afore we go on to Oxford. We'm to go to Exeter College next.'

'Do you think I could make them well enough?'

'Aye. Not the big moulded altar candles. They've to be perfect, for they light God's altar. But the dipped candles, wax or tallow, they're for ordinary use. 'Twon't come amiss if some are lopsided.'

She spoke with perfect seriousness and Emma at once determined that her candles would not be lopsided.

'If you can teach me,' she said, 'I'll do my best.'

Aelwith smiled at her. 'Ye'll soon learn, my dear. Come the mornin', I'll have you makin' them, easy. Edgar and I learned as children. My man came to it late. He was a carpenter to trade, but there was not enough work for him and his brother both, so after we wed, he joined us. He learned quick enough.'

'Abbey ahead,' Edwin called from the front of the cart.

Emma picked her way carefully forward, past Jak, who was curled up asleep. Her feet were gradually healing, but they were still painful. She looked out over Edwin's shoulder. Thomas and Edgar were walking with the horses. Ahead of them, Osney Abbey stretched out. A vast place, it was, more like a village than an abbey, beside which Godstow, itself far from small, seemed hardly more than a toy. Beyond the perimeter wall, Emma could make out some of the monastic buildings, and rising above all was the abbey church with its enormous tower.

'A fine sight,' she said.

'Aye.' Edwin nodded, reining in the horses at the gate. 'They say the bell – Great Tom her's called – is the loudest thing nearby Oxford.'

As if to prove him right, the abbey bell began to ring. The cart trembled and Emma could feel the vibration through her feet, echoed by a tremor in her breastbone. It was impossible to speak, impossible to hear, impossible to think.

Great Tom was ringing for Vespers.

Chapter Nine

I had never driven Rufus so hard. Whether Jordain and Philip were close behind me or not, I neither knew nor cared. By the time we reached the North Gate, I realised that the horse had nearly foundered, so I held him back, though everything in my heart cried out for me to hurry. That devil Malaliver was going to loose his alaunts on Emma, I was sure of it. They would rip her apart, then he would have some plausible excuse – it was an accident, his men had exceeded his orders. He might even hang one of his men to demonstrate his good faith, but it would all be too late. Too late.

I tried to think clearly. Malaliver was determined to rid himself of Emma so that he could claim her inheritance; I was sure now that there could be no doubt of this. Yet even Philip had not been entirely certain of the niceties of the law. If Emma's grandfather died and she inherited before taking her final vows, then the property was hers and went with her to the nunnery, provided she became a nun. If she took her final vows before her grandfather died – which seemed to be what lay behind Malaliver's plan to force her to become a nun, then I *thought* – or so Philip had implied – she would not inherit and Malaliver might be able to claim the inheritance through kinship by marriage, though his claim could be disputed. Her only blood kin were the Farringdons and they were on her mother's side, no kin of the Thorgolds.

Jordain and Philip caught up with me as I entered the

North Gate, and we forced our way along Northgate Street.

'That horse of yours is nearly done,' Philip said.

'I know,' I said, feeling guilty. 'I needs must take him straight back to the Mitre. You must go to the Castle without me. If the sheriff is not there, ask for the deputy sheriff, Cedric Walden. He will not ask too many questions, and he has the good sense to act swiftly when necessary. Be sure he understands that Malaliver intends to use alaunts against the girl. That is as good as murder.' My voice cracked, despite my efforts to stay calm.

'What shall you do?' Jordain asked. He reached out and caught hold of my reins to detain me.

'I shall return Rufus and hire another mount from the Mitre,' I said, 'and I had best warn my family that I may not come home today. I mean to ride with the sheriff if I can catch up with him, and then continue the search for Emma. Surely she cannot be far.' I said it as much to reassure myself as to convince them.

Jordain released my reins. 'The sheriff will stop Malaliver,' he said.

'If he is not too late,' I said grimly.

'Aye.'

I twisted in my saddle. 'Philip, after you have been to the Castle, can you draw up the document for Emma's grandfather to sign? I think I must ride there tomorrow, whether we have found her or not. Once we have evidence that Sir Anthony approves Emma's departure from the abbey, I think it will be difficult for anyone to force her to take the vows.'

Philip nodded. 'I will do so.'

'However,' Jordain said, manoeuvring his horse past a street vendor of hot pies, 'once the maid is out in the world and free to inherit, does that not mean that she stands all the more clearly in Malaliver's way? Will he not have even more reason to wish her dead? In the abbey, she is unhappy but safe from him. Out of the abbey, she is in danger every minute of every day.'

I ran my hand over my face. Jordain was thinking

more clearly than I was.

'You have the right of it,' I said hoarsely. 'All she would be thinking of was escaping before she was forced to take her vows. I do not suppose she has ever thought about the Thorgold property and Malaliver's intentions.'

'Is she so naïve?' Philip said.

'Nay, I would not say so,' I said, 'but she is young, and I do not think she cares much for wealth. She has not lived with her grandfather for some years. I suppose she must know that all the rest of her Thorgold family is dead, but perhaps she has not considered how that affects her.'

At Carfax I turned Rufus into the High. 'You must hurry to the castle. And Philip, I will come to Merton first thing on the morrow for the document.'

They headed in the opposite direction, down the slope of Great Bailey to the castle, while I made my way to the inn, at a gentle pace to spare the horse. Once there, I unsaddled Rufus myself, rubbed him down, and gave him a substantial feed of oats, by way of apology. The stable lads at the Mitre were good fellows, but they did not know how hard I had ridden Rufus. Yet all the while I was burning with impatience. Having ordered another horse to be ready for me when I returned, I ran all the way down the High to my shop, to the astonishment of those I passed, and of Walter and Roger when I burst in, out of breath.

They were not at their desks, but crouched on the floor with Alysoun and Rafe, all of them clustered around the puppy Rowan. Alysoun was sobbing. Rafe had his thumb in his mouth and his face was very white.

'What's afoot?' I said, kneeling down beside Alysoun and putting my arm around her. 'Don't cry, my pet. Tell me what has happened?'

'It wasn't Rowan's fault.' She turned up a face blotched with tears.

'Calmly now,' I said. 'Tell me what has happened.' I saw that there was blood, and the puppy lay very still.

'We were going past that butcher in St Mildred Street. We'd been with Juliana. And there were sausages hanging down from the counter.' She gave a sob that was part hiccough. 'He shouldn't leave sausages hanging like that, should he, Papa? How is a dog to know?'

'What happened?' I said, though I had a shrewd idea.

'Rowan gave a little tug at them. It was just a little tug, wasn't it, Rafe?'

Rafe nodded solemnly, without taking his thumb from his mouth.

'She didn't steal the sausages?'

'Nay, but somehow it made a jug fall off the counter, and it smashed.' She gulped. 'He's a horrible man, Papa, that butcher.'

'Tell me quickly, my pet, so I can help Rowan.' I noticed now that there was also blood on Alysoun's gown.

'He took a piece of the broken jug and slashed her with it. All along her side. I carried her home, but I think she's going to die. Oh, Papa, please don't let her die!'

'Where is your aunt?' Margaret would know best what to do.

'Gone to the market,' Walter said.

There was nothing for it. Despite my desperate need to ride in search of Emma, I could not leave the dog lying injured.

'Roger,' I said, 'fetch me a bowl of water and a rag from the kitchen. I think I know what Margaret would use to clean the wound and salve it.'

I got to my feet and hurried to my sister's stillroom. There were bottles of the tinctures of cleansing herbs Margaret used when the children fell and scraped their knees, and small pots sealed with melted wax of the salve she applied afterwards. I was not sure what herbs she used, but whatever was healing for humans could do a dog no harm. As an afterthought I caught up a piece of the fine linen she used for bandages.

The puppy lay quiet while I cleaned the wound, which was a nasty deep gouge running along her side. Unnecessarily cruel, I thought. I knew the man, greedy for money, careless of cleanliness, and short of temper. He was known to beat his wife and children. An errant dog could expect little mercy.

Alysoun watched me with her hands gripped tightly together, looking as if she might be sick at any moment. I thought it best to make a return to normal.

'Thank you, Roger. You and Walter may go back to work. Alysoun, you and Rafe may prepare something for Rowan to eat when I have finished here. I am sure she will be hungry after the shock. There is some gravy in a jug on the shelf by the back door. Put it in her bowl and crumble some bread into it to soak.'

They ran off, clearly glad to have something to do. Margaret might have had other plans for that good beef gravy, but I thought she would not begrudge it.

'How bad is it?' Walter asked quietly, once they were out of earshot.

'Nasty,' I said, 'but fortunately her ribs stopped it going too deep. If the shard of pottery had slid between her ribs it would probably have killed her. Damn the man!'

Hearing the anger in my voice, Rowan lifted her head and licked my hand apologetically. I stroked her and rubbed her behind her soft spaniel ears.

'Not you, poor imp. Now, stay quiet while I finish.'

I smeared the jagged gash with the salve, then wound the bandage right round her body and secured it with a knot at her back. She might well try to pull it off, but for the moment it would offer some protection. I gathered her up and carried her into the kitchen. Set on her feet, she sat down suddenly, then managed to walk, somewhat shakily, to the dish of bread and gravy, which she began eating with enthusiasm,

'There, you see,' I said to the children, 'she is not going to die, but I think you should keep her in the house until that heals. And Alysoun, you'd best put that gown to soak in a bucket of cold water. I am going to clean the floor in the shop, then I am afraid I must go out again. We are searching for a missing girl. Tell Aunt Margaret I am not sure when I will be home.'

'Oh, Papa, you saved her!' Alysoun flung her arms around my waist and buried her face in my chest. I tousled her hair, swallowing a tendency to weep myself.

'Nay, my pet,' I said. 'I do not think she was going to die.'

However, when I had washed away the blood on the shop floor I realised that the puppy had lost a good deal. She would need care for the next few days. I flung the bloody water out into the garden, abandoned the bucket and rag outside the door, and hurried back to the shop, where I explained briefly what was to-do at Godstow.

'Alaunts?' Walter said, shocked.

'Aye. I hope that the sheriff may come in time.'

With that, I left, running back up the High to the Mitre.

The horse they had saddled for me was Merrylegs, a poor choice of name, for he was an ill-tempered beast, inclined to bite, so I had no compunction at kicking him up to a good speed once I was out of the town and heading up St Giles. Dealing with the puppy had delayed me, so the sheriff's men must be well ahead of me, if they had started as soon as Jordain and Philip had alerted them. I suppose I had ridden about two miles when I came up with the party of horsemen from the castle. To my relief, the deputy sheriff was in charge. I had never had dealings with the sheriff of Oxfordshire, but Cedric Walden I knew and liked.

'Any sign yet of the girl?' I asked.

He shook his head. 'Not yet, but first we will make sure of this Falkes Malaliver and his dogs. Once they are secure, then we can begin the search for the novice.'

Looking across at me, he said, 'Why do you suppose she has run away from Godstow?'

'She feared being coerced into becoming a nun,' I said. 'It was not her wish to enter the nunnery, she was forced into it by this stepfather of hers.'

'She's not the first, and won't be the last. It was his

right, if he is her guardian.'

'There is more to this than a wish to dispose of an unwanted stepdaughter,' I said grimly. 'There is the matter of a large inheritance.'

'Ah.'

'Master Olney is investigating the legal side, but there seems to be some evil intent on Malaliver's part. And since he is bent on hunting her down with dogs who can kill a wolf or a boar–' I shrugged, leaving Walden to draw his own conclusions.

'Then the sooner we put a stop to it,' Walden said, 'the better for all, including the man himself, if he has no wish to face a murder charge.'

With that he spurred his horse on, and we all galloped up the road to Woodstock like cavalry going to war.

We came face to face with Malaliver and his men where the track to Wolvercote joined the road to Woodstock. I was surprised that they had not ranged further, but pressed my horse close up behind Walden so that I could hear what passed between the two men. At first Malaliver shouted at Walden to clear the way, as flushed and angry as he had been earlier at Godstow, but Walden stood firm, his disciplined men formed up in ranks beside him, and asserted his authority as deputy sheriff of Oxfordshire.

All the time, the lymers ranged about the feet of the horses, aimlessly scenting the undergrowth on either side of the track. The alaunts, to my great relief, were still held on chains by the huntsmen.

'God curse the wench!' Malaliver shouted, barely lowering his voice from his first arrogant orders to Walden. 'She was well cared for amongst those women. She would soon have been safely made a nun. Wherefore has she gone running off?'

'It is my understanding,' Walden said quietly, 'that she is quite opposed to taking the veil. It seems that she has taken drastic measures to avoid it.'

'That is not for her to decide,' Malaliver yelled,

growing, if possible, even redder in the face, 'when her legal guardian has decreed otherwise. She has been given to God, and with God she must remain. It is God's will.'

I wondered that he could so twist the intentions of the Deity, to follow his own desires, and at the same time call upon Him to curse the girl.

'All of this may be settled in time,' Walden said calmly, 'and may need a decision in the courts, but nothing is of account until the maid is found. Since you have not travelled far from Godstow, do I understand that your tracking dogs have not yet picked up her scent?'

'We scouted in the opposite direction first, in case she had taken that way, avoiding the road.' Malaliver had lowered his voice from a shout now, perhaps reasoning that he needed to placate Walden. 'After that we searched the home farm, lest she was hiding out there, but there was no sign.'

'Your lymers have something to give them the scent?'

'Aye, the women gave me a blanket from her bed. Or so they claimed. It would be no surprise to me if it was a trick.' He glowered. 'The dogs have found no scent, so how can that be? If she came this way out of the abbey, she must have left a scent. My lymers are the finest in the kingdom. If there was a scent, they would find it. It was probably some other woman's blanket and those women sought to frustrate me. More fools they! They need the wench back, and quickly, or they will regret it.'

His tone was threatening, and I wondered what he meant. Merely the demand that Abbess de Streteley return Emma's monastic dowry? Or something else?

'Well, it seems that this is the only way out of the abbey,' the deputy sheriff said, 'through the gatehouse, which I understand was left unbarred that night. The maid is most likely to make for Oxford, since she has kin living there.'

He laid a slight emphasis on the word 'kin', as if to show that he knew Emma had blood kin, which Malaliver was not.

'Therefore,' Walden continued, 'we will make an enlarged party to search all the way from here to Oxford, and in the meantime you will tell your huntsmen to take those alaunts back to the abbey, where they will request a secure outbuilding in which the dogs may be lodged. To hunt a woman with killing hounds is against the law, and you are fortunate that they were still held on chains when we found you. Otherwise I should have put you under arrest.'

Walden too could sound threatening when he chose, and I was pleased to see that Malaliver was somewhat taken aback. Sullenly he ordered the men holding the alaunts – three dogs to a man, nine in all – to return with them to Godstow.

The deputy sheriff now took charge of the search, commandeering Malaliver's chief huntsmen and ordering the careful search by half the lymers on each side of the road, while his men scoured the woods, following behind the dogs. Malaliver's men were distributed amongst the groups of the sheriff's men, but not permitted to range off on their own. Walden had taken the measure of Emma's stepfather and clearly did not trust either him or his men.

Thus began our slow progress back to Oxford, with diversions into farmland where the woods had been cleared, and then the search of every barn and cottage we passed. Night was falling when we reached the town, but we had found no trace of Emma.

I hardly slept that night. Though I would not admit how much Emma Thorgold was beginning to matter to me, I argued with myself that any decent man would be concerned at the thought that a gently born girl was lost and alone, somewhere out in the uninhabited country around Godstow. Since England had been torn apart by the Great Pestilence, the numbers of outlaws and masterless men had soared. Some were escaped villeins, seizing the opportunity of a world turned upside down to flee their bondage and their lords. Although there were those amongst them who had found work as free labourers with new masters in countryside or town, many still roamed the land, living wild. As well, there were outlaws, driven from their own parishes for crimes too minor for the death penalty, but too serious to be ignored. Both groups lived not only by poaching illegal game but by preying on any travellers not strong enough to withstand them. Even merchants took care to travel in large parties, with armed retainers. A girl, alone and unprotected, could no more resist them than a fledging bird can resist a hunting cat.

Abandoning any hope of rest, I rose and dressed before dawn, taking care to don my best cotte and a cloak of fine azure blue wool, for I wanted to make a good impression on Sir Anthony Thorgold, to ensure his support for his granddaughter. On my way home the previous evening I had stopped at a barber in Northgate Street for a better shave than my usual rough and ready efforts at home. I ran my hand over my chin now. There was no marring of stubble yet. I am fortunate that my beard grows slowly.

Margaret, of course, was up before me, just drawing her new baked loaves out of the bread oven. She raised her eyebrows when she saw me.

'You are early astir, Nicholas.'

'I want to set off for Long Wittenham as soon as I may, once I have the document from Philip Olney in hand. It will take most of the day to ride there and back, with seeing Sir Anthony between. I do not know how I will be received. It may take time to persuade him to sign Philip's document. Indeed, I may fail to persuade him at all, but I must make the assay.'

'Dressed like that, you could persuade the king himself,' she said.

I laughed, but felt somewhat flattered, until she added, 'You have forgot to comb your hair.'

My feelings of apprehension over approaching Sir Anthony, as well as the worry over Emma, robbed me of any appetite, so I left soon after this for the Mitre. To my relief, Rufus appeared none the worse for his hard usage the previous day. I could rely on him to take me to Sir Anthony's manor and back without mishap. With so early a start I need not force the pace.

After mounting Rufus I rode him down to Merton and was surprised but pleased to see that Philip had come out to the gatehouse to meet me.

'Here is the document we discussed,' he said, handing me a scrip with the parchment rolled up safely inside. I buckled the scrip to my belt.

'And all he needs to do is to sign it?' I asked.

'Aye, but you will need to explain its purpose to him first, and what I judge to be the position in law. The position, that is, of his granddaughter in relation to taking the veil.'

I nodded. 'Of course. I only hope the man is not too ill to see me or to understand why I have come. If he cares for his granddaughter, surely he must want to support her wishes.'

Philip shrugged. 'Who's to know? Families can be strange in their ways, and not all kin love each other.'

'True.'

'However, if you find him in his right mind, and willing to sign, I think you might go further.'

'What do you mean?' I said.

'If it is possible to do so discreetly, I think you should warn him about what we suspect of Malaliver's intentions. It may be unseemly for you, as a stranger, to speak to a dying man about his will, but were I his man of law, I would urge him to so word his will that the Thorgold estate cannot fall to Malaliver. If you can think of a way to do it, warn him.'

'Aye.' I nodded. 'We know that he was opposed to his daughter-in-law, Emma's mother, marrying Malaliver after the death of his son. It may be that he was not simply opposed to her remarriage, but to her intended husband. And of course he may not even know that Emma was forced into the nunnery. He may believe that she went of her own choice. I will do my best to make everything clear to him.' I grimaced. 'Including Malaliver's use of killing dogs.'

'There has been no word of her, I suppose, since you spoke to me yesterday?'

I shook my head. 'None. I would prefer to stay here and help with the search, but I must see Sir Anthony first. Cedric Walden is going to cover the ground north of Godstow today, sending one party to Woodstock and another along the road to Witney and Burford.'

'Why should she go to any of those places?'

'Why indeed? But where can she be?'

'Do you know what Malaliver intends?'

'I do not.' I frowned. 'I hope Walden will keep a close watch on him. He and his men – and his dogs and horses – were to spend the night in the guest house at Godstow. I do not envy the Reverend Mother the task of entertaining them.'

'Nor I. Well, I shall not delay you further, Nicholas. If it is not too late when you return, come and tell me how you fared.'

'Aye, and I will bring you, I hope, the signed document for you to retain as Emma's man of law.'

He gave a rueful smile. 'A client I have never met, and who has quite vanished. God go with you, Nicholas.'

'And you.' I turned Rufus to cut through the back alleys to reach Fish Street, saving me the distance of riding round by Carfax. Philip gave me a wave and withdrew into his college.

The way to Long Wittenham was familiar to me from my recent trip with Jordain to fetch the Farringdons and their goods, but riding a sturdy horse I could travel at a much brisker pace than we had done with our lumbering horse and cart. I had not thought to bring any vittles with me, but I still felt the nausea of apprehension which robbed me of hunger. However, the weather had turned sunny again after the thunderstorm. The crops would be drying in the fields and those I passed did not appear to have suffered too much of a beating. As the sun rose further, I began to feel too warm in my cloak, and I wished that I had at least brought a flask of ale with me.

When I reached the river ferry at Clifton, I hoped the ferrymen would not remember me as one of the passengers with the stubborn-minded carthorse, but they showed no sign of recognition. No doubt so many people passed this way, travellers as well as locals, that they took no particular notice of us, except when a passenger added an extra penny to the fare.

One change was clear. The rain had filled the Thames and all its tributaries, so that the water level at the ferry landing was at least a foot and a half higher than it had been on our previous visit. It was possible to lead Rufus straight from the wooden landing stage on to the ferry without the unnerving slither down an exposed muddy bank which the carthorse had to negotiate. We were soon across, despite the rapid flow of the river, and I rode up to the inn on the southern bank.

I was not surprised to see the same two ancient villagers once again seated on the bench overlooking the ferry. Probably they spent every day of fair weather there. In winter no doubt there was a good fire in the inn parlour, where they could enjoy a little peace from wives and daughters sweeping around their feet and scolding them for idleness.

'God give you good-day, friends,' I said, as I dismounted.

'And to 'ee.' It was the more loquacious of the two who responded.

'Have you a thirst on you?' I asked. It hardly needed saying.

'It do be warmer weather,' he volunteered politely.

I hitched Rufus and went within, where I bade the cheerful innwife to bring a flagon of ale for three, then rejoined the villagers on the bench.

'I seen 'ee beforetimes,' the ancient said, with an air of discovery.

'Aye, we came to convey a family to Oxford with their household goods.'

The other man laughed, with a noise like a creaking door. 'Horse don't take to the ferry. Near had you in the river.'

'He did that.' I smiled as I poured him a cup of ale. 'And now I am back again. I have business with Sir Anthony Thorgold. Tell me, have you news of his health? Before, you said he was near his end.'

'Ah,' the first man said sadly, shaking his head. 'Poor old gentleman. Not long for this world.' He crossed himself, and we did likewise.

The innwife had come out with a plate of little meat pasties, which she set down on a stool in front of us.

'Will you try these, sir?' She turned to the sorrowful faced villager. 'What tales you do tell, Jacob. Sir Anthony is younger than you by at least five years, mebbe more. And he was ill in the spring, but I've heard from my cousin's girl, who works up at the manor, that Sir Anthony is much better, and like to be with us yet a while.'

This was encouraging news. In fact, I even felt able to sample one of the innwife's pasties, which were fresh from the oven and still warm.

'Excellent, mistress,' I said. 'You have a light hand with your pastry.'

She blushed with pleasure. 'I thank you, sir. You're for seeing Sir Anthony today?'

'I am. About two miles along the turn to the left, did you say? On the way to Long Wittenham?'

'That's it, sir. Mebbe not as much as two miles.'

I stayed a little longer, much refreshed by the ale, and even ate another pasty before bidding the three of them a courteous farewell and mounting Rufus again. I wondered whether the inn had any other customers than the two old men, but reasoned that all the men and women of working age would be out in the fields. They probably ended their tiring days of farm labour here in the evening.

The turning to Sir Anthony's estate was not far and I

rode down it in a state of high curiosity. All this time we had been talking about Emma's probable inheritance, but I had no real idea of the extent of the property.

Then – in less than two miles, I was sure – the road took a turn through a belt of woodland and emerged at the lip of a shallow valley, meticulously cultivated to right and left of the road, while in the distance there appeared to be the beginning of a wooded hunting ground. Straight ahead, on a slight rise, stood what was clearly Emma's ancestral home.

It had started life as a small castle, a square keep standing on a man-made motte, but later generations had built on to this austere tower a comfortable timber house above a stone undercroft, well provided with windows, whereas the tower had only arrow embrasures. It was a substantial building with three bays and roofed with slates. On such an extensive roof, those slates spelled wealth. As did the glazed windows. Villeins were working in the fields, hoeing the weeds out from amongst the grain crops and beans. A water meadow lying beside what must be a tributary of the Thames was filled with sleek cattle. The whole was busy, well maintained, and prosperous.

If this was Emma's inheritance, it placed her in rank far beyond the reach of an Oxford shopkeeper.

❧∘❧

Once the wide gate to Osney Abbey was opened, Edwin drove the cart without hesitation to a space close to the stables, where Thomas and Edgar unhitched the horses and led them within, following one of the abbey grooms. It seemed that even here the candle-makers would live in their cart, not the guest hall, but Emma was interested to see that when the monks were served their supper, a generous portion was sent out to the travellers from the abbey kitchen.

'It do save our time,' Aelwith explained. 'I can be makin' candles, not cookin' food. 'Tis part of our agreement – meals while we be here and coin at the end.'

'Do you supply the wax?' Emma asked. She had not thought it right to explore the working section of the cart.

'Aye, if the customer has not their own. Here at Osney they will have wax enough from their own hives.'

'But where do you obtain the wax, if they do not?' Emma said.

'Most folk keep a skep of bees and are glad to sell us the wax for coin, using rush dips or tallow candles themselves.'

'And do you make tallow candles too?'

Aelwith gave a scornful sniff. 'Only when times are hard. We'm wax candle-makers, my dear. My father is a member of the Guild of Wax Chandlers in London Town. He was apprenticed there as a boy, rose to Master Chandler, but my mother fretted to come back to Oxfordshire after Edgar was born, and I was born here. Mostly we serve the monasteries, and a few of the great houses, who've no call for tallow dips – foul, stinking things – though sometimes they do want them for servants' quarters.'

Emma nodded. She had noticed that the lantern in the cart the previous night had been lit by a good wax candle, not tallow, as she had expected.

Once they had eaten the supper provided by the abbey, they had all retired early to bed, planning an early start in the morning. Emma did not sleep so well as on the previous night, after a lazy day sitting in the cart. And the sound of the abbey bell ringing for Matins and Lauds woke her with the accustomed reaction. She had half risen, sleepily preparing to descend the night stairs for service, when she remembered where she was, and what she had become. When she woke again, she found she was the last to rise.

Edgar and Thomas had set up a large rectangular brazier in the cobbled yard, well away from the stables, and were feeding it with sticks, while Edwin and the boy Jak emerged from the front of the cart, carrying between them a tin tub, rectangular like the brazier, which they fixed above it. Aelwith was rummaging in a sack and drawing out irregular pieces of wax honeycomb, from which all the honey had been extracted.

Emma carefully eased her sandals over her feet, which were healing, but left the straps loosely buckled, then climbed down the steps at the rear of the cart to join Aelwith, who smiled at her. Emma noticed that the wax contained quite a few impurities, mostly dead bees or fragments of the wings or bits of leaves and petals.

Before she could ask how the candle-makers could obtain the pure wax needed for the best quality candles which the abbey would demand, Edwin returned from the cart with a mesh of woven wires, which he set over the tin tank.

'Now ye may help, my dear,' Aelwith said. 'Lay the combs flat along the mesh. As the wax melts in the heat, this rubbish be left behind, see?'

Emma did see. A very simple but effective way of cleaning the wax.

While she and Aelwith worked with the wax, the men set up more equipment, which they arranged on two of the stools. She saw that it consisted of a row of brass moulds, the size and shape to make almost the largest of the church candles, about two feet high and four inches in diameter. Then they stood another set of moulds directly on the ground, the largest of all, three feet high and six inches in diameter. For the altar candles.

Aelwith went back to the cart and returned with a large bundle of dried rushes. Seeing Emma's puzzled face, she laughed.

'Wicks for the candles. Ye can easily help with this. Watch, now.'

She took one of the rushes and cut off the head with a knife from a sheath at her belt, leaving it with a small length of stem. It was the same knife she had used for eating. The rush head she set aside. Then she began to peel the rush, revealing the pith. She laid it down and picked up another.

'Will you throw the rush heads away?' Emma asked.

'Nay, they can be used for rush dips.'

'You have left a bit unpeeled,' Emma pointed out, picking up the first rush.

'Aye. That's meant. If we do take off all the peel, so there's nothing but pith, it would bend and fall apart. No use for a wick.'

'Oh, I see.' Emma felt foolish. Of course that would happen. 'I think I could do that.'

Aelwith cut the heads off several more rushes and handed them to Emma, who found that it was not quite as easy as she had supposed to leave that one neat strip of peel remaining. She persisted, and began to make a better show of it. From time to time as they worked, Aelwith got up to check on the progress of the filtered wax, adding more combs when there was room. Edwin took some of Aewith's peeled rushes and began securing them in the moulds.

Once there was a good pile of prepared rushes, Aelwith cut them into different lengths, working entirely by eye. She now seemed to have decided there was enough wax melted in the trough, and called to Thomas to remove the wire grid, which he did gingerly, holding it with a thick cloth wrapped round his hand.

'That's how my fool brother burnt himself,' Aelwith said. 'Always in a hurry. Did not use a thick enough cloth. That gets main hot, that do.'

Emma was beginning to feel a little nervous herself about working with so many scalding hot objects.

'Now,' Aelwith said, taking up a length of rush in each hand. They were about a foot long. 'Ye must keep about an inch or so clear at the top, for to hold by. As ye are just startin', mebbe two inches. Then 'tis dip and cool, dip and cool. Like this.'

She dipped the two lengths of rush into the hot melted wax, held them there for a moment, then lifted them out and held them well above the heat. The thin skin of wax shone wet, then slowly turned dull. She dipped again and repeated the process. Gradually the wax began to build up around the wicks until it assumed the thickness of a standard household candle.

'Do ye think ye can do that, my dear?' Aelwith laid down her candles on a large cloth Edgar had spread on the ground.

'I'll do my best,' Emma said, taking up two lengths of rush and dipping them in the wax. The heat rushed up toward her hands and she jerked them back.

'Ye'll not burn if you stay clear of the wax.'

Emma nodded, ashamed of her cowardice. This time she managed to hold the wicks in the wax about as long as she thought Aelwith had done. When she lifted them out, to her delight they each had a fine covering of molten wax. She plunged them in again.

'Too soon,' Aelwith said. 'Ye must wait for the wax to cool, or the next layer will not stick.'

Emma tried again, and this time received a nod of approval. Aelwith watched until the candles were thick enough to satisfy her.

'Now wait until they are hard, then lay them down next to mine.'

Emma did as she was bid. She had been so absorbed in her own work she had not noticed that Aelwith had made three more pairs of candles. Her own pair were somewhat uneven, but perhaps not totally lopsided. Aelwith watched while Emma made two more pairs, each a little more even than the ones before.

Aelwith nodded. 'Ye'll do fine. Thomas, ye may take my place. And where's that scamp Jak?'

Jak, it seemed, was in the stables talking to the grooms, but was soon fetched to his work, joining Emma and Thomas at the dipping. Emma saw that Jak finished two pairs of candles to her one, and determined to catch him up. Aelwith and Edwin now set to work on the big moulded candles, using long handled dippers to collect wax from the trough, then pouring the molten wax into the moulds.

'Have to work quick, see,' Edwin said, as he politely eased her aside to reach more wax. 'Otherwise it leaves a ridge on the candle, between pourin'. Can't have that on the altar candles.'

Emma realised that only the Master Chandler and his daughter had the skill to make the moulded candles of the quality required for the abbey. She had never thought about the many processes required in the making of something so essential to life as a candle, or so vital to the due worship of God. Whenever she lit a candle in future, she would treat it with more respect.

They paused in their labours to eat the dinner provided by the abbey, and Aelwith laid out more combs on the mesh to filter into the tank, while Edgar, who could do little else with one hand bandaged, fetched more fuel from the abbey store for the brazier. As they were preparing for the afternoon's work, a plump little monk came bustling across from the church.

'The sacristan,' Edwin murmured. 'Come to check whether our candles do meet with his approval.'

It was Edwin who went forward to meet the monk and display the candles which had been made in the morning. Although it was Aelwith who had appeared to direct the work, clearly the monk would not recognise a woman as being in charge. It seemed he was satisfied, and gave them all a quick nod. Just before leaving them to their work, he noticed Emma for the first time, frowned as if he did not know what to make of her, then turned away. She found she was holding her breath. Thomas had thought her a boy at first. She could only hope the monk thought so as well, or he might have punished her for assuming men's garb. At all costs he must not see her shorn head, or he would recognise her for what she was. Suddenly it occurred to her that word might have gone out from Godstow to the other religious houses in the neighbourhood, since they were the principal providers of hospitality to travellers. They might be expected to encounter Godstow's wandering renegade.

The work seemed much harder in the afternoon. Emma found that her arms and shoulders had begun to ache, shooting pains ran up the top of her spine and into her neck every time she held her candles in the air, waiting for them to cool enough to dip again. The repeated motion, though holding nothing heavier than a pair of candles, was more wearing than working in the laundry. By the time they had finished, when the long summer daylight at last started to fade, Emma had begun to hate the sight of wax, though by then there was a large heap of the dipped candles. The third batch of the great moulded candles had been carefully laid with the others in a wide, shallow basket provided by the abbey.

Even the others were tired, although they did not seem to be in such pain as Emma, so there was little talk over supper, although Aelwith regarded the completed candles with satisfaction.

'I think us'll need just one more day, Father.'

'Aye. The weather is holdin'.' He gestured vaguely at the sky, which was entirely cloudless, dotted with the first of the evening stars. 'Make an early start tomorrow, finish by evenin', be off next mornin' for Oxford.'

That would suit Emma very well. She would travel with the candle-makers to Exeter College, and ask there for her aunt. What she was to do thereafter, she was not sure. Would her aunt have found work in Oxford? She would need some source of income, although Emma could not picture what her aunt might do. In the past she had helped her husband run their yeoman holding, herself often instructing the manager her uncle hired after the death of their elder son, little Maysant's father, but there could be no call for Mistress Farringdon's country skills in a town like Oxford. Would she be able to help Emma find work?

Jocosa had spent the day making friends with the candle-makers' elderly hound and following him about the abbey enclave, but when Emma lay down exhausted to sleep, she curled up happily under her mistress's arm. Both slept soundly until called to an early start by Edwin.

Chapter Ten

Although the manor of Sir Anthony Thorgold seemed steeped in rural tranquillity, his people kept a sharp look-out in these somewhat lawless times. A boy who had been scaring crows away from the bean field left his task and went running ahead of me toward the house, so that by the time I reached the gate in the perimeter wall a dignified elderly man, carrying a staff of office, was already making his way out to meet me. Sir Anthony's steward, no doubt.

'God give you good greeting, sir,' he said, with old fashioned dignity.

'God's blessing on this house and its people,' I responded, taking my cue from his manner. 'I am Master Nicholas Elyot of Oxford. I wrote to Sir Anthony, requesting the favour of a meeting.'

He bowed a head of thick grey hair in acknowledgement. 'You are expected, Master Elyot.'

I dismounted, and almost before my feet touched the ground there was a smart young groom at my elbow, ready to lead Rufus to the stables set against the inside of the perimeter wall. The steward bowed me in through the open gate and across a cobbled yard to a wide outside stairway. This led up to the upper, timber-framed portion of the house. In the stone built undercroft a wide doorway stood open beyond the stairway, allowing a glimpse of a partitioned storeroom inside. Like the farmland without, within the manor's compound everything was orderly and well managed.

The steward led the way up the steps, then opened a heavy oak door and stood aside for me to enter. After the bright sun outside, it took a few moments for my eyes to adjust themselves to the dimmer interior, although the room was relatively well lit by the ample windows. The manor was a curious mixture of styles. Although the exterior of the house seemed modern, the interior had a curiously old fashioned look. We had entered a large hall with a dais at one end, and doors leading to the family's private quarters at the other. But for the windows, it might have been built two hundred years ago. Perhaps this had been the first extension to the old castle, and the windows had been added more recently by knocking out some of the wattle and daub between the oak framework. Clearly this was a family which clung to some of the old ways, while embracing certain modern comforts. The house did not retain the old habit of a smoke hole amongst the rafters, though the signs of soot amongst the high roof beams showed that originally smoke had escaped that way. There were now two large and handsome fireplaces, and outside I had observed the modern stone built chimneys.

The steward did not pause in the great hall but led me at the same dignified pace toward a door at the far end, where he knocked and was bidden to enter.

'Master Nicholas Elyot of Oxford, Sir Anthony,' he announced.

Once again he stood aside for me.

It was a comfortable modern room, not unlike the Warden's lodgings at Merton which I had visited recently. However, here the walls were hung with Flemish tapestries depicting scenes from the Old Testament, far too expensive even for a wealthy college like Merton. Despite the warmth of the day, a small fire was burning in an elaborately carved fireplace. There were chairs with arms, made even more comfortable with cushions, although I noticed that their needlework was somewhat faded with age. The work of Sir Anthony's late wife? A low table held a wax candle in a silver candlestick and four books, one of which lay open, with an *aestle*, a gold and ivory page turner, laid across it to keep the place. All the books had excellent bindings of beautifully tooled leather, and the parchment of the open book was of the very finest quality. The room smelled fresh and clean. Somewhere there was lavender.

The man who rose from the chair which stood between this table and the fireplace was perhaps in his seventies, but still strongly built, although his flesh was a little sparse on the bones, perhaps as the result of his illness in the spring. He had an upright, knightly bearing, which caused me to wonder whether he had seen service in the French wars at a younger age. Despite this, I saw that a stick was propped against the side of his chair, as though he might need its aid in walking.

'Sir Anthony,' I said, bowing deeply, 'I thank you for agreeing to see me.'

He returned my bow. 'You are most welcome, Master Elyot, although I am at a loss as to this matter of my granddaughter which you wish to discuss.' His manner was not unfriendly, but it was marked with a certain reserve.

He motioned me to a chair facing him and lowered himself carefully down into his own chair, as though his back pained him. I remembered my grandmother seating herself with the same wincing care.

'Hawkley,' Sir Anthony said, 'have wine and refreshments sent up. Master Elyot has had a long ride.'

The steward bowed. 'At once, Sir Anthony.' He withdrew, closing the door softly behind him.

While waiting for a servant to appear, Sir Anthony led the talk to commonplace matters – the recent storm, the prospects for the harvest, the latest news of the king's campaigns. Once we were served with a fine golden wine in silver gilt cups and a plate of almond and fig sweetmeats, he sat back in his chair, clearly prepared for the serious business of my visit.

'Now, Master Elyot, you said in your letter that it was a matter of my granddaughter's final vows. Has she then changed her purpose? I am not of a mind to listen to any shilly-shallying on her part. If she has chosen to take the veil, she must stand by her choice.'

The tone of his voice had shifted from the polite to the bitter, and his mouth was set hard. I was momentarily taken aback, so that I blurted out without choosing my words with any care, 'But, Sir Anthony, Emma was forced into the nunnery by her stepfather! She never sought to take the veil.'

He frowned. 'What is this? I was told – a year ago, it must be – that after losing her mother, who was my former daughter-in-law, Emma was so bereft that she sought the peace of the enclosed life.'

'Forgive me, Sir Anthony, but did she tell you this herself?'

'Nay. I had seen her not long before. There was no mention of it then.' His voice was even more bitter. 'She came here on a visit with her mother's relatives, the Farringdons. Her aunt and uncle, and her cousins. They went on to Malaliver's manor. It adjoins mine, just touching on the southern boundary of my land.'

He made an abrupt gesture with his hand, as much a dismissal of Malaliver as an indication of the direction. 'Her mother died shortly afterwards and I have not seen her since.'

'And when did you hear that she had chosen to become a nun?'

He frowned again, and his hands, which had lain loosely in his lap, suddenly came together in a fierce grip.

'It was a few weeks later. A letter from her stepfather. She had already left for Godstow. She did not even care to come and bid me farewell before withdrawing from the world forever.'

Despite his dignity and his formal manner, I could hear the hurt underlying the words. I leaned forward.

'Sir Anthony, your granddaughter was sent under armed guard and against her will to the abbey. Moreover, Falkes Malaliver signed documents to say that he was giving her as an oblate, provided with a substantial dowry.

He did everything he could to ensure that she was locked up in the nunnery for life.'

His whole body stiffened. 'You are sure of this?'

'Completely. I have had it from Emma herself.'

'How can that be?' He frowned again, full of doubt. 'You were allowed to see her?'

'Through a curious set of circumstances, I have come to know her.'

I set out as swiftly as possible how I had met Emma through the murder of her cousin William, my growing involvement with the Farringdon family, and Emma's work in the scriptorium at Godstow. My purchase of the book of hours she had made. I knew that Mistress Farringdon must have told him something of this in her letter, but I wanted to make all clear. As he listened, I saw that Sir Anthony's initial look of disbelief gradually vanished.

'And you say that she is afraid she will be forced to take her final vows against her will?'

'She is. On her behalf I consulted a lawyer I know, and he advises that if you are prepared to support her in leaving the nunnery, the vows can be delayed until the matter is settled in court. Despite the stepfather's actions, your will should override them, you being her blood kin, and more properly her legal guardian.'

I took Philip's document out of the scrip at my belt.

'The lawyer has drawn this up for me to bring to you, a statement that you support Emma's wish to leave the monastic life.'

'In that case, I will gladly sign.' He reached out his hand, but I did not immediately hand him the document.

'However,' I said, 'matters have changed since I saw Emma four days ago. Or is it five?'

I swallowed. I was unsure how Sir Anthony would take the latest piece of news.

'When I returned to Godstow with the lawyer yesterday, planning to see the abbess and tell her that Emma's friends would be disputing her confinement to the nunnery, it was to learn that she had disappeared more than a day earlier, most probably during the night. Extensive searches have been made by the deputy sheriff of Oxfordshire as well as all those about the abbey, but when I left Oxford this morning there had still been no sign of her.'

The old man turned pale, and his hands gripped more tightly together.

'Anything might have happened to her,' he said hoarsely.

I nodded, but said firmly, 'As far as we can tell, no harm has come to her yet. But–'

He leaned forward. 'What are you not telling me?'

Once again, I swallowed uncomfortably. 'The abbess sent word to Falkes Malaliver, to inform him of Emma's disappearance. I was at Godstow when he arrived there, with a troop of armed men, and a pack of huntsmen bringing lymers and alaunts.'

At this he sprang from his chair with more vigour than I would I thought possible.

'The devil he did! Was he proposing to hunt her like a wild animal?'

'It seems so. That is when we fetched the deputy sheriff, who ordered him to kennel the alaunts, though they are still using the lymers in the hope of tracking her. I spent the day with them hunting for her yesterday. The hunt continues today. And will do until she is found.'

He picked up his stick and walked to the window, limping slightly, his back bowed. Before he turned away from me, I saw the glint of tears in his eyes.

'This is my fault. I should have acted sooner, after her mother died.' He was speaking softly, to himself. 'I should have sent for her to come and live with me at once. But it happened so quickly.'

'I think that was done on purpose, Sir Anthony,' I said. I knew I must tell him of our fears about Malaliver's intentions to seize Emma's inheritance, but it felt wrong to intrude upon his grief with such worldly matters. However, he picked up my remark at once.

Returning to his chair, he sat down and confronted

me, in command of himself once more. 'What do you mean by that, Master Elyot?' he said.

'We need to ask ourselves why Falkes Malaliver was so anxious to thrust Emma into a nunnery immediately after her mother died,' I said. 'Also – and I had not thought of this before – why did he choose Godstow.' I paused. 'There are nunneries closer to here, are there not? Littlemore? Bromhale? Even Goring or Burnham? Perhaps he wished to send her well beyond your own country.'

'There are many reasons why girls are sent to nunneries,' he said, 'and not always malicious. He has daughters himself. But if it was a question of lacking a dowry on my granddaughter's marriage, the fellow must have known that I would provide it. Emma is the only kin I have left.'

Again I caught that echo of loneliness and sorrow.

'Forgive me, Sir Anthony. This is not my affair. I ask only because I feel it has a bearing on Malaliver's actions. Is Emma your heir?'

'Until she entered the nunnery, certainly.'

'But now?'

He looked uncomfortable. 'I should have made my will anew. I realised that, but I have been ill, and have taken no action yet.'

'I believe,' I said bluntly, 'that Falkes Malaliver is scheming to seize Emma's inheritance. The situation is confused in law, but he might be able to make a case, through kinship by marriage to her mother.'

'You think that was his reason for putting Emma in Godstow?'

I saw that his earlier doubtful look had given way to thoughtfulness.

'I do. So does the lawyer I spoke of.' I hesitated. I was reluctant to speak to such a man about his will, but it was he who had mentioned it. 'He also said,' I added, 'the lawyer, that is – said that if he were your man of law, he would advise you to word your will carefully, so that under no circumstances would Falkes Malaliver ever be able to inherit. He thinks this would be necessary for Emma's safety, especially now she is no longer within the walls of Godstow. There, although she was restrained against her will, her life at least was safe.'

Even as I spoke, a sudden thought came to me. How safe was Sir Anthony himself? If Malaliver were to suspect that the will might be changed to bar him, was there a danger that he might take action against Sir Anthony before that could happen? If Sir Anthony were to die now, Emma would inherit, as she had not taken final vows. Then were she to disappear completely, or to die, Malaliver might still be able to seize the estate. I remembered again the sight of those vicious killing dogs. They could make short work of Emma, but was there any way Malaliver could attack her grandfather? My head had begun to ache with trying to work out all the possibilities.

'Sir Anthony,' I said, 'I think you should send at once for your man of law to draw up a new will. And ensure that your own person is safe. Malaliver seemed to me a man bent on desperate measures.'

He nodded slowly. 'That may be. I have heard rumours that the man is in debt. I shall do as you advise. My lawyer lives in Oxford, but I can send for him to come tomorrow. In the meantime I shall make sure that I am well protected.' He smiled grimly. 'I have faced men in battle often enough, but the devilish snake that works by dark means, of him I have little experience.'

He rang a small brass bell which stood on the table beside the books. Almost at once the steward appeared and Sir Anthony instructed him to send word immediately for his lawyer to come the next day from Oxford.

'Now,' he said, when the man was gone, 'let me see this document you wish me to sign. Then I hope you will dine with me.'

I handed him Philip's document, which he perused carefully before signing it and sealing it with wax stamped with a seal taken from his pocket. He returned it to me.

'That should be sufficient to delay the process of

making my granddaughter a nun, and may serve to put a stop to it altogether.' He gave me a wan smile. 'I am grateful to you, Master Elyot, for all you have done for the girl, who seems to have fallen in your way quite by chance.'

'Had it not been for the tragedy of her cousin's murder, we would not have met,' I said, with wonderment as I did so. How frail the threads of mere chance.

'And you are a bookseller, you say, though originally destined for scholarship or the law yourself?'

'That was my father's wish, and mine too until I met and fell in love. With a bookseller's daughter. A married man cannot remain a scholar. I chose marriage.'

'You and your wife have children?'

'A boy and a girl, but my wife was taken in the Great Pestilence.'

'Ah, I am sorry to hear that, and you so young. May God give her rest.' He crossed himself. 'You have not remarried?'

'Nay.'

'I too have lost many. My wife, my children. A man should not outlive his children.'

He sighed, then made a visible effort. 'Tell me what you think of these books,' he said, clearly uncomfortable that he had touched on the subject and wishing to change it. 'I am not a scholar, but I saw to it that my sons were lettered. Emma learned from her father and also from her cousin William's tutor. 'Tis pity in many ways that she was not born a boy. However, if she marries a man of good standing, he will be able to run this estate for her when I am gone.'

I inclined my head, but did not point out that I thought Emma would be well able to do so herself. If she was ever found. If she survived. My stomach twisted, and I pushed the thought aside. Instead I began to praise Emma's skill in making the book of hours.

'I hope that some day, when this is over, you will bring it to show me,' he said.

Our talk turned to books until dinner was announced and we adjourned to the great hall, where I discovered that Sir Anthony kept to the old ways. We sat upon the dais with his steward, bailiff, and clerk, while his lesser servants and the men and women I had seen working in the fields were seated below us at trestle tables set up for the meal.

After we had dined, I made my farewells to Sir Anthony.

'I want to return to Oxford in time to learn from the deputy sheriff how today's search has fared,' I said. 'They were moving north to Woodstock and northwest to Witney and Burford. If that has proved fruitless, I expect they will try ranging over to the east.'

'I cannot see why Emma would have gone anywhere but Oxford,' he said, 'since Mistress Farringdon is now living there.'

'It does seem strange that no trace of her has been found on the nearest road from Godstow to Oxford. She would have known that was the way to go.'

'You have not mentioned any search to the west. Could she have gone that way?'

I shook my head. 'Unlikely. Godstow stands on an island, the only way out is over the bridge to Wolvercote. To go west she would have had to cross the river, and no boat is missing. And on the far side of the river the countryside is desolate, deserted since the Pestilence laid waste all the cottages and farms there. I see no reason why she should have gone that way.'

He accompanied me down to the manor courtyard, and a groom now brought Rufus, who wore the complacent look of a horse well fed and rested. When I had mounted, Sir Anthony laid his hand on Rufus's neck.

'You will send word if Emma is found?'

'At once. You may be sure of it.'

'And if you are able to speak to her, tell that I would be glad for her to come here to live with me.'

'I will so.'

Then I bade him farewell again and rode away from

the manor on the road back to the ferry. I wondered whether Emma would want to live here. I knew from Maud Farringdon that during her father's lifetime Emma had lived at her grandfather's manor, with frequent visits to her cousins, but how would she view the prospect now? I could see that her grandfather was lonely and would welcome her company, but half formed already in his mind were plans to find her a suitable husband to take over the running of the estate. Would that seem any better a future to Emma than remaining within Godstow? Would she have any greater freedom tied to her lands instead of to God, and bound fast by an arranged marriage instead of bound fast by her monastic vows?

It seemed to me that Elizabeth, daughter of an Oxford burgess, had had greater freedom to choose her own future than ever Emma Thorgold would have, whichever path lay ahead of her.

This time I did not stop at the inn by the ferry, although I waved to the two old men who still sat on the bench outside as though they had grown there. Once across the river on the Clifton side I set Rufus to a brisk but undemanding pace, yet it was nearly nightfall by the time we reached Oxford, since I had remained with Sir Anthony far longer than I had intended.

On reaching the town, I went first to the castle, to enquire about the day's search.

Cedric Walden shook his head. 'Nothing. Neither man nor beast could find any trace.'

'You are still using Malaliver's lymers?'

'Aye. Best to keep him under my eye. Tomorrow we will try going east, along the road to Otmoor, but I tell you in confidence, Master Elyot, I am beginning to lose hope. I fear the maid has suffered some mishap.'

His words chilled me. 'But surely, sheriff,' I protested, 'if she had come to harm, you would have found some trace by now. Could she have taken refuge in some cottage, and that is why you cannot find her?'

'We have searched every house, cottage, barn, stable

and hen house over all the ground we have covered. Never a sign.'

'I shall come with you tomorrow,' I said.

He looked at me curiously. 'You have a mighty interest in this maid, Master Elyot.'

I felt the blood rising to my face.

'I have spent most of the day with her grandfather, an old man who was very ill in the spring. She is his only kin. I have promised him not to abandon the search.'

'Of course,' he said, though I saw that he still eyed me speculatively.

I returned Rufus to the Mitre, then walked to Merton, where I climbed the stairs to Philip Olney's small kingdom of books.

'Did he sign?' he asked, barely pausing to greet me.

'He did. And has taken your advice about his will. His man of law will be there tomorrow. He did believe that Emma had gone of her own will to Godstow and was bitter that she had not even troubled to bid him a last farewell.'

'You undeceived him?'

'I did. He wants her to live with him.' I did not mention my misgivings to Philip.

'Here is the signed document.' I drew it from the scrip and laid it on his desk. 'You had best keep it safe, under lock and key if you can, as Emma's man of law. Until it shall be needed.'

He unrolled the scroll and studied the signature and seal. 'A fine bold flourish,' he said. 'So he is not so frail and ill after all.'

'Indeed he is not. The illness which laid him low in the spring was not fatal. Talk of his dying seems to have been exaggerated local gossip.'

'I see,' he said. 'Well, now all that remains is to find the maid and bring her to safety. There is no news from the searchers. I have just returned from the castle.'

'And I. You must have been not long ahead of me. I will have a word with Jordain tonight, tell him how I fared with Sir Anthony, then tomorrow I will join the search. The sheriff plans to go northeast to Otmoor. I have little hope of discovering anything there.'

By the time I had visited Hart Hall and told Jordain of all that had happened that day, I found I was remarkably tired and went to my bed soon after the children. Margaret regarded me with concern, but said nothing.

Early the following morning I joined Cedric Walden and his men at Carfax, where we had agreed the previous evening to meet. I thought that both the deputy sheriff and his men looked tired and discouraged. They rode up St Giles at a slow amble, showing none of the eagerness that had animated the search on the first day. As we headed right handed on to the road to Banbury, I moved Rufus forward until I was beside Walden.

'Where do you plan to search today? Do you truly believe the maid could have headed this way?'

He shrugged. It was clear that he was losing enthusiasm for the task, but he had given his word that he would continue. I wondered how long he would reckon that promise should be valid. Perhaps until he was called away to deal with some other crime or emergency.

'I thought we would head over Otmoor way, then work south along the far side of the Cherwell to Shotover, then back through the East Gate.'

I looked at him dubiously. 'I cannot think why she should have gone that way. What could have been her aim? Her aunt is in Oxford. Her grandfather lives further south, and her way to either would lie in or through Oxford.'

'Yet we have twice searched the direct road from Godstow to Oxford,' he said. 'We returned that way yesterday, after our fruitless search to the north. In case we had missed something the first time, we quartered every field and copse, turned villeins out of their hovels and harried the yeoman farmers. I am convinced she never came that way.'

'Has Malaliver taken himself off?' I had seen no sign of Emma's stepfather, but did not believe he would abandon the search so easily.

'Nay, he will ride across from Godstow on the road east, and meet us where our roads cross. He claims his lymers are the best in England, but I have brought some of our own as well.'

I nodded. I had noticed half a dozen of the tracking dogs following behind us, though I doubted they would prove any more successful than Malaliver's hounds. As more time passed, I was beginning to share Walden's fear that some accident had befallen Emma.

While we continued to ride north I told Walden in more detail about my visit to Sir Anthony.

'So you now have evidence that he supports his granddaughter's desire to leave the nunnery?'

'We have.'

'Although it will be of little use unless we can find the maid. It seems you were right. She is indeed an heiress. Grounds enough for that stepfather of hers to be tempted.'

'Of course, we have no proof against him,' I admitted reluctantly.

'I suppose proof will be difficult to find. Giving the maid as an oblate is no proof. He could claim that he was doing his best for her.'

'Against her will. And, it seems, without the knowledge of her grandfather, her blood kin and a man of much higher rank than Malaliver.'

'That does smack of subterfuge,' he said. 'Unless there was an arguably good reason not to tell him. When did he suffer this severe illness?'

'Not until the spring of this year. Long after Emma had been sent to Godstow.'

'Then it seems to me that Malaliver will have some serious questions to answer, should the matter go to court. Ah, and here is the gentleman in question.'

Falkes Malaliver was indeed approaching from our left, surrounded once again by his armed retainers, who slightly outnumbered Walden's men. His huntsmen followed with the lymers but, I was relieved to see,

Malaliver was continuing to obey the deputy sheriff's orders and had left the alaunts behind at Godstow. I wondered what the gentle nuns like Sister Mildred would be thinking of those vicious beasts.

Malaliver gave a cursory nod in Walden's direction, ignored me, and spurred his horse to the head of the company. Walden would not tolerate that and soon overtook him, but I had no wish to ride near Malaliver. I dropped back amongst the men from the castle.

Before long we approached the edge of Otmoor, a strange area of marsh and standing pools, surrounded by what are known at the 'seven towns' of Otmoor, though none are more than villages: Oddington, Beckley, Fencott, Murcott, Noke, Charlton-on-Otmoor and Horton-cum-Studley (though the last might count as two). My scrivener Roger came from Beckley and his widowed mother lived there still. An ancient road built by the Romans crossed it on higher ground, some of it a man-made causeway. I have always supposed that the name meant 'Otter Moor', but some learned scholars in Oxford, who study these things, assert that it is 'Otta's Moor', but dispute the identity of this Otta.

We had a long day of it, riding around the moor, searching the seven villages and questioning the villagers. We even made a foray on to the moor itself, a bleak place inhabited by wildfowl who took to the air with a clatter of wings as we approached. No doubt the villagers snared them and caught fish in the streams and pools dotted over the whole moor, but no one would ever farm here, for it was forever flooding.

There were bullaces and blackberries, not yet ripe, amongst the tangled undergrowth below willow copses around the edges of the marshy ground. I even caught sight of a pair of young otters tussling in one of the pools. The place had its own distinctive smell, compounded of water and mud, peat bog, rotting vegetation, and a kind of ferocious fertility. Despite this fertility, Otmoor would never make farmland. However much puny Man tried to drain it, Nature's irresistible hand would raise the waters from some secret source, deep underground. The fertility here was of a much wilder, more ancient kind, the land's own vigorous cycle of rebirth and growth, quite untouched by human hand. I found the place disturbing, yet somehow exciting, uninhibited.

As I expected, there was no sign of Emma, for why should she ever come to this lonely place? I suppose Cedric Walden was right to be thorough, extending the search for Emma in every possible direction radiating out from the gatehouse of Godstow Abbey, but I had never believed that today's foray into Otmoor would yield any evidence that Emma had come this way.

Weary and discouraged, we began the long ride back to Oxford. We had spent so long about Otmoor there was no time left to ride south to Shotover. Our horses were as exhausted as we were, for they had laboured through the boggy ground across and around the moor. Even where some attempt had been made to improve the trackways, the moor had a way of insidiously undermining them. The recent storm had not improved matters. The heavy rain had raised the level of the meres and increased the flow of the river Ray and its tributaries. We were a muddy, dispirited troop when we halted at the crossroads where Falkes Malaliver and his men would take the westward road across to Godstow, while the rest of us turned south along the Banbury road to Oxford.

With no clear intention of doing so, I found myself near Malaliver as he took an abrupt leave of the deputy sheriff.

'There is one direction in which we have not ventured,' he said. His tone was arrogant, as if instructing Walden in his duty. 'Across the river to the west of the abbey.'

'The maid could not have gone that way,' Walden explained patiently. 'There was no boat taken. And there is no other way to cross the river. On that side of the Thames there is nothing but ruins and deserted farms. Nowhere to find food or shelter or help from humankind.' He glanced uneasily over his shoulder at me. 'Even supposing she could have gone that way – and, as I say, I do not believe she could – then I fear she would have little chance of surviving.'

A curious expression flickered over Malaliver's face. I thought: *He is calculating how his plans will be affected if Walden is right. And if she is* . . . I shied away from the word . . . *if she has not survived, he will need proof.*

I eyed the man. What would he do next?

As if he had read my thoughts, Malaliver cast a patronising look at Walden.

'I, at least, shall not leave the task unfinished. Tomorrow I shall demand a boat to take me with my men across the river from the abbey. We will see whether there is any sign of my stepdaughter to be found there. I shall establish whether she could have gone that way.'

'You must do as you wish.' Walden spoke with cold politeness. 'I shall not be able to accompany you. I have duties in Oxford tomorrow which cannot be neglected. I wish you God speed. Should you discover anything, you will of course report to me.'

It was clear that Malaliver did not care to be spoken to in such a way, like some minion receiving orders from the deputy sheriff. He gave a grunt, a curt nod, and turned away on the road to Wolvercote, followed by his men, who had overheard the exchange and looked disgruntled at the prospect of yet another day like today. They were followed in turned by the huntsmen with the lymers, now on chains. Dogs and huntsmen, who had walked all day, seemed scarce able to move one foot before the other as they trailed wearily after the horsemen. I hoped the kitcheness at Godstow would feed them well on their return, for I ached with exhaustion myself, and I had been mounted.

Walden and I, followed by his men and dogs, headed south, and were both too tired to speak for a long while, but as we came to St Giles, I roused myself.

'I wonder,' I said, but then broke off, thinking that

what I had been about to say sounded foolish.

'You wonder . . . what?' Walden raised his eyebrows and waited for me to continue.

'This idea that Emma Thorgold might have crossed the river. I have discounted it from the start, but after our failure to find any trace elsewhere, I am not quite so sure. If you remember, after all those weeks without rain, the rivers were running quite low. I know that Emma had been punished for wading in the river on the far side of the island, just off the meadow where they keep the goats.'

'Go on,' he said, as I hesitated.

'The night she disappeared was the night of that thunderstorm. Until the storm filled the rivers again, the level was low. The lowest it has been all year. Could she have waded across? Gone that way from the abbey?'

He looked at me thoughtfully. 'It would explain why the dogs have not been able to pick up her scent outside the gatehouse. I have always been puzzled by that. Everyone says that was the only way she could have gone. And that there was no boat at the time which she could have used to cross the river. But I wonder whether you might be right. Even with the level low, would it have been low enough for her to wade?'

I shrugged. 'Who can tell? And it would be impossible to judge now, for everywhere the water level is higher since the storm.'

'So you think Malaliver has the right of it, to search along that bank tomorrow?'

'It is possible.'

We were coming to the North Gate, and our ways would soon part.

'I think I might make a small search of my own,' I said, assuming a careless tone of voice, which I do not suppose deceived Walden for a moment. 'I will not join Malaliver, never fear! Nay, I think I might start from the other end. If I ride out past the castle, across Bookbinder's Island, and take the road toward Osney, I think there is a way up the far side of the Thames, all the way until you are level with Wolvercote but on the other side. I might go that way. Try to find that path.'

'It can do no harm,' Walden said. 'Shall I lend you some men? Dogs?'

'Nay. It is probably a foolish notion. No need for your men to waste their time. And no need for dogs either. I have nothing to give them the scent. You have business of your own tomorrow. I shall make assay by myself, and if it is fruitless, it troubles no one but myself.'

We had reached Carfax. Walden halted his horse and smiled quietly.

'I think she must be a very remarkable maid, this Emma Thorgold,' he said.

I looked him steadily in the eye.

'She is,' I said.

᪥

The second day at Osney went much as the first. Emma's shoulders continued to ache and, growing careless in the afternoon she splashed herself slightly with hot wax. Aelwith smeared it at once with a salve of febrifuge herbs, which she kept to hand.

'There always be one or two scalds,' she said. ''Tis not to be helped. Ye be growin' tired. Rest for a while.'

Emma shook her head. 'Nay, 'twas my own carelessness. I want to help you finish today.'

She set to again, with more circumspection this time. At first today she had been slow, still even slower than the boy Jak, but now she was beginning to develop some skill. It took practice to judge both how long to dip the candle in the molten wax and when the wax, cooling out in the air, had turned to the right shade of dull cream before it could be dipped again. For a short time she stopped to watch Aelwith and Edwin making the altar candles. By now she realised that what appeared simple certainly was not. The wax in the moulds must not be allowed even to begin to harden before each new layer was added, or the candle would have an irregular, striped look. At first she wondered why they did not pour all the wax into the mould at once, but now she realised that for these huge candles it would be far too heavy to handle with the skill required. As each of the great candles was finished, it was freed from the mould – with bated breath, lest it break – then Aelwith polished it with a silk cloth to remove any imperfections and produce a gleaming surface as fine as the silk itself.

They did not stop this second day to eat a cooked dinner, but made do with bread and cheese while they worked. Edwin was anxious that all should be completed before the end of the day, so that there would be no need to light the brazier and melt more wax the next morning. That would mean waiting until all was cool again before they could pack up the cart, causing a delayed departure. And by Vespers they were finished. Edwin and Thomas made three trips to the sacristan's office, carrying the everyday candles in sacks and the huge basket of church candles, coming away with a heavy purse of coin. After a final meal provided by the abbey, the candle-makers packed up as many of the tools of their trade as they could. The brazier and melting trough would cool overnight, now that the fire in the brazier had been extinguished when they finished work. A layer of wax was congealing in the bottom of the tin tank, but would be left to be used in a few days at Exeter College. Everything else was ready for a prompt start in the morning.

The sky was overcast the next day, and the candle-makers were gloomy at the prospect.

'Us cannot work if it do rain,' Aelwith said.

Emma nodded. The danger from fire and hot wax meant working out of doors, unless the customer could provide a place sheltered from the rain. It seemed unlikely that such would be available at an Oxford college. However, it was not raining yet.

When they were all but ready to leave, Jak could not be found anywhere. Edwin was angry, his plans frustrated, for he had hoped to reach the college in time to make a start during the afternoon, for fear that rain might come on later. While the men finished loading the cart and saw to the horses, Aelwith and Emma went in search of the boy.

'He'll surely not have gone a-huntin',' Aelwith said crossly. 'That lad goes everywhere with his bow, but the abbot will not be pleased, if he's shootin' rabbits from the abbey's warren.'

Fortunately for Jak, he had not embarked on any poaching of the abbey's game, but was discovered in the kitchen, where one of the servants had treated him to a slice of seedcake and a handful of raisins. Aelwith thanked the servant somewhat grimly, took Jak by the collar of his cotte and marched him back to the cart. Jak looked in no way abashed. Emma suspected this was not the first time he had found his way to a friendly kitchen.

As soon as they returned with the truant, Thomas and Edgar hitched up the three horses in line and led them toward the gatehouse, Edwin once again driving, with Jak at his side, where he could be watched. Aelwith sat near the back of the cart, having taken up her spinning again. Emma perched at the top of the rear steps, looking for the last time at Osney Abbey. Her feet, resting on the uppermost step, were almost healed, though she would need to be careful not to allow her sandals to rub again. She had kept the cloths bound round the worst places and had tied her bundle again at her waist, leaving her hands free to carry Jocosa when she parted with the candle-makers after reaching Oxford.

They were through the gate and fairly on the road to Oxford, when she caught sight of a party of mounted men preceded by hunting dogs riding toward the abbey, coming from the same direction as they had themselves come, two days earlier. It struck her as odd, for there was no hunting ground hereabouts, apart from the abbey's private park. Perhaps they hoped for a day's hunting there. The party – which also included huntsmen on foot with chained alaunts as well as the other dogs running loose – rode boldly up to the abbey gatehouse and were clearly demanding admittance, when two of the dogs – she recognised them now as lymers – veered away and began to run after the cart.

The mounted men milled about, as if uncertain what to do. The huntsmen in charge of the tracking dogs began whistling, but the two lymers ignored them, and instead the rest of the tracking dogs followed them. One of the keepers of the lymers was holding a bundle of black cloth.

There was a heavy built man at the head of the horsemen, who appeared to be shouting at the men on foot to call back the dogs. Then he jerked his horse viciously round until he was facing the retreating candle-makers' cart, which was just reaching a bend in the road.

'I can see Oxford Castle!' Jak called from the front of the cart. 'Over there.'

Behind them, the big man seemed to make up his mind. He gestured to his men, set his heels to his horse, and began to gallop after the slow moving cart. The men with the chained dogs were stooping over their charges.

Emma was suddenly afraid.

That bundle of cloth. It looked like the habit she had left behind, thrust under a bush far back up the bank of the river.

The killing dogs were loosed. The big man was drawing nearer.

She knew him now.

It was her stepfather, Falkes Malaliver.

Chapter Eleven

The long rides of recent days must have tired me more than I had realised, for I overslept the next morning. My intention had been to ride out toward Osney Abbey early, as soon as I had settled Walter and Roger to their work, then pick up the riverside track on the far side of the many-branched Thames and work my way north. I was unfamiliar with the track, but knew of it by repute. Even allowing for the many diversions caused by the winding course of the river, I thought the total distance could not be more than eight or nine miles, perhaps a little more, before I would find myself opposite the island on which Godstow Abbey stood. Although originally I had discounted this as the way Emma might have left the abbey, our failure to find a single trace of her in any other direction was beginning to convince me that it was just possible she had managed to cross the river somehow. Besides, if Falkes Malaliver carried out his intention of going that way, I wanted to make sure that there was at least one person to witness his actions. The more I had seen of the man, the less I trusted him.

Therefore, it was with some shame that I dressed and descended to the kitchen long after the sun was up, to find it deserted and spotless, with no sign of Margaret or the children. When I went through to the shop, Walter and Roger gave me 'Good day, master,' with smirks of conscious virtue, both clearly busily occupied at their desks for some time. Rowan was with them, and bounced over to me, the only one to greet me without implied criticism of my slug-a-bed behaviour. She seemed not to be suffering any ill effects from her injury.

'Mistress Margaret has taken the children to visit Mistress Farringdon,' Walter volunteered, in response to my baffled look at finding the house deserted. 'She said they would also go to the weekly market, and return in time for dinner.'

He grinned. 'If you were awake by then,' he added.

So much for my early start. In that case, I might as well break my fast before setting out. The kitchen was still filled with the intoxicating scent of Margaret's new baked bread, so I cut myself generous slices, found fresh butter bought yesterday from Mary Coomber's dairy, some soft cheese from the same source, and a pot of our own honey. A jug of ale kept cool in the stillroom completed my preparations, so I drew up a stool to the table and settled myself for an ample breakfast, a pleasure I had not been able to enjoy for some days.

An expectant Rowan soon joined me in the kitchen. Her forlorn demeanour suggested that no one had fed her before abandoning her to the scriveners, which I did not believe, but I shared some of the bread and cheese with her. The bandage I had wound around her body was long gone, probably tugged off in irritation, but when I checked the gash in her side, it did not seem to have suffered. It was scabbed over, but dirt-free, and she seemed none the worse for it. Young animals, like young children, have fresh, clean flesh which heals quickly. It was fortunate the vile butcher had not cut more deeply, and I hoped that Rowan would have the sense to avoid his shop in the future.

After I had eaten and explained my plans to the men, I set off up the street to the Mitre. It was indeed beginning to seem to me that it would be cheaper to buy Rufus outright, instead of constantly hiring him, although that did not solve the problem of having no stable. When I reached the inn, I found one of the stable lads in the act of removing Rufus's saddle.

'Why, Master Elyot,' he said in surprise, 'us thought as how ye'd changed yer plans.'

'Nay,' I said, 'I still want the horse. I was delayed.' I did not explain that it was due to my own slothfulness.

As soon as the saddle was back in place, I mounted and rode out through the archway into the street, under a lowering sky which threatened rain before nightfall, but perhaps not yet. The streets of the town were remarkably busy, considering that most students had left for the summer. The weekly market in St Giles always draws in country folk to sell their produce, whether it be a cottager's wife with a basket of eggs or a farmer with a bullock to sell to the butchers. Some had regular stalls, some merely spread out a cloth on the ground to display a row of cheeses or piles of beans and onions. Of course, some of these people came on other days, if they lived nearby, to sell small goods on the street – with or without a licence from the town – but the weekly market was a bigger affair. Afterwards, money earned would often be spent on goods which could not be made at home, but were to be found in Oxford, like a fine pair of gloves, or stout boots for the winter. Less provident young men had been known to spend the whole day's earnings in the town's taverns, reeling home to be met by the scoldings of mothers and young wives.

Fortunately today I did not need to force my way through the buyers and sellers in St Giles. My way took me from Carfax west down the slope of Great Bailey and through the small rebuilt West Gate of the town, under the shadow of the castle walls. Glancing up at it, I wondered whether Cedric Walden had really had urgent business today, or whether he was growing tired of the fruitless search for Emma Thorgold. Circling the castle moat, which had been contrived by diverting part of the Thames, I crossed the Castle Bridge to the first of the many islands in the river. After reaching the island, the road ran north along the bank of the river to the Quaking Bridge. This bridge in turn led off on the right hand to another, smaller island, but

I headed left, across the island to Bookbinders' Bridge. I passed Henry Stalbroke's bindery, calling a greeting to his principal journeyman, Tom Needham, and on the far side of Bookbinders' Island, crossed the river again by the bridge known simply as the Small Bridge.

Free of the Thames for a short distance, I rode past small houses on either side of the road. Probably built not long before the Great Pestilence, many were deserted now, although those which were occupied – about one in three – were clean and tidy enough, with long gardens behind them providing sufficient room to grow most food (except grain) for a family, and to keep a pig for autumn slaughtering. Beyond these houses there was just St Thomas's Bridge. I skirted St Thomas's itself and headed toward Osney Abbey. I had been here a few times, supplying parchment and inks, and even a few books, so I knew that the riverside track met the road somewhere near here. On previous visits to the abbey I had never thought about how many branches of the Thames one must cross to reach here from the town, but now I realised just how confusing it must be for anyone making for Oxford from this westerly direction, and how baffling the skein of waterways must seem to strangers. It made matters no easier that the river had a disconcerting habit of changing direction from time to time, with some branches drying up and others cutting new courses through this low lying land. It was a veritable Minotaur's labyrinth, only in water instead of stone.

Mindful of Rufus's wearisome travails on the previous day, I had kept him to an ambling pace, but after I had passed the group of houses lying between Bookbinders' Island and St Thomas's, it occurred to me that I should turn back and enquire there whether anything had been seen of Emma in these parts. There were few people about, for it was likely that most of them would have work away from here – many of the men probably plied the boats that carried goods up and down the reaches of the river round about the town and the nearby countryside. Such people as I met were courteous enough, but had nothing to tell me of a lost maid.

'Nay, maister,' said one old woman, sweeping dirt from the single step leading to her cottage. 'There be no strangers hereabouts. Nobbut them as come and go every day 'cross the river and 'long the river. And he do be high this day, since that storm.'

I could see that she was settling in for a long discussion about the weather, and was turning away when I remembered what John Barnes had told me of his borrowed cap and the likelihood that Emma had filched clothes from the laundry at the abbey, so I asked also whether any youth had been seen, a stranger in these parts, and I mentioned the small white dog, but the old woman and everyone else I spoke to gave a shake of the head and a polite but clear 'nay'.

As I turned back again toward Osney, I felt I had been wasting my time, but it was necessary to be thorough. I skirted round St Thomas's Church and headed for Osney. There was farmland here, arable and meadow, bordered by stands of coppiced woodland and some taller trees left to grow straight to provide timber for building. All of this probably belonged to the abbey, which was generally said to be wealthy. I was uncertain whether this was the best way to pick up the riverside path leading north, or whether I should have turned the other way at St Thomas's, the opposite direction from Osney. I was not familiar with this area, apart from the direct road to Osney, and the meanderings of the river are enough to confuse any man. I wondered whether the best plan was to continue on my way to Osney and ask the porter there to set me on the right road.

On the other hand, I reflected, Rewley Abbey lay further north along the river, and although I had been there, I had never approached it from this direction. I had always gone the more direct way: out of the North Gate of Oxford, then immediately left, along the road between the town wall and Broken Hays. There were then only two bridges to cross, Hythe Bridge and little Hythe Bridge, followed by a turn north over the abbey's own small bridge leading to its gatehouse. Like Godstow, Rewley stood on an island, but I had always supposed this to be a man-made one, since it seemed to have been contrived at some time in the past by digging a square moat around the abbey enclave, like the circular moat around the castle, which the Thames had also obligingly filled. Despite this appearance of a withdrawn and enclosed monastery, Rewley was in fact part college, a place for Cistercian monks to dwell while studying at the university. It could well be that the Rewley monks would be more familiar with the riverside path than the monks of Osney.

I reined Rufus in and pondered which would be my best course. I knew that there must be a road through to Rewley if I went back to St Thomas's Church, but I was not sure of the way, and might simply waste more time, even though I might be given better directions once I reached there than I would at Osney. Remembering my hesitation now, I still feel a moment of cold panic at what might have happened, had I made the wrong choice and gone to Rewley.

In the end, I judged it best to continue with my original plan and head for Osney. I was just urging Rufus on from a walk to a trot, to make up for the time spent enquiring at the cottages and debating which way to go, when I rounded one of the clumps of coppiced trees and became aware of a disturbance and many people on the road ahead, coming toward me.

In the lead was an exceptionally large cart, an extraordinary vehicle, covered with a colourful cloth and drawn by three horses harnessed one behind the other. I took it for some kind of mountebank's vehicle, though larger than most. We see such things in Oxford at the time of St Frideswide's Fair, although this was not the time of the fair, so that could not be the reason it was heading toward the town. An elderly man was driving the cart, with a boy sitting beside him, and two more men were walking along beside the horses.

I paid little attention to the cart, for I was looking beyond it toward a large party of horsemen just rounding the bend further away, beyond which I could glimpse the roofs of Osney and the great tower of its church. I had ridden during two whole days with that company of riders. There was no danger of my being mistaken. Falkes Malaliver had made unexpectedly good time to have reached this point from the north, even if he and his party had been set ashore at dawn to the west of the Thames, brought over on boats hired or (more likely) commandeered from Godstow.

Malaliver himself was in the lead, as usual, except for his lymers which – unlike their behaviour on previous occasions – appeared to be following a clear trail. One of the curious things about these dogs is that they have been bred to be voiceless. Unlike other tracking hounds, they will follow a trail in total silence, an excellent attribute for any hunter who makes use of them to track deer or boar, for the quarry is unaware that it is being followed. However, I have always found it somewhat unnerving. It is natural for a dog to give vent to its feelings in sound. A joyous bark should signal the discovery of its prey. But these creatures padded after their prey in total silence, like hunting cats. It was unnatural.

Their prey?

Suddenly the figures before me took on a new significance. There was only one prey Falkes Malaliver would be hunting with his lymers, and for the first time the dogs appeared to have found a scent. Then I saw one of the huntsmen thrust a bundle of black cloth at the nearest dogs, who smelled it eagerly, then leapt away from him with increased speed and enthusiasm. Oddly, they seemed to be pursuing the mountebanks' cart.

But wait! That dark cloth.

Emma would have left the abbey wearing her black habit, but would have changed into secular clothes soon afterwards and had probably abandoned the habit somewhere along the way. It looked as though Malaliver and his men must have found the discarded habit, which had given the tracking dogs a fresh scent to follow. So his guess – and mine – had been right. Somehow Emma had crossed the river to the west bank and left her habit there.

But why were they pursuing this seemingly harmless if bizarre cart? Unless it was merely blocking their way, so that both dogs and horses needed to force their way past it. And that meant that Emma must already have travelled this way, and was now behind me, between me and the town. Perhaps she was hiding in one of those abandoned houses this side of the Small Bridge. I should have searched those as well, not merely enquired whether anyone had seen her.

I was on the point of turning Rufus about and heading back once again to the group of houses in search of her, when many things happened at once.

The lymers did not run past the long cart, as I had expected, but began to circle it, some rising on their hind legs and resting their forefeet on its sides. The man at the reins twisted around and shouted something over his shoulder into the cart, although I was too far away to make out his words, then he whipped up the horses. Startled, they broke into a shambling canter, causing the cart to rock perilously from side to side, for it was too top heavy and too unwieldy to be driven at speed. Seeing their own danger of being run over or crushed if the cart went out of control, the two men who had been walking at the horses' heads broke away and began to run in my direction.

Behind the cart, Malaliver and his men, on their less burdened horses, were closing the gap between the two groups. I saw that Malaliver was shouting and gesturing to a second group of huntsmen, who had come up from behind the riders. With a shock I realised that they were the men who handled the alaunts.

And they were bending down to release the killing dogs from their chains.

I let out an involuntary cry, waving my arm at the driver of the cart in warning, but I could not tell whether he understood.

The men running from the cart had almost met me, with the cart itself careering crazily behind. I expected at any moment to see it topple over and crash into a ruin of broken timbers and ripped cloth. The alaunts were now galloping after the lymers, and unlike the tracking dogs they came on in full cry. They were huge dogs, heavily muscled, with strong jaws and broad chests, and the hunting cries that rang out from them, echoing from these chests, were deep and thunderous. Rufus shied suddenly in fear, and would have thrown me, had I not already been clinging tightly with my knees as I urged him forward. He shied again, dancing sideways, and no blame to him, being driven by me straight at those fearsome beasts.

Suddenly someone leapt from the back of the cart, clutching something white and fluffy, and ran at desperate speed, zigzagging away from the pursuing alaunts and heading for a copse of beech trees, with thick undergrowth below. It looked like a slender long legged youth, but I knew at once it must be Emma.

Fool girl! Why had she not stayed in the cart? Precarious as it was, it would have offered some protection from the alaunts. Now she was out in the open and would not stand a chance. Those dogs could outrun her, drag her to the ground, kill her, long before anyone could reach her.

But perhaps I was mistaken. The alaunts could easily have jumped into the cart, and for the moment it was the cart which drew them, as they followed by instinct and training after the lymers, but if Emma could burrow into those thick bushes, or better still, climb a tree, she might escape their jaws. Yet how could she climb a tree? I realised that she was holding her little dog, Jocosa, and it would be impossible to climb one handed, even supposing the girl knew how to climb a tree. And the little dog – clearly as terrified as Rufus – was struggling.

I drove my heels hard into Rufus's flanks and headed straight for them.

As soon as Emma had seen Falkes Malaliver leading his

company of armed men, with his hunting lymers pursuing the cart, she knew that she was being tracked as relentlessly as a hunted deer. At any moment the dogs would lead her stepfather and his men to the candle-makers' cart. She would be captured, dragged back to Godstow, humiliated and ashamed. And these people, Aelwith and her family, who had taken her in and befriended her, never questioning who she was or why she was wandering the countryside alone – they would suffer the full force of Malaliver's wrath. He could destroy them, if the dogs had not killed them first..

'Father!' Aelwith had also realised that they were being pursued. 'A band of armed men after us. Whip up the horses! Us'll be safe, come us get near the castle.'

'Outlaws, is it?' Edwin yelled back over his shoulder, as he whipped the horses to a speed that was dangerous.

'Aye,' Aelwith shouted.

'Nay.' Emma laid her hand on Aelwith's arm. 'Those are no outlaws. It is me they are hunting. That man in front is my stepfather, and he means me nothing but evil. See, he is releasing his alaunts for the kill. I will not let him harm you.'

She caught up Jocosa under her arm, then leaned forward and kissed Aelwith lightly on the cheek.

'Go as fast as you may for the castle. The dogs will follow me.'

Without another word, she leapt from the cart and began to run for the copse of beech trees.

At the front of the cart, Edwin had not seen her go, but continued to drive as fast as he dared, faster by far than was safe. Aelwith threw down her spindle and stumbled forward along the perilously rocking cart, trying to reach him.

It was not far to the copse, and Emma had noticed the thick undergrowth of bushes and brambles beneath. She flew across the beaten turf between, clutching a struggling and terrified Jocosa to her chest. At first the lymers did not notice her. They had fixed on the cart as their quarry, and were still following it, the huge alaunts coming up behind, trained to follow where the lymers led and to finish off the quarry unless the huntsmen called them off.

Emma threw herself to the ground and began to crawl into the thickest part of the bushes, dragging Jocosa with her, despite the dog's yelps of protest. The thorns of the brambles snagged her clothes and she spared one hand to clamp John Barnes's cap to her head. Glancing back, she saw both lymers and alaunts still following the cart, but any minute now the lymers would pick up her fresh trail and follow her here. If only she could burrow into the tangle of brambles and ivy, where they might hesitate to follow her. Surely her stepfather would call off the dogs, would he not? He wanted to find her, to bend her to his will. How could it profit him if the dogs were to kill her?

Then through a gap in the bushy undergrowth she saw that there was another horseman approaching from the Oxford road. Was this another of her stepfather's men, and she to be trapped between them, caught like a lamb in the jaws of a wolf? If Malaliver had another troop on the road ahead, she was surrounded. For a moment she felt nothing but black despair and gave a great sob. Her grip on Jocosa weakened and the dog, who was now in a blind panic, struggled free from her arms and fled out from under the bushes by the way they had come. She tore away, running as fast as her short legs would carry her, away from the hunting pack and toward the solitary horseman.

The vicious brutes would kill Jocosa at once. They must be ten times her weight. They would break her neck, or tear out her throat. Emma began to drag herself backwards out of the bushes. Only she could save Jocosa. She must reach the dog before the hunt did.

I had passed the cart now. The tracking dogs were still following it, the alaunts coming up behind, but any moment now they would realise that their quarry was no longer there. I headed Rufus toward the bushes where Emma had taken refuge. If I could reach her before the dogs, before

Malaliver . . . If I could get her away from this horror of the hunt . . .

Suddenly a ball of white fur burst from under the bushes right in front of Rufus, who reared in fright. I struggled to keep my seat and to bring Rufus down without crushing the dog, which had stopped suddenly, confused. Rufus's near fore missed her by inches. Leaning down from the saddle, I grabbed the dog by the scruff of her neck and scooped her up before she could be crushed by one of Rufus's hooves.

The bushes thrashed wildly, and Emma crawled out, white but defiant, ready to challenge me.

'Emma!' I called. 'It is Nicholas Elyot. Come quickly.'

Already the lymers had picked up her scent in the grass and were wavering uncertainly between the cart they had been following and this new trail. Emma hesitated only a moment, then tore across to me.

'Put your foot on mine,' I ordered, shifting the dog to my right arm, but keeping a hold on the reins, for Rufus was beginning to circle nervously. There was sweat on his neck and his ears were laid back.

Emma tried to do as I bid, but Rufus kept moving. At last she managed it.

'Give me your hand. Nay, the other one.'

I gripped her hand, lost it, grabbed her upper arm so hard I knew I was hurting her, and dragged her on her stomach across the horse's withers. Both dogs and men were nearly on us now. Somehow she understood what to do and managed to fling her leg over so that she was sitting in front of the saddle.

'Take the dog.'

We were in a tangle of reins and dog and horse's mane, but I managed to turn Rufus so that we were facing back the way I had come. Just as I urged him forward, one of the alaunts made a leap for Emma's leg. She shrieked as the brute sank his teeth in. I swung the slack of the reins to whip them across the dog's face and it dropped to the ground. Rufus kicked out and the animal let out a yelp, then we were galloping back toward Oxford, following the fast disappearing cart.

Emma gave a shaky laugh. 'It near had me then.'

'Aye. I think it had not managed a proper grip. They are trained never to let go.'

There was blood running down her leg, and the dogs were still following. I could hear the thunder of the horsemen behind them, but did not look round. I had my arms around Emma, holding the reins in front of her, while the dog Jocosa trembled in her arms.

'Can you lean your head to the side?' I said. 'I find it difficult to see through John Barnes's cap.'

She turned her head round to look at me, ignoring my request. 'You know about John Barnes?'

'Aye. Now will you move your head? We need to reach the castle before they catch us. I must be able to see the road.'

This time she lowered her head, but also managed to twist and look behind.

'My stepfather is shouting at you to stop. Does he know you?'

'Unfortunately. Let him shout.'

Despite the hunt, I was suddenly, gloriously happy. Emma's body was pressed up against mine. I could feel the warmth of it, and her weight against my chest. I would probably never again hold her like this, but I would savour every moment while I could.

Rufus had nearly caught up with the cart and despite his double load had managed to outrun Malaliver and his men, who were hampered by the crowd of dogs milling in confusion about their legs. I could hear the huntsmen sounding their horns: 'Come away, come away'. It would be some time before all the dogs, lymers and alaunts, had been called to order. I hoped it would give us time to reach the castle first and report to Cedric Walden.

'Why were you in that mountebanks' cart?' I asked, once I believed that Malaliver was too much hampered to catch us. We were passing the cart, and I saw that Emma waved and smiled at a woman who was now sitting between the old man and the boy. The driver had slowed his horses to a steadier pace, but they were still alarmed, snorting and blowing, gobbets of foam flecking their jaws.

'They are not mountebanks,' Emma said indignantly. 'They are travelling candle-makers and very respectable people. They have just been at Osney Abbey. They taught me to make candles, so if I needs must earn my keep, I can become a candle-maker.'

I smiled into the back of John Barnes's cap, thinking of Sir Anthony's estate. 'I do not think it will come to that,' I said.

As we reached the first of the bridges, I slowed Rufus to a sober pace. I was fairly certain Malaliver would not try any tricks with dogs now that we were amongst houses and workshops. By going more slowly, I could prolong my time close to Emma. She sighed and leaned back against my chest. Her body had gone slack and I realised she had lapsed into that time of weakness and exhaustion that follows sudden terror and flight.

'It was brave of you to lead the dogs away from those people,' I said. 'The candle-makers.'

She yawned and curled up closer to me. 'Aelwith was very good to me. And Jak is just a child. I could not let them be hurt.'

'You still have ink on your fingers,' I said.

'Aye, and wax under my nails. I must not forget, I have something for you.'

She patted an untidy bundle of oiled cloth, tied at her waist with a length of rope. I opened my mouth to speak, then closed it again. Time enough for that later.

'Where are we going?' Then she stiffened. 'You will not take me back to Godstow?'

'Never fear. We will go first to the castle, and report to the deputy sheriff. He must be told that Malaliver has disobeyed his orders and loosed his killing dogs against a human quarry. After that, I will take you to your aunt.'

'Good.' She relaxed, her head falling on to my shoulder.

'And your leg must be seen to. Are you in pain?'

'Not much.'

She yawned again. By the time we reached Bookbinders' Bridge, she was asleep.

Chapter Twelve

'So you have found the maid.' Cedric Walden himself had spied us as we neared the castle and had come out into the bailey to meet us. The guards at the gate had admitted us without question and with considerably more courtesy than I had received on a previous occasion.

'Aye.' I smiled grimly. 'Found her being pursued by Falkes Malaliver not only with lymers but with alaunts. He loosed them, and one has torn her leg.'

I nodded toward Emma's blood-stained hose. My hands were full, for I was not only stopping her from sliding off Rufus's back but keeping a precarious hold on the little dog, which had very nearly slipped to the ground when Emma fell asleep.

'The cart you see coming along behind us,' I said, 'let them be received courteously. They will bear witness to what I have to tell you.'

Shortly before we had reached the castle I had reined in Rufus and waited for the cart to catch me up, before asking the driver that he should follow us to the castle in order to explain what had happened.

'Aye, maister, willingly,' he said, 'but we'm expected to Exeter College. 'Twon't mean bidin' long?'

'Only long enough to tell what you saw – the chase, and the dogs loosed after the maid.'

'Wicked, that was,' the woman sitting beside him said. 'Wicked.'

Falkes Malaliver, I observed, had dropped back, but

was still following, his men now riding in immaculate order, the lymers walking docilely on chains with the huntsmen. The alaunts, I saw, had disappeared.

Now in the bailey of the castle I felt we were safe at last. Malaliver would not dare to make any attempt to hurt Emma before such witnesses as the deputy sheriff and the garrison, but I was sure he would not give up his claims on her person at all easily.

'Take the dog from me,' I said to Walden, who was too surprised to refuse as I lowered Jocosa into his arms. Having fully recovered her spirits, she licked him on the nose, which he took in good part, although he lost no time in setting her on her feet.

As though she felt the loss of the dog's soft fur against her arm, Emma stirred and woke. For a moment she stayed limp in my arms, then she sat forward and looked over her shoulder at me.

'Where are we? Is this Oxford castle? By Jesu, it is uncomfortable riding on a horse's shoulders without a saddle.'

I laughed. 'I apologise, my lady, but we lacked the time to find you a pillion.'

As though she suddenly realised that I was still holding her close in my arms, she blushed a fiery red.

'I had best dismount,' she said.

'Aye,' I said, although I did not immediately release her. 'How is your leg?'

She considered, bending her knee slightly. There was a long gash in her left calf.

'It does sting,' she admitted, 'more than it did before.' She rubbed the back of her hand across her face. 'Had I not best get down?'

'Stay there a moment.'

Reluctantly I swung myself out of the saddle, then reached up and took her about the waist to lift her down. When her feet touched the ground she did not immediately pull away, but stood facing me, my hands still at her waist, her hands on my shoulders. We stared at each other, and I ran my tongue nervously over my lips.

'I owe you my life, I think, Master Elyot.'

She was so close I could feel her breath on my cheek.

'A life worth saving, Mistress Thorgold,' I said, and chided myself for a tongue tied fool.

There was no time for more. The candle-makers' cart had rumbled into the bailey, and now Falkes Malaliver and his men were crowded through the gate behind it. Emma and I drew apart. The dog Jocosa, who had been exploring the bailey, ran back to Emma in alarm at the sight of the lymers and was caught up into the safety of her mistress's arms.

'There she is!' It was Malaliver shouting and pointing at Emma. 'The shameless wench, humiliating the family, reneging on her religious vows, stealing away from the house of God, turning the shire upside down in the hunt, running about the countryside in those – those – villein's rags!'

His face was so red I thought he might have an apoplexy.

'And as for you, fellow.' He swung round on his heel and pointed at me. 'I called to you to stop. You know she is mine, and you ignored me. You had no business riding off with her like that. What did you mean by it?'

'What I meant by it,' I said quietly, 'was to save her before she was killed by your dogs. And to bring her to the safety of the castle and the deputy sheriff.'

He made a scoffing noise. 'Killed by my dogs? They would never harm man or beast. Gentle as doves, they are, but skilled in finding her out.'

The lymers, who were now stretched out asleep on the beaten earth of the bailey, did indeed look as harmless as they were.

'I grant you,' I said, 'that your lymers were no danger to her. I am speaking of your alaunts.'

'My alaunts? My alaunts are shut up in kennels at Godstow. You are weaving a web of lies, Elyot.'

'There are plenty here who saw you loose your

alaunts on the maid. If your men are too afraid to admit it now, these good people saw what happened.' I gestured toward the candle-makers' cart. They were standing beside it: a woman, three men, and a boy who was clearly enjoying every minute of his adventure.

'And for further proof,' I said, 'one of the alaunts tore the lady's leg before I could get her away.'

I pointed to the gashed leg, which was still bleeding. Walden came closer to observe it better.

''Tis all true, sir.' The older man stepped forward and addressed Cedric Walden. Apart from one sharp glance, he ignored Malaliver. 'This man come after us with his trackin' dogs first. Chasin' after the maid, they was, usin' that for scent.'

He pointed to the bundle of black cloth which one of the huntsmen still held tucked under his arm. The man, suddenly aware of it, tried to hide the bundle behind his back, but Walden walked over and took it away from him. He shook it out. As I had guessed, it was a novice's habit, creased now and somewhat torn, but unmistakable.

'Is this yours, mistress?' he said.

Emma nodded.

Walden turned to the man. 'And then?'

'Then they brought up them killin' dogs. Alaunts, is it? Let them off their chains. I thought we was for it, and whipped up the horses. The maid, she jumps from the cart, runs for the bushes, see, drawin' them away from us. Tells us to drive on. Dogs follow us for a bit, then turn aside after her. And they'd have had her too, if this gentleman hadn't come along.'

'Well, Master Elyot?' Walden said. 'Does that agree with what you saw?'

'It does,' I said, 'in every detail. One of the dogs caught the lady's leg in his jaws as I was lifting her on to my horse, but we managed to drive it off. Then I rode here as fast as the horse could carry us. In the meantime it is clear that Malaliver sent his alaunts away, so that you would believe he had still kept to your orders.'

Malaliver glowered at me. 'All lies. These vagabonds have been bribed to tell some tale. I sought only to find my stepdaughter. And now that I have found her, I demand that you hand her back to me, churl.'

Emma had slipped behind me, still holding Jocosa, who favoured me with a lick on my ear. It was difficult to keep my temper when I was so insulted, but I knew it would be no help to Emma if I lost it.

'Sheriff,' I said, addressing Walden but staring hard at Malaliver, 'it is clear from the evidence of all of us, and from the injury to the lady, that this man has disobeyed your orders and broken the law, by hunting an innocent and helpless girl with killing dogs. I am sure, also, that his men, in private, and with the right persuasion, will be prepared to admit what happened.'

Several of the huntsmen turned pale at this, and the armed horsemen shifted uneasily in their saddles. I doubted whether Walden would need to use force to persuade them to admit the truth. The suggestion alone would probably be enough.

'Moreover,' I said, 'the day before yesterday, as you know, I paid a visit to the lady's grandfather, Sir Anthony Thorgold.'

I heard Emma catch her breath behind me. Malaliver suddenly looked taken aback, less sure of himself.

'Sir Anthony told me that Malaliver lied to him, reporting that Mistress Thorgold had chosen to enter a nunnery of her own desire, whereas it is quite clear that she has always protested against it. He has signed a document asserting that he supports her wish to leave the monastic life. He has also expressed a wish that she should return to live with him and resume her proper station in life.'

I am sure that I managed to banish my own feelings from my voice, but even so I felt the soft touch of Emma's hand on my back.

'Lies!' Malaliver blustered. 'All lies! Let the fellow produce the document if this is true.'

'There is no difficulty in that,' I said. 'The document

is currently lodged with the lady's man of law.'

Malaliver gaped at me. It seemed I had silenced him, at least for the moment.

Emma moved closer to me, until her body brushed mine. I could feel her breath on the back of my neck. Unless, of course, it was Jocosa.

Events moved swiftly after that. Sheriff Walden ordered Malaliver and his company to be held in the castle for questioning, thanked the candle-makers and sent them on their way, and finally turned to me.

'Well, Master Elyot,' he said, 'it seems you have succeeded in finding the lady and at the same time exposed what may have been an attempt at murder.'

He was speaking softly, to avoid being overheard by Emma, but if he thought she was unaware of the danger she had been in, then he was much mistaken.

'The most urgent matter now,' I said, 'is to take Mistress Thorgold to her aunt's house, so that her leg may be dressed. A bite from one of those vicious brutes might well become infected.'

We both glanced over at Emma, who was leaning wearily against Rufus's side, with her eyes shut. She had gone very white. Jocosa was curled up at her feet, seeming none the worse for her own ordeal.

'Certainly,' Walden said, 'do you wish to borrow a mount for the lady?'

'Nay. But if you have a pillion saddle to fit behind mine . . .?'

He smiled. 'We do not often need to accommodate ladies, but I believe there is one sometimes used by the sheriff's wife.'

The pillion saddle was found after a brief search in the stables and strapped on to Rufus's rump, who seemed resigned to anything I might demand of him today. I remembered with some pleasure how he had kicked the alaunt which had tried to savage Emma.

Once I had mounted, Walden himself helped Emma

on to the pillion and passed up Jocosa, who seemed to have taken quite a fancy to him, and would have washed his entire face had he not handed her over quickly to her mistress. I looked back as we passed through the gate and saw that he was wiping his face on his sleeve.

Emma wrapped her arms tightly around my waist, cradling the dog between us, and laid her cheek against my back.

'Is it far?' she said.

'Not far,' I answered, but thought, *Not far enough.* 'Do you know Oxford?'

'I rode through when I was brought to Godstow, but that is all I have seen of the town.'

'This is Great Bailey we are riding up,' I said. 'At Carfax – that is the main crossroads – we enter the High Street, then the first street on the left, just after the Mitre Inn, is St Mildred Street. Your aunt's house lies a little way along it.'

'My aunt will be most astonished to see me.'

'Perhaps. She knows we have been hunting for you.'

'I am sorry to have given you so much trouble,' she said formally.

'I did not find it a trouble,' I said. I shifted the reins into my left hand and laid my right hand over both of hers, where they were clasped at my waist.

She tightened her grip on me. 'There is no need to rush.'

'Your leg . . .'

I felt her face move against the back of my neck. I thought she was smiling.

'It will wait.'

Yet however slowly I rode, it did not take long to reach Mistress Farringdon's house.

'Wait there,' I said, swinging my right leg over the horse's head so as not to dislodge her and sliding to the ground. 'I will break the news first.'

I knocked on the door, but received no reply. When I tried to open it, I found it locked.

'She is not here.' I was a little dismayed. I had looked forward to bringing them together. 'I will take you to my own house, if you do not think . . . that is, if you . . . my sister Margaret should be there. She will be able to see to your leg. And lend you a gown.'

Secretly, I liked Emma dressed in her hose and cotte, with John's overlarge cap on her head. The clothes made her look very young and somewhat vulnerable. In her novice's habit she had been slightly intimidating.

'How will you mount again?' she said, looking down at me from Rufus's back. 'I do not think you can reverse that very original way in which you dismounted.'

She was right. In the end, she slid down from the pillion, I mounted in the normal way, took Jocosa from her, and then she hoisted herself on to the pillion saddle without assistance.

'This is proving quite a performance,' I said. 'We seem to have been getting on and off this horse all day.'

'We have.' This time I was sure that she muffled her laughter in the back of my cotte.

'Pass me Jocosa,' she said. 'Is it far to your house?'

'Not far enough,' I said.

I took Rufus back down St Mildred Street and along the High as slowly as I could, my whole body conscious of Emma's arms embracing me. I kept my hand laid over hers at my waist. I had not been so close to a woman since Elizabeth died, and at the memory of Elizabeth I felt suddenly ashamed. What was I thinking of, to take pleasure in the warmth of the girl's body against mine? She was hardly more than a child, and an heiress as well. And I was a widower, a man who still loved his lost wife, the father of two children.

I started to draw my hand away from hers, but she seized it and pressed it hard between both of hers, so that I could not withdraw it without hurting her. In this unresolved situation, we reached my shop. Emma did not at once release her grip on my hand or my body.

'Tell me about your sister. Will she frown upon me,

dressed – as Malaliver said – in these villein's rags? No respectable woman will want to have to meet me.'

'Margaret knows that you fled from enforced confinement in the nunnery,' I said. 'She knows that we had been searching for you for days, while you lived rough in the countryside. She will not expect you to be dressed primly in your novice's habit.'

I paused. How could I explain about Margaret?

'My sister is five years older than I, and was married off at the age of fourteen to an older man, who seemed prosperous and respectable, but he beat her, made her life wretched. The only joy that arose from that marriage was the birth of her two sons. Then the Pestilence came. It freed her from a cruel husband, but it also robbed her of her sons. Since the death of my wife, she has kept house for me and helped me look after my children.'

It was but a bare sketch of my sister's life, but Emma tightened her arms around me. 'Poor Margaret,' she said. 'Poor Nicholas.'

There was no answer to that.

I noticed that both Roger and Walter had caught sight of us through the shop window, open to the street, with the wide shutter lowered. It is a fine, big shop, one of the best in the High Street, the width of two normal town messuages, but what a humble place it appeared, now that I had seen Sir Anthony's manor, with its ancient keep and its modern comfortable house, set in wide acres of fertile farmland. I was suddenly ashamed that I had brought her here.

'Are those your scriveners?' Her tone was interested. Of course she would be interested. Had she not deplored the fact that her sex debarred her from becoming one?

'They are,' I said abruptly, 'and they have had quite long enough staring at us.'

Walter has risen and was coming to the door, clearly intending to help Emma down so that I could dismount in the normal way. Jealousy prompted me to make my awkward scrambled descent, and I reached up for Jocosa, set her down, then took Emma about the waist. She laid her hands lightly on my shoulders and slid to the ground.

She smiled uncertainly. 'You have met my family, what is left of them. Now I must meet yours.'

I had not seen matters in the same way, but I nodded. 'Just Margaret and my children. Alysoun is six and somewhat pert. Rafe is four and shy.'

I hitched Rufus beside the door and opened it for her. Jocosa ran ahead of us into the shop, then stopped and looked about her with interest.

'My scriveners,' I said, 'Walter Blunt and Roger Pigot. You see that we have found Mistress Thorgold.'

They both bowed, and Walter said eagerly, 'It was you made Master Elyot's book of hours! It is a fine piece of work.'

Emma looked surprised and pleased, and her hand went to that odd bundle which still dangled from her waist.

'I thank you,' she said, and I noticed that she seemed less tense, though I had feared that Walter's familiarity might offend her..

'Is Margaret here?' I asked. 'Mistress Thorgold has been hurt and needs help.'

'Aye,' Walter said, 'she's through in the kitchen.' He hesitated. 'And–'

I did not wait to hear any more. The injury to Emma's leg had been left too long already. I ushered her through to the kitchen, all the while conscious and embarrassed that I was leading a landed heiress into a shopkeeper's humble kitchen.

At first I stopped on the threshold in astonishment. The room was full of people. Margaret and the children were there of course, but also Mistress Farringdon with Juliana and little Maysant. Jordain was lifting a cookpot from its hook over the fire and Philip was seated at the table with a cup of ale in his hand. Emma had shrunk back at the sight of so many people, but could not retreat, since Roger and Walter had followed us through from the shop. It occurred to me that for a year, apart from the last few days, she had lived in the quiet and familiar surroundings of Godstow Abbey, and had mixed little with strangers.

'A welcome party indeed,' I said, quite taken aback.

Seeing Jocosa, Rowan trotted forward and the two dogs began to size each other up. Although Rowan was larger, she was younger, and seemed to sense that she should defer to the older dog. She sat down, her tongue hanging out, and allowed herself to be examined.

'Where have you been?' Margaret asked briskly. 'The messenger from the castle was here near half an hour ago.'

I stared at her blankly. 'Messenger? I suppose . . . we went first to St Mildred Street. He must have passed while we were there. A messenger from sheriff Walden?'

'Aye,' Jordain said. 'He was to tell you that Malaliver's men have confirmed your story, whatever that purports. And he wishes Mistress Thorgold's man of law to call on him without delay with the document signed by Sir Anthony, so that he can set matters in motion. I had already come to ask Margaret whether there was any word from you, so I sent Roger to fetch Philip.'

Without speaking, Philip lifted the rolled document which lay beside him on the table. Emma took a few steps forward, then halted. She also was silent, but I saw that her eyes were fixed on the parchment.

'Forgive me, Mistress Thorgold,' I said formally. 'May I present my sister, Mistress Margaret Makepeace? The gentleman by the fireplace is Master Jordain Brinkylsworth, Warden of Hart Hall, and the gentleman seated at the table is Master Philip Olney, Fellow of Merton College and now your man of law, if you are agreeable.'

Margaret dropped a curtsey. Philip rose from his seat and both men bowed. Emma curtsied in her turn, which looked strange in cotte and hose instead of a gown. Alysoun had wriggled past Jordain and was studying Emma with frank interest. I beckoned her forward and took her by the hand.

'This is my daughter Alysoun. Make your reverence to Mistress Thorgold, Alysoun.'

She did so, although she wobbled a little, and continued to stare at Emma as though fascinated. I suppose she found the clothes disconcerting.

'Over by the door is my son Rafe,' I said. Rafe had his thumb in his mouth again. I must stop that habit. He threw a swift look at Emma, then began to back away through the open door into the garden.

'Your own family of course you know,' I concluded.

As if released by my words, Juliana flew across the room and threw her arms around her cousin, closely followed by her mother. Both were tearful.

'Are you truly come back to us?' Juliana cried. 'Will you come to live with us in St Mildred Street? It is not very large, the house, but it is very comfortable. Master Elyot and Master Brinkylsworth got it for us, and painted it, and fetched our furniture. And Mama is become a cheese maker at a dairy in the High Street, so we eat cheese very nearly every day, but it is very good cheese. You can share my bed, it is big enough, or you can have it all to yourself and I shall share the truckle with Maysant.'

'Hush, child,' her mother said. 'Give Emma room to breathe and time to think. She shall come to us at first, of course, but her grandfather wants her to return to him.'

Already I felt that Emma was slipping away from me, toward all these other people who had a better claim on her than I had.

'Before anything else,' I broke in, 'Mistress Thorgold has been injured. She was bitten by one of Falkes Malaliver's alaunts. It was a savage bite and it needs dressing.'

I turned to my sister. 'Meg, can you take Mistress Thorgold to your bedchamber and see to her injury? And perhaps you have a gown she might borrow?'

'Of course,' Margaret said. 'Come with me, my dear.' She turned to Mistress Farringdon. 'Maud, will you fetch cleansing tincture and wound salve from my stillroom? And bandage? Juliana, could you take the children and dogs into the garden? I think Mistress

Thorgold is somewhat tired.'

I was thankful to hand matters over to my capable sister. Emma was indeed looking pale again, as she had at the castle. I hoped the bite was not more serious than I feared.

'You may return to your work,' I said quietly to Walter, as the women headed for the stairs. 'I think Margaret was preparing dinner. You may join us when it is ready.'

The two scriveners withdrew to the shop. It seemed extraordinary that it was barely past time for the midday meal. I seemed to have lived through a lifetime since I had left the house.

Then suddenly there were only the three of us left in the kitchen. Jordain and I joined Philip at the table and he poured us ale.

'So what is this tale of sheriffs and killing dogs?' Jordain said.

'And candle-makers,' Philip prompted. 'The messenger from the castle made some mention of evidence from candle-makers.'

As briefly as I could, I recounted the events of the morning, up to the time we had left the castle. The ride back with Emma I was keeping to myself.

We were on our second cup of ale when we heard the women's voices from the stairs, Margaret and Maud Farringdon came down first, and they were smiling.

'The injury?' I said 'How bad is it?'

'Fortunately not too deep,' Margaret said. 'I have cleaned and salved it, but I have left it open to the air. I think that way it will heal more quickly.'

Maud Farringdon nodded her agreement.

'And have you found something for her to wear?' I was conscious that while Margaret had been slim as a girl, two pregnancies had filled out her figure. Her gowns would hang loose on Emma.

'I found one of my old gowns I was keeping for Alysoun to wear later,' she said. 'It will do well enough for now.'

The two women smiled at each other, and glanced at the stairs.

She had taken off her clumsy sandals and walked barefoot, so I had not heard her coming. I had seen her heavily swathed in a novice's black habit, and lithe as a boy in rough cotte and hose. Now she descended the stairs transformed.

The gown was a deep blue, like her eyes, clinging tightly from shoulder to hips, then flaring out to a gold embroidered hem. The neck was low and square, the sleeves were narrow at the top, then fell, bell-shaped below. The effect was simple and slightly old-fashioned. Her head was swathed in a plain white wimple.

She was remote, beautiful, and untouchable.

Incongruously, she was carrying John Barnes's cap and the ugly bundle, both of which she laid on the table. Jordain, Philip, and I had all risen to our feet, speechless.

She blushed faintly at our continued silence, then cleared her throat.

'I should like this to be returned to John Barnes,' she said, touching the cap with her forefinger, 'but I think it best I should not go to Godstow myself.'

I managed to find my voice. 'I shall see to it.'

'And this,' she began to untie the bundle, 'this is for you, Master Elyot.' She raised a radiant face to me. 'I hope it has not suffered..'

She drew out from the oiled cloth a sheaf of parchment. I saw that the sheets were written over in her neat, distinctive hand. The initials and borders were drawn, but no colour had been added yet. A few corners had curled up, but parchment is a tough material. They could be flattened again.

'Your new book of hours.' I said.

She nodded, looking sad. 'I shall not now be able to finish it. But perhaps one of your scriveners? And I must send parchment to Sister Mildred at the abbey, to replace what I have . . . stolen. Perhaps you could help me?'

'I should be glad to provide Sister Mildred with parchment myself, in exchange for this,' I said. We were both speaking formally. 'But as for another completing your work, that seems like a kind of sacrilege.'

A spark of hope sprang in her face, but died again. She shook her head, but said nothing.

Margaret had gone to the fire and replaced the cookpot Jordain had removed from the heat. ''Tis a good hour past dinner time,' she said. 'There is plenty here for all. Jordain, will you call the men from the shop? Maud, the dishes are there on the shelf. Nicholas, you had best put those pages safe in the shop. The children may take theirs into the garden, for this one time, else there will not be seats enough.'

The whole party sat down to a hearty meal of stewed bacon, onions, and cabbage, and the bread I had seen baked that morning before I set out from home, followed by Meg's preserved plums from last year. It was a lively meal, with the children running in and out, and the two dogs, who had become allies, begging for – and getting – scraps.

Yet both Emma and I were quiet. I did not know what she could be thinking. Would she stay here in Oxford with her aunt? Or would she return to her grandfather's estate, as he hoped? Our ride, clinging together, from Osney to Oxford, was slipping away from me. Already it had taken on the appearance of a dream. Once, she caught my eye and smiled, then looked hurriedly away.

I needed time to think. After we had eaten, Jordain and Philip both left, Jordain to return to Hart Hall, Philip to attend the sheriff at the castle and show him Sir Anthony's signature and seal. By then it was halfway through the afternoon and I decided to give Walter and Roger leave to go home early.

At last there was no one left but my family and the Farringdons. And Emma.

'Will you come home with us now, Emma dear?' Maud Farringdon said. 'It is a humble house, but very comfortable. You may stay with us until you decide what you wish to do.'

'Aye,' Emma said quietly. 'I will come.'

Alysoun fetched her sandals and I watched her put them on. I had not noticed before the damage to her feet, but they bore traces of the salve Meg had spread there in addition to what she must have used on the injury from the dog.

We walked with them to the street door.

'I thank you for all your kindness, Margaret,' Emma said, and kissed her swiftly on the cheek. 'I will return the gown.'

'Nay, you will keep it,' Meg said firmly, 'and with my good will. It never looked as well on me as it does on you.'

The Farringdons were in the street now. In a moment Emma would be gone. Yet she hesitated.

Then she took both my hands in hers.

'And you, Nicholas. I owe more than my life to you.'

She leaned forward and I felt her lips on my cheek. The kiss lingered, and for a moment our hands clung together.

Her hands slid from mine, and I thought I saw tears in her eyes as she turned away. Slipping her arm though Juliana's, she walked up the High Street, not looking back.

'I shall never see her again.'

I was hardly aware that I had spoken aloud, but my sister slipped her arm about my waist.

'And why do you say that?'

'Emma Thorgold is now the lady of a manor,' I said. 'In rank far above a mere Oxford shopkeeper.'

Margaret smiled.

'Do not be too sure of that, Nicholas,' she said.

Historical Note

If you visit the site of Godstow Abbey today, you will find that it no longer stands on an island. As Edwin tells Emma, the course of the Thames, with its many branches and tributaries, has been constantly changing over time. The building of canals in the area in the eighteenth and nineteenth centuries also had an effect on the river. Some branches have moved, some have dried up altogether. Some have even been culverted and now run underground, like much of the Trill Mill Stream. In fact friends have told me that they have seen a change in the course of the river beside Godstow in quite recent years. Driving around Oxford now you will hardly notice that you are crossing the successors to the bridges which were already in place in Nicholas's day.

It is indisputable that many women who chose the monastic life had a genuine religious vocation. For others, it must have offered the prospect of a tranquil life, away from a possible forced marriage and the endless dangers of childbirth, at a time when so many women died from simple complications or puerperal fever. Virtually all the girls who entered nunneries came from the upper classes, since a fairly substantial 'dowry' was required on entering. Had they remained in the secular world the likelihood was that they would be given in marriage as part of some property or political deal. In a nunnery, on the other hand, a woman could have a safe and comfortable life, and if she had talent, could rise to be one of the *obedientiaries* or office-holders of the institution. I have written about the management of medieval nunneries here: http://bit.ly/2bBEGOk

However, the system could be abused. What is beyond doubt is that some girls *were* forced into the monastic life against their will. Sometimes these were redundant daughters. If a family ran to a large number of girls, the cost of marrying them all off advantageously could ruin an estate. (Presumably even larger dowries were demanded for a secular marriage than a marriage to God.) Sometimes they might be the daughters of their father's earlier marriage, thrust out of the manorial nest by the cuckoo of a second or third wife, bent on securing the greatest advantages for her own children – the seed of so many fairy tales about wicked stepmothers. And in a number of documented cases which have come down to us, the girl was shut away in a nunnery so that someone else could seize her inheritance.

From time to time, some of these girls fought back, managed to leave the nunnery, claimed their inheritance, married, and had children.

And what of those candle-makers? Nowadays, when at the mere flick of a switch we can have all the light we desire, it is difficult to comprehend the huge importance of candles in the Middle Ages. The poorest people rose with the sun and went to bed when it set, but in northern Europe even they needed some illumination during the long dark hours of winter, if they were to manage all their daily tasks. For those not so poor, some form of lighting was essential merely for a comfortable life, and for churches candles were a part of the ritual and a means for showing true devotion.

The cheapest form of lighting was the rush dip, which could be made at home by dipping the head of a rush (gathered in a nearby boggy area) into melted tallow (animal fat). This would then be clipped into a wooden or metal stand and gave off a poor, smoky light and an unpleasant smell. Next in quality was the tallow candle.

Like a modern candle this had a wick and was made by dipping until a coating of tallow was formed. It would have given a better light than a rush dip, but still had the unpleasant smell.

The best form of lighting, used by anyone who could afford them, was provided by wax candles, consisting of a rush stem wick, dipped in successive layers of pure beeswax. The finished candle would be held in a candlestick made of anything from wood to gold. So valuable were the stub ends that they were generally the perk of one of the servants. Most expensive of all were the great moulded candles, often of enormous size, used by the Church on various altars and sometimes carried in processions. Made by skilled craftsmen, these were the highest form of the candle-maker's or *chandler's* craft.

So important was the business of candle-making that there were *two* guilds in London: the Worshipful Company of Wax Chandlers and the Worshipful Company of Tallow Chandlers. These still exist to this day, though I suspect few of their members do much candle dipping themselves.

Since wax was expensive and the making of candles quite a skilled craft, groups of candle-makers travelled about the country. They would call at the larger houses and the monastic institutions perhaps once a year, stay for some days, and make a year's supply of candles. In addition to these itinerant candle-makers, there were, of course, chandlers in all the towns, who supplied the local townspeople and those who came in from the surrounding countryside on market day. As late as 1840 there was still a tallow chandler in the large village of Weobley in Herefordshire.

As standards of living rose (for some) under the Tudors, better lighting began to be demanded, and the royal family required staggering amounts of candles for their palaces, the nobility not lagging far behind. The supply of wax in England began to be insufficient to meet the need, and was one of the major imports from Russia, by the Muscovy Company, as I mention in *Voyage to Muscovy*. The merchants might have begun by thinking exotic goods like furs would be most profitable, but in reality humble ship's cordage and wax for candles were to prove their most valuable imports!

The Author

Ann Swinfen spent her childhood partly in England and partly on the east coast of America. She was educated at Somerville College, Oxford, where she read Classics and Mathematics and married a fellow undergraduate, the historian David Swinfen. While bringing up their five children and studying for a postgraduate MSc in Mathematics and a BA and PhD in English Literature, she had a variety of jobs, including university lecturer, translator, freelance journalist and software designer. She served for nine years on the governing council of the Open University and for five years worked as a manager and editor in the technical author division of an international computer company, but gave up her full-time job to concentrate on her writing, while continuing part-time university teaching in English Literature. In 1995 she founded Dundee Book Events, a voluntary organisation promoting books and authors to the general public.

She is the author of the highly acclaimed series, *The Chronicles of Christoval Alvarez*. Set in the late sixteenth century, it features a young Marrano physician recruited as a code-breaker and spy in Walsingham's secret service. In order, the books are: ***The Secret World of Christoval Alvarez, The Enterprise of England, The Portuguese Affair, Bartholomew Fair, Suffer the Little Children, Voyage to Muscovy*** and ***The Play's the Thing.***

Her *Fenland Series* takes place in East Anglia during the seventeenth century. In the first book, ***Flood***, both men and women fight desperately to save their land from greedy and unscrupulous speculators. The second, ***Betrayal***, continues the story of the dangerous search for legal redress and security for the embattled villagers, at a time when few could be trusted.

Her latest series, *Oxford Medieval Mysteries*, is set in the fourteenth century and features bookseller Nicholas Elyot, a young widower with two small children, and his university friend Jordain Brinkylsworth, who are faced with crime in the troubled world following the Black Death. The first book in the series is ***The Bookseller's Tale***, the second is ***The Novice's Tale.***

She has also written two standalone novels. *The Testament of Mariam*, set in the first century, recounts, from an unusual perspective, one of the most famous and yet ambiguous stories in human history, while exploring life under a foreign occupying force, in lands still torn by conflict to this day. *This Rough Ocean* is based on the real-life experiences of the Swinfen family during the 1640s, at the time of the English Civil War, when John Swynfen was imprisoned for opposing the killing of the king, and his wife Anne had to fight for the survival of her children and dependents.

Ann Swinfen now lives on the northeast coast of Scotland, with her husband, formerly vice-principal of the University of Dundee, and a rescue cat called Maxi.
www.annswinfen.com

CPSIA information can be obtained
at www.ICGtesting.com
Printed in the USA
FSHW010002061221
86714FS